THE

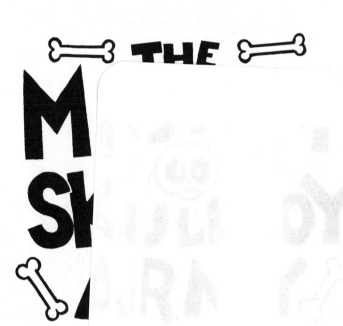

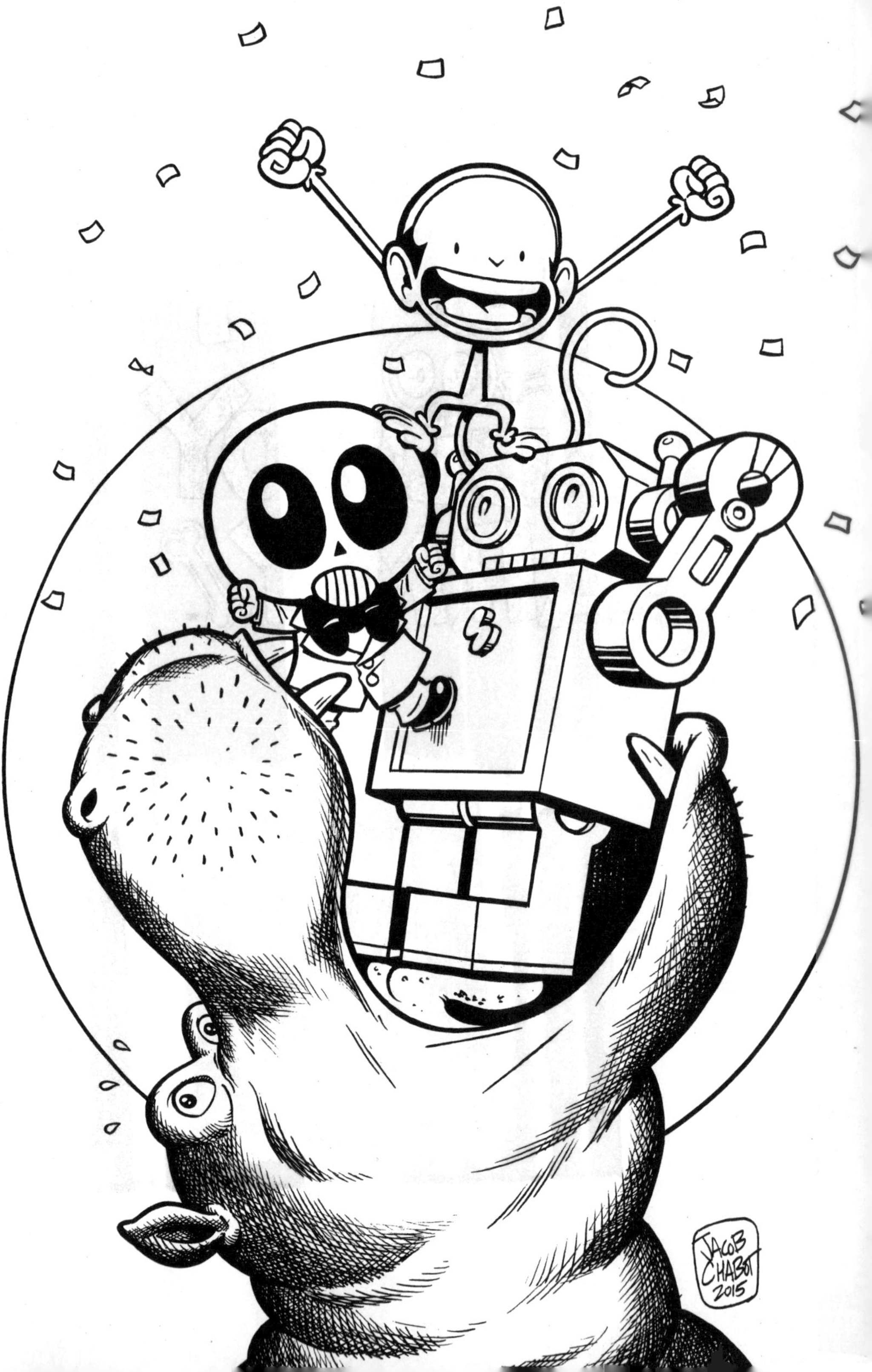
JACOB
CHABOT
2015

THE MIGHTY SKULLBOY ARMY

By JACOB CHABOT

DARK HORSE BOOKS

President and Publisher **Mike Richardson** Editor **Philip R. Simon**
Assistant Editor **Roxy Polk** Designer **Brennan Thome**
Digital Art Technician **Ryan Jorgensen** Special thanks to **Mike Carriglitto**

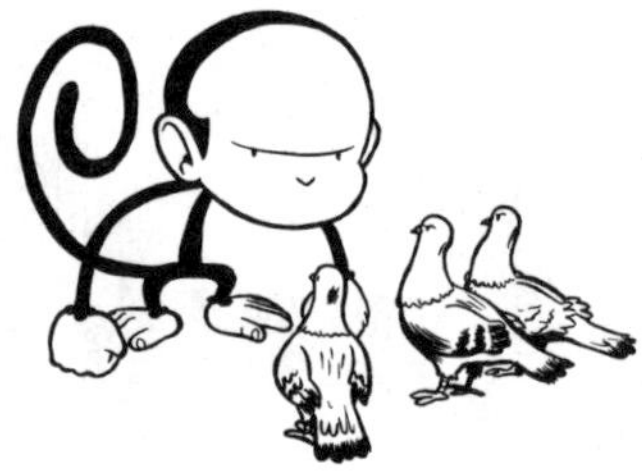

Published by Dark Horse Books
A division of Dark Horse Comics, Inc.
10956 SE Main Street, Milwaukie, OR 97222

DarkHorse.com

To find a comics shop in your area, call the Comic Shop Locator Service toll-free at 1-888-266-4226.

THE MIGHTY SKULLBOY ARMY VOLUME 1

This volume collects issues #1–#7 of the *Mighty Skullboy Army* minicomics, self-published from 2000 to 2006 by Jacob R. Chabot, along with comics from *Strip Search* (2004) and *New Recruits* (2006).

First edition: February 2007 | Second edition: August 2015 | ISBN 978-1-61655-734-8
1 3 5 7 9 10 8 6 4 2

Printed in the United States of America

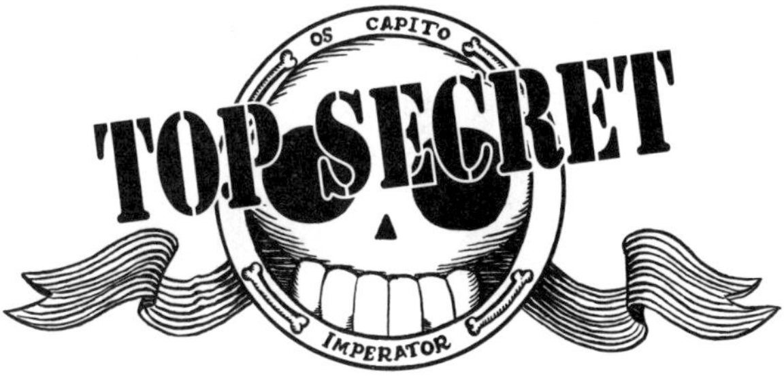
OS CAPITO
TOP SECRET
IMPERATOR

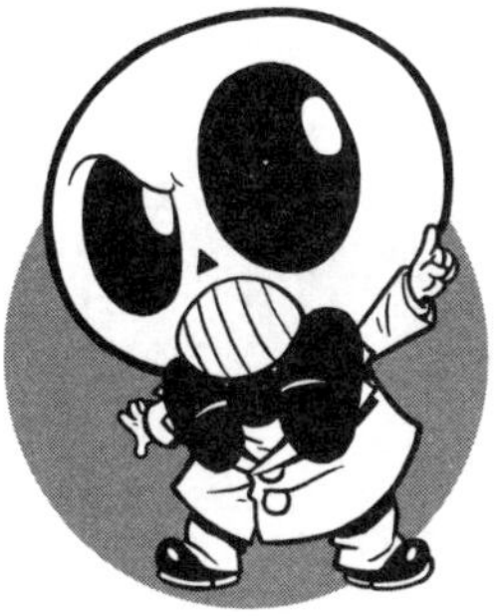

SKULLBOY

This is Skullboy, your commander in chief. He's the owner and CEO of Skull Co. Unfortunately, due to his young age, he also has to attend elementary school. When he grows up, he would like to be the richest man in the world.

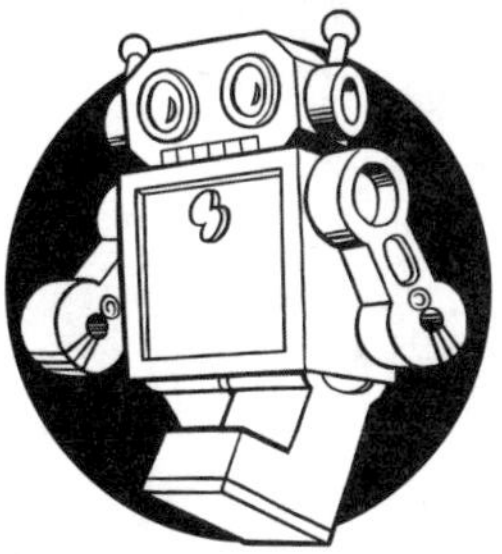

UNIT 1

Unit 1 was the first member to be officially inducted into the Mighty Skullboy Army. He feels that this makes him the most superior, as well. This belief is backed up with the many gadgets packed into his robotic frame. Such devices include plasma cannons, rocket skates, telescopic vision, a secret compartment, and more.

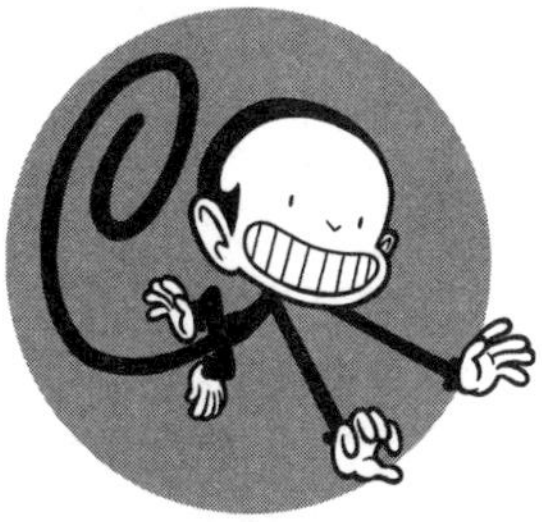

UNIT 2

Bred in the Skull Co. labs to be superintelligent, this primate may actually be the smartest member of the Mighty Skullboy Army. However, most of the time he'd rather chase bugs and eat flowers than carry out a secret mission. Provoke with caution, because beneath that innocent exterior lurks a devious mind.

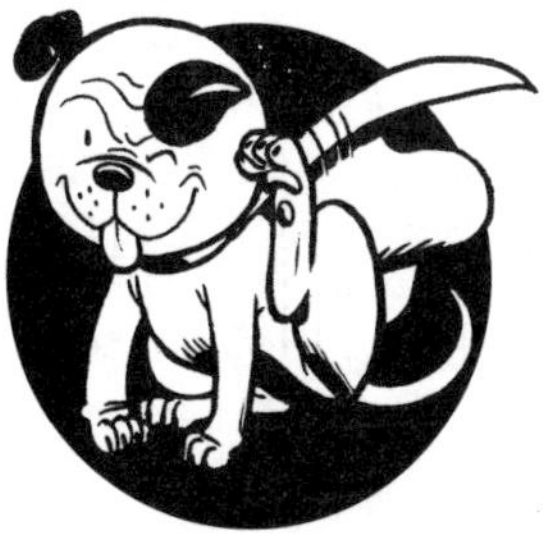

MOD DOG

Very little is known about this mysterious mutt. All we know is that he seems to have some sort of superpowers that enable him to fly. That, and he has some sort of vendetta against Skullboy. Although experts say that he acts just like a normal dog and probably isn't any sort of mastermind. As far as the Mighty Skullboy Army is concerned, though, Mod Dog is a jerk and should be antagonized whenever possible.

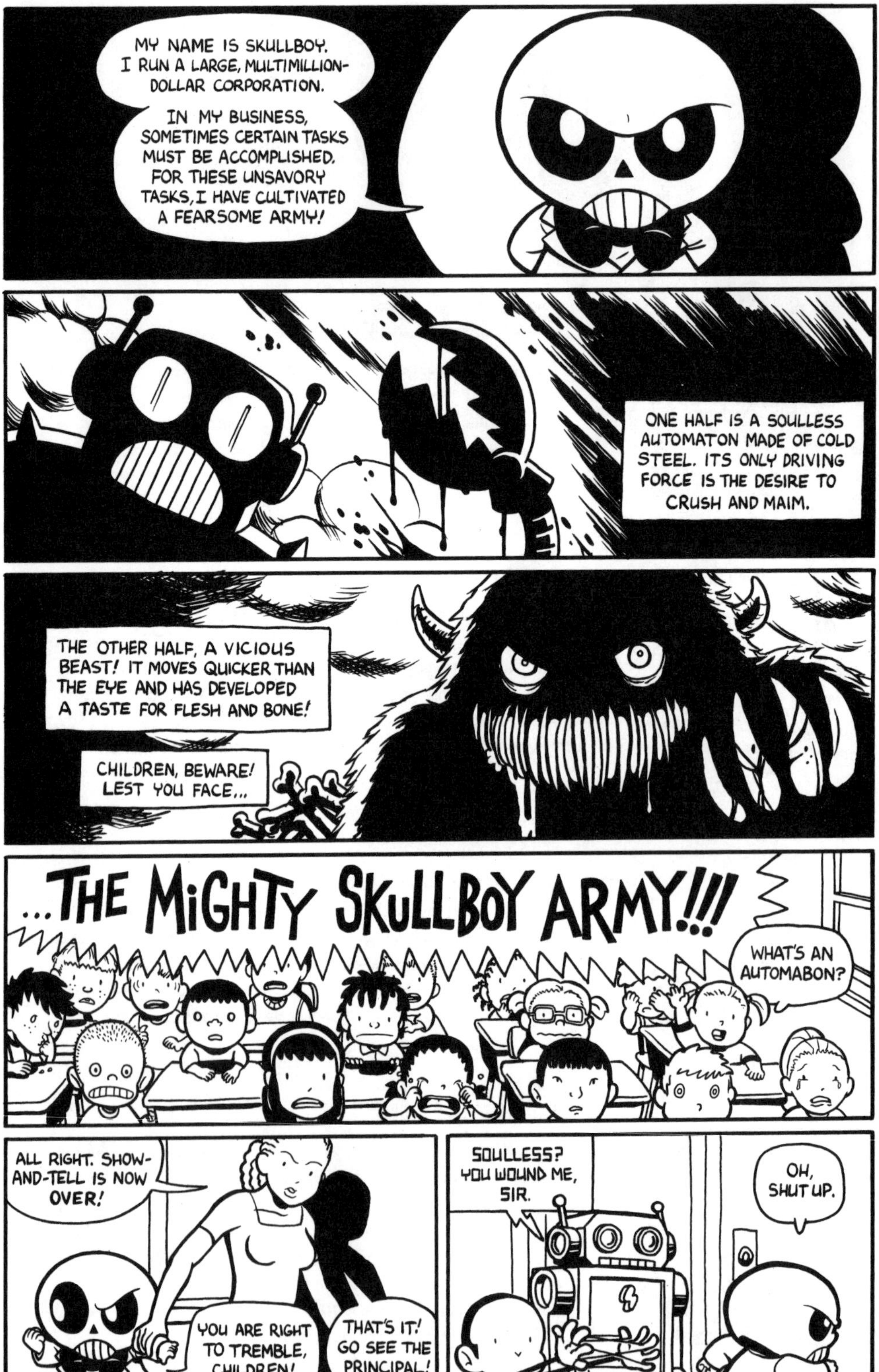
MY NAME IS SKULLBOY. I RUN A LARGE, MULTIMILLION-DOLLAR CORPORATION.
IN MY BUSINESS, SOMETIMES CERTAIN TASKS MUST BE ACCOMPLISHED. FOR THESE UNSAVORY TASKS, I HAVE CULTIVATED A FEARSOME ARMY!
ONE HALF IS A SOULLESS AUTOMATON MADE OF COLD STEEL. ITS ONLY DRIVING FORCE IS THE DESIRE TO CRUSH AND MAIM.
THE OTHER HALF, A VICIOUS BEAST! IT MOVES QUICKER THAN THE EYE AND HAS DEVELOPED A TASTE FOR FLESH AND BONE!
CHILDREN, BEWARE! LEST YOU FACE...
...THE MIGHTY SKULLBOY ARMY!!!
WHAT'S AN AUTOMABON?
ALL RIGHT. SHOW-AND-TELL IS NOW OVER!
YOU ARE RIGHT TO TREMBLE, CHILDREN!
THAT'S IT! GO SEE THE PRINCIPAL!
SOULLESS? YOU WOUND ME, SIR.
OH, SHUT UP.

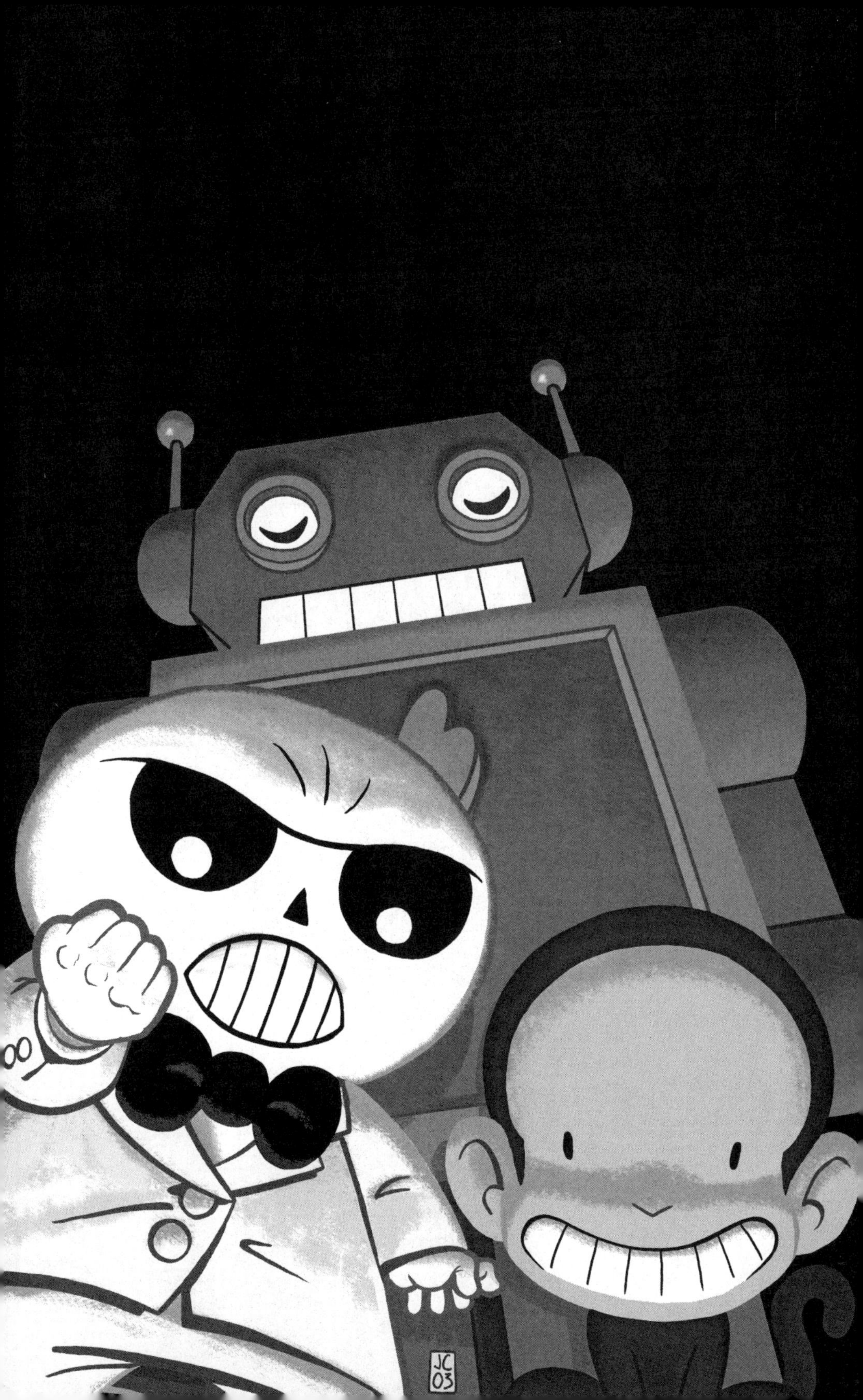
JC
03

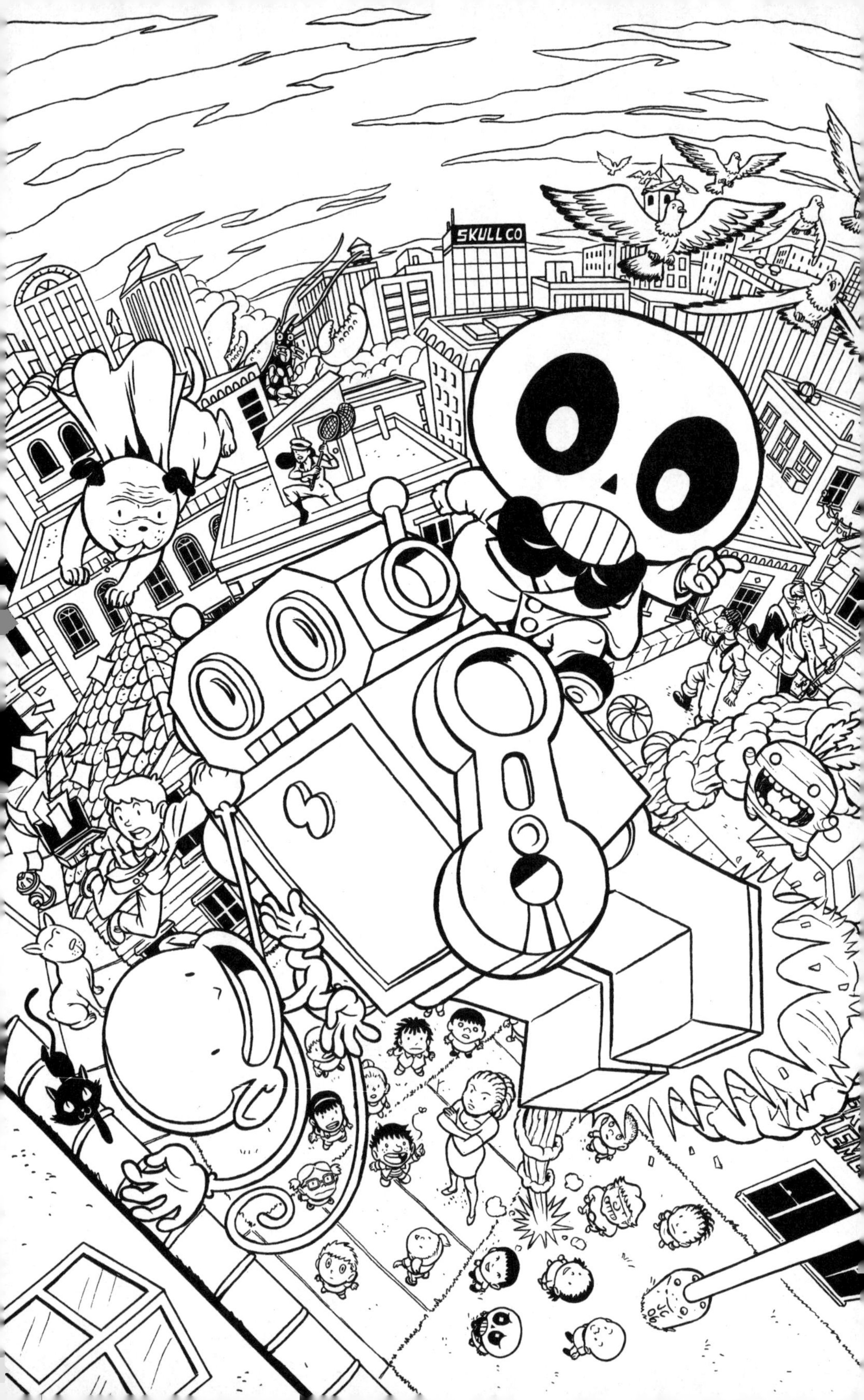
SKULL CO

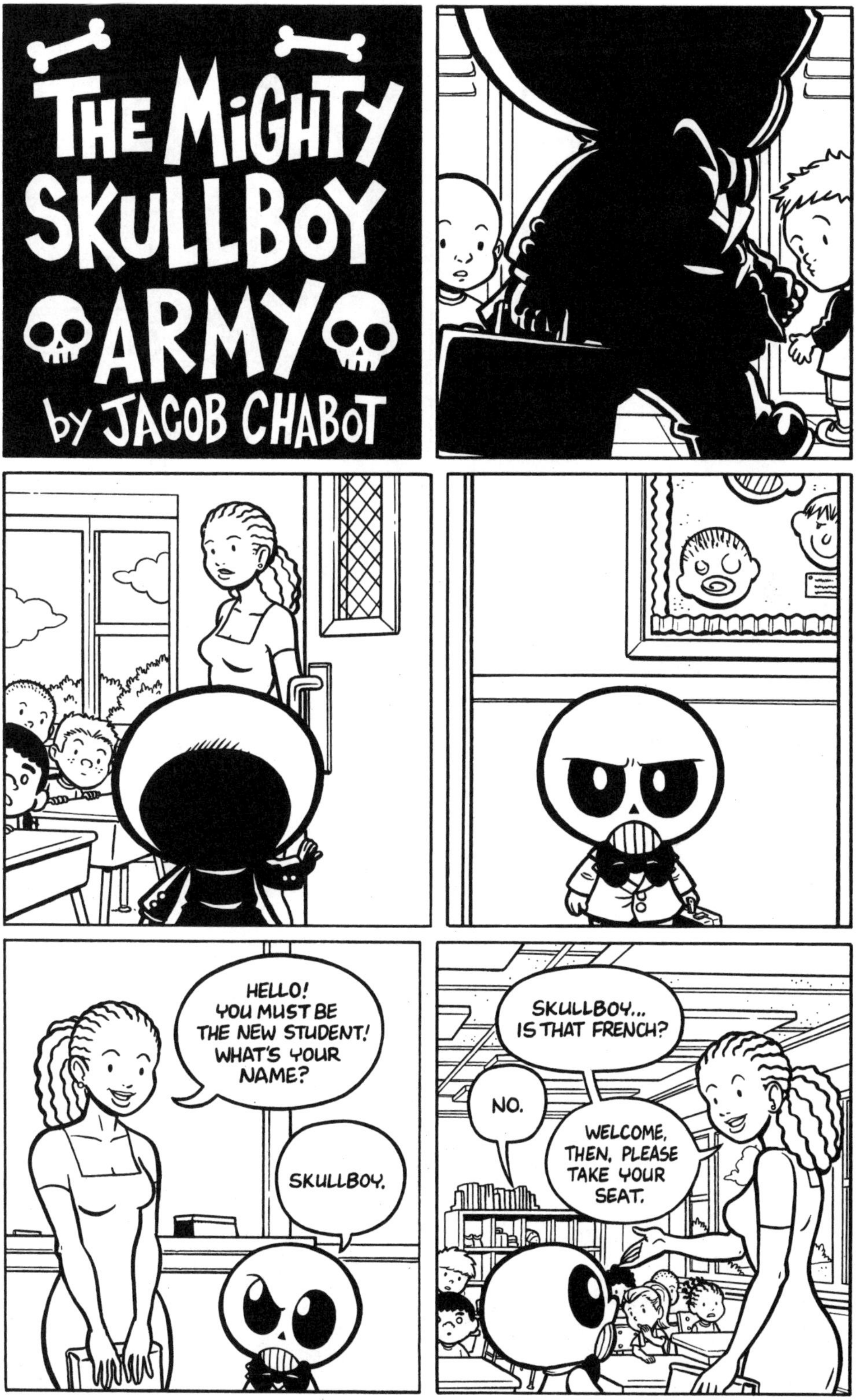
THE MIGHTY SKULLBOY ARMY
by JACOB CHABOT
HELLO! YOU MUST BE THE NEW STUDENT! WHAT'S YOUR NAME?
SKULLBOY.
SKULLBOY... IS THAT FRENCH?
NO.
WELCOME, THEN. PLEASE TAKE YOUR SEAT.

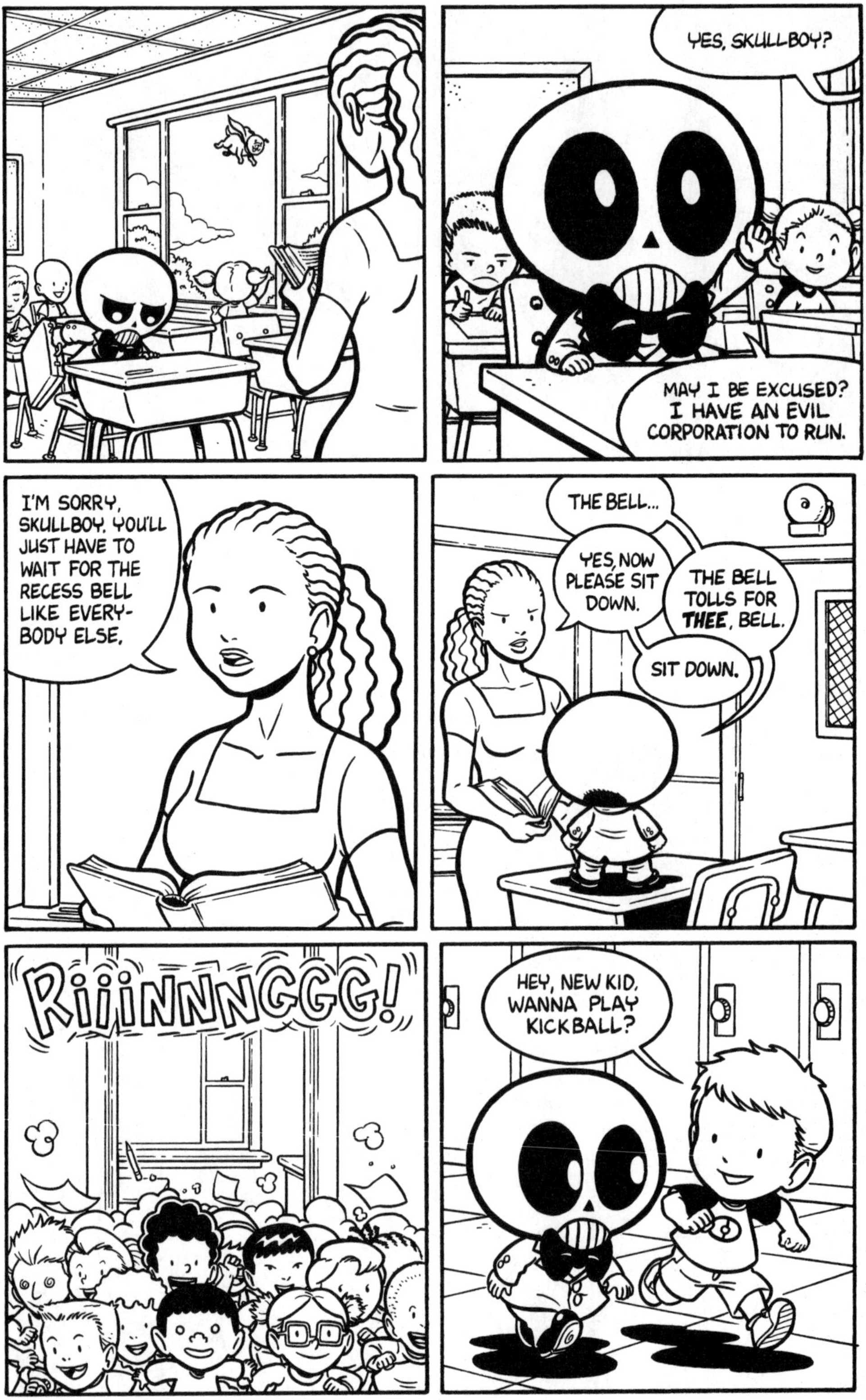
YES, SKULLBOY?
MAY I BE EXCUSED? I HAVE AN EVIL CORPORATION TO RUN.
I'M SORRY, SKULLBOY. YOU'LL JUST HAVE TO WAIT FOR THE RECESS BELL LIKE EVERY-BODY ELSE.
THE BELL...
YES, NOW PLEASE SIT DOWN.
THE BELL TOLLS FOR **THEE**, BELL.
SIT DOWN.
RIIINNNGGG!
HEY, NEW KID, WANNA PLAY KICKBALL?

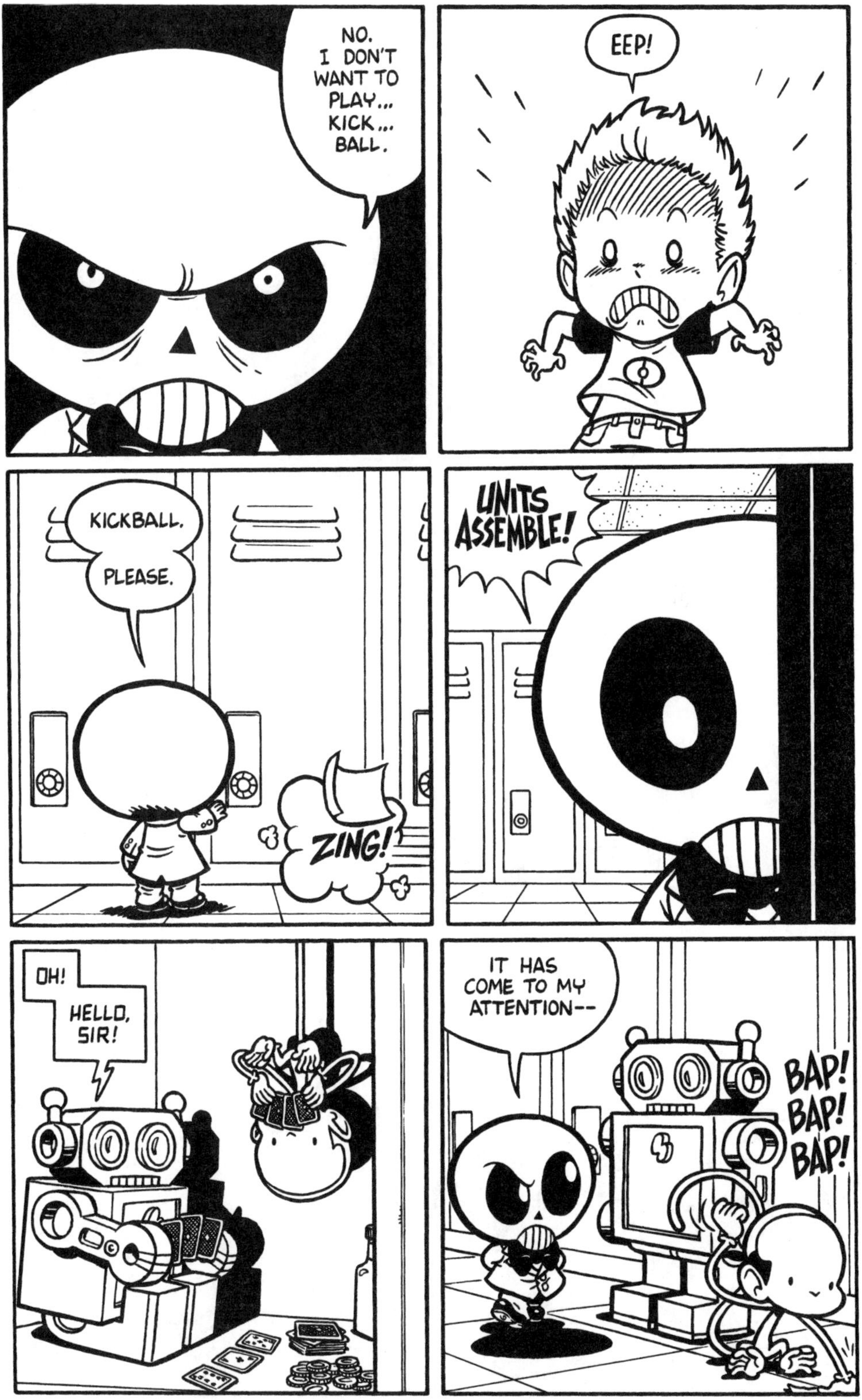
NO. I DON'T WANT TO PLAY... KICK... BALL.
EEP!
KICKBALL.
PLEASE.
ZING!
UNITS ASSEMBLE!
OH!
HELLO, SIR!
IT HAS COME TO MY ATTENTION--
BAP! BAP! BAP!

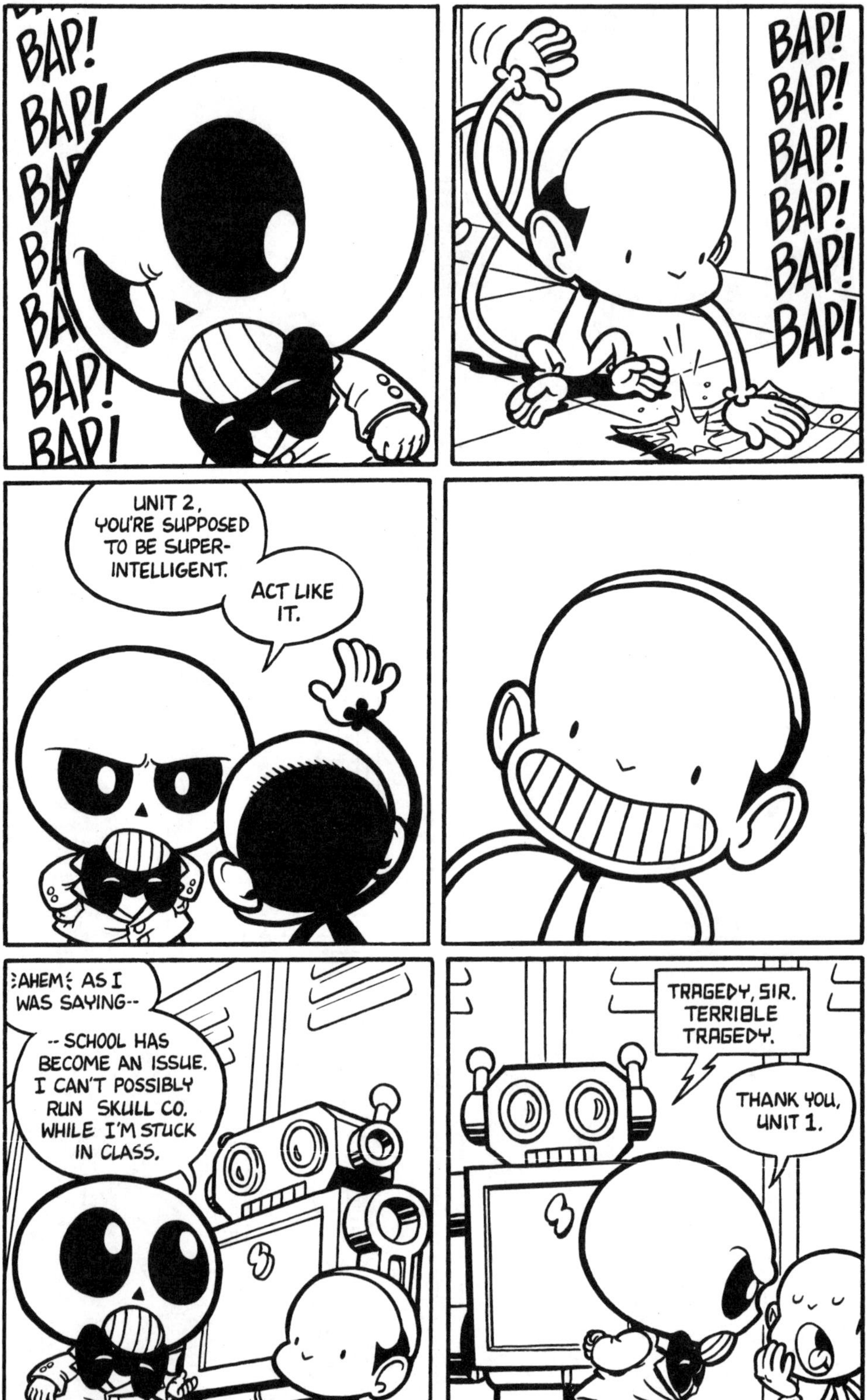
BAP!
BAP!
BAP!
BAP!
BAP!
BAP!
BAP!
BAP!
BAP!
BAP!
BAP!
BAP!
UNIT 2, YOU'RE SUPPOSED TO BE SUPER-INTELLIGENT.
ACT LIKE IT.
:AHEM: AS I WAS SAYING--
-- SCHOOL HAS BECOME AN ISSUE. I CAN'T POSSIBLY RUN SKULL CO. WHILE I'M STUCK IN CLASS.
TRAGEDY, SIR. TERRIBLE TRAGEDY.
THANK YOU, UNIT 1.

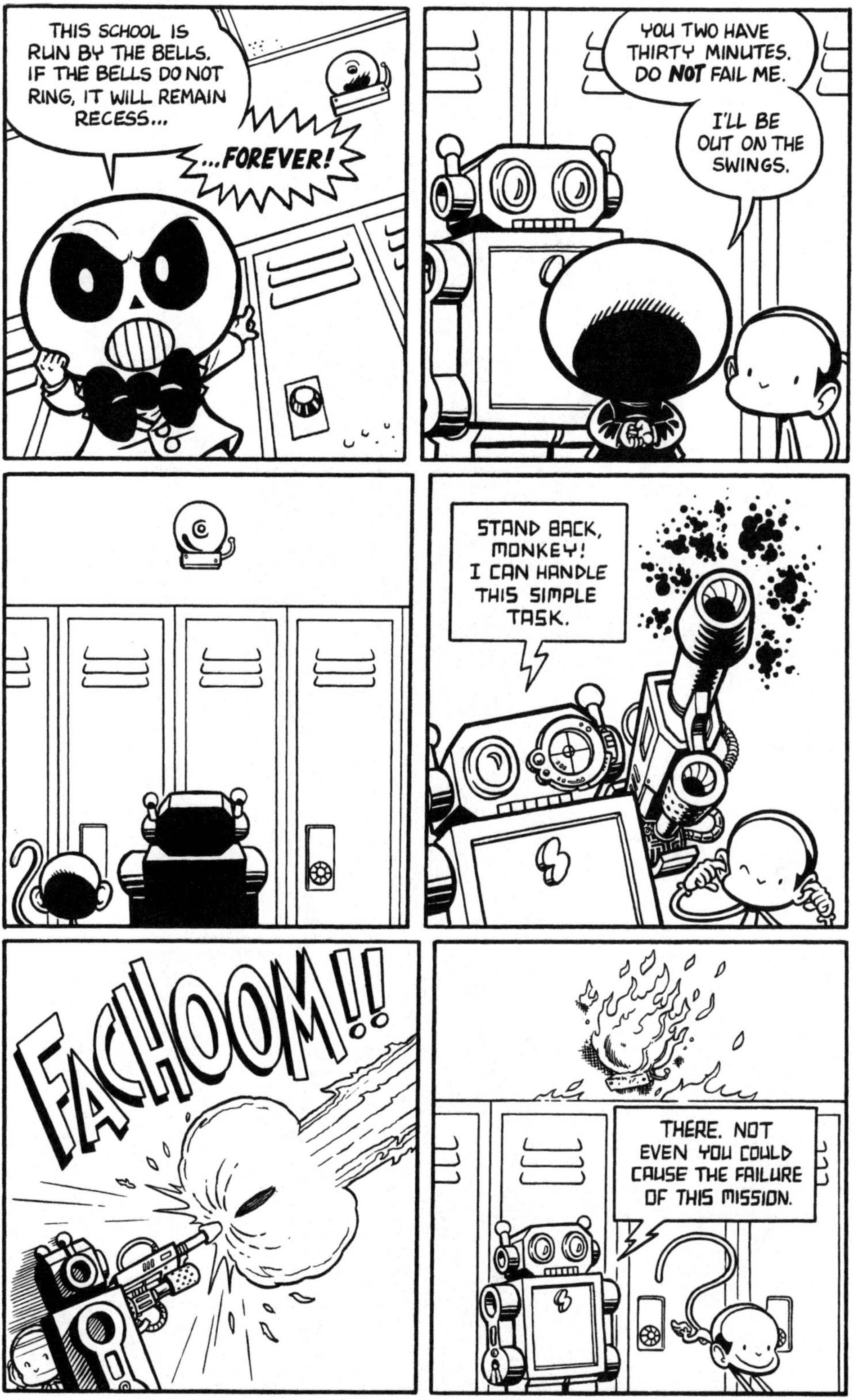
THIS SCHOOL IS RUN BY THE BELLS. IF THE BELLS DO NOT RING, IT WILL REMAIN RECESS...
...FOREVER!
YOU TWO HAVE THIRTY MINUTES. DO NOT FAIL ME.
I'LL BE OUT ON THE SWINGS.
STAND BACK, MONKEY! I CAN HANDLE THIS SIMPLE TASK.
FACHOOM!!
THERE. NOT EVEN YOU COULD CAUSE THE FAILURE OF THIS MISSION.

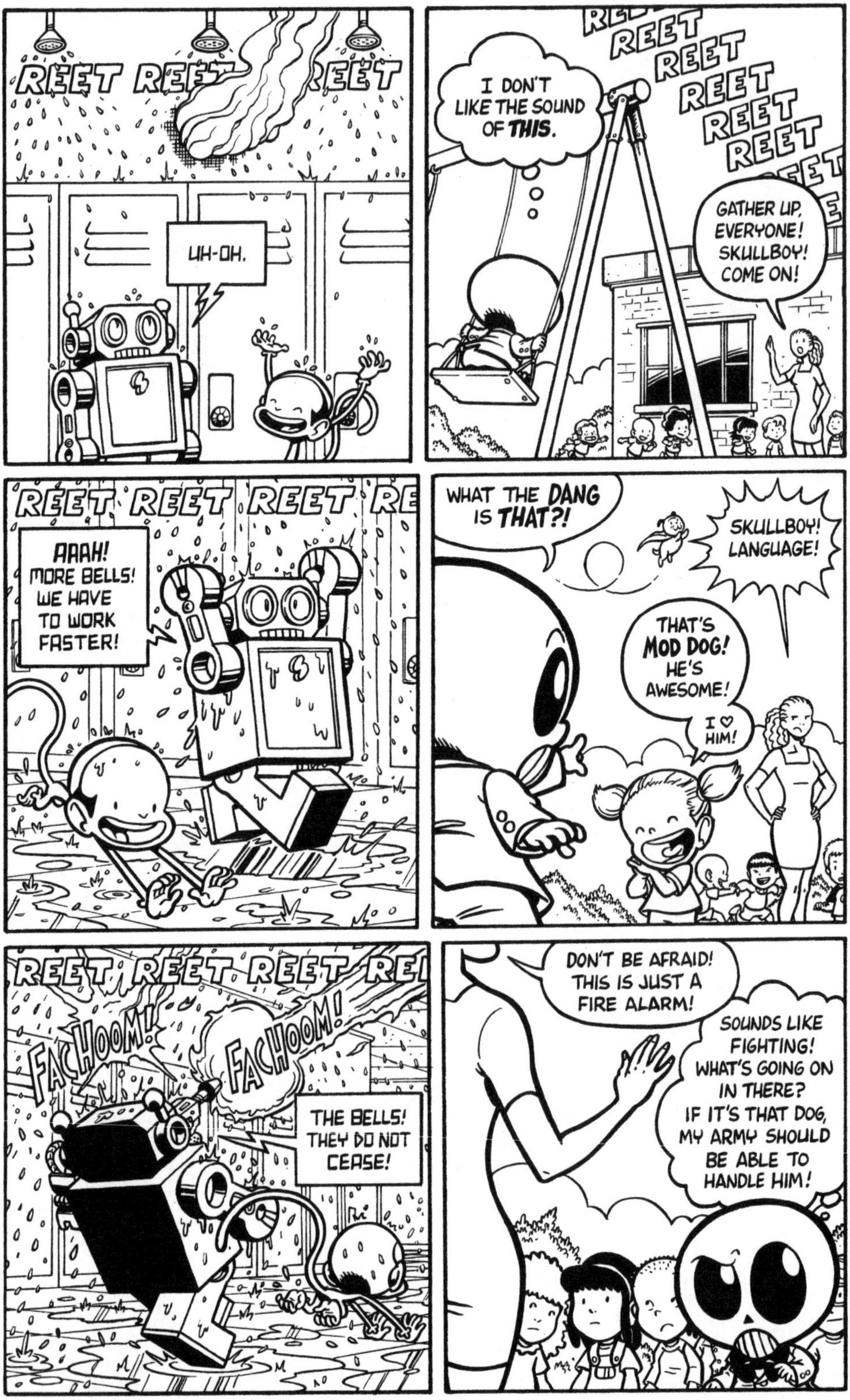
REET REET REET
UH-OH.
REET REET REET REET REET REET
I DON'T LIKE THE SOUND OF THIS.
GATHER UP, EVERYONE! SKULLBOY! COME ON!
REET REET REET
AAAH! MORE BELLS! WE HAVE TO WORK FASTER!
WHAT THE DANG IS THAT?!
SKULLBOY! LANGUAGE!
THAT'S MOD DOG! HE'S AWESOME!
I ♡ HIM!
REET REET REET
FACHOOM!
FACHOOM!
THE BELLS! THEY DO NOT CEASE!
DON'T BE AFRAID! THIS IS JUST A FIRE ALARM!
SOUNDS LIKE FIGHTING! WHAT'S GOING ON IN THERE? IF IT'S THAT DOG, MY ARMY SHOULD BE ABLE TO HANDLE HIM!

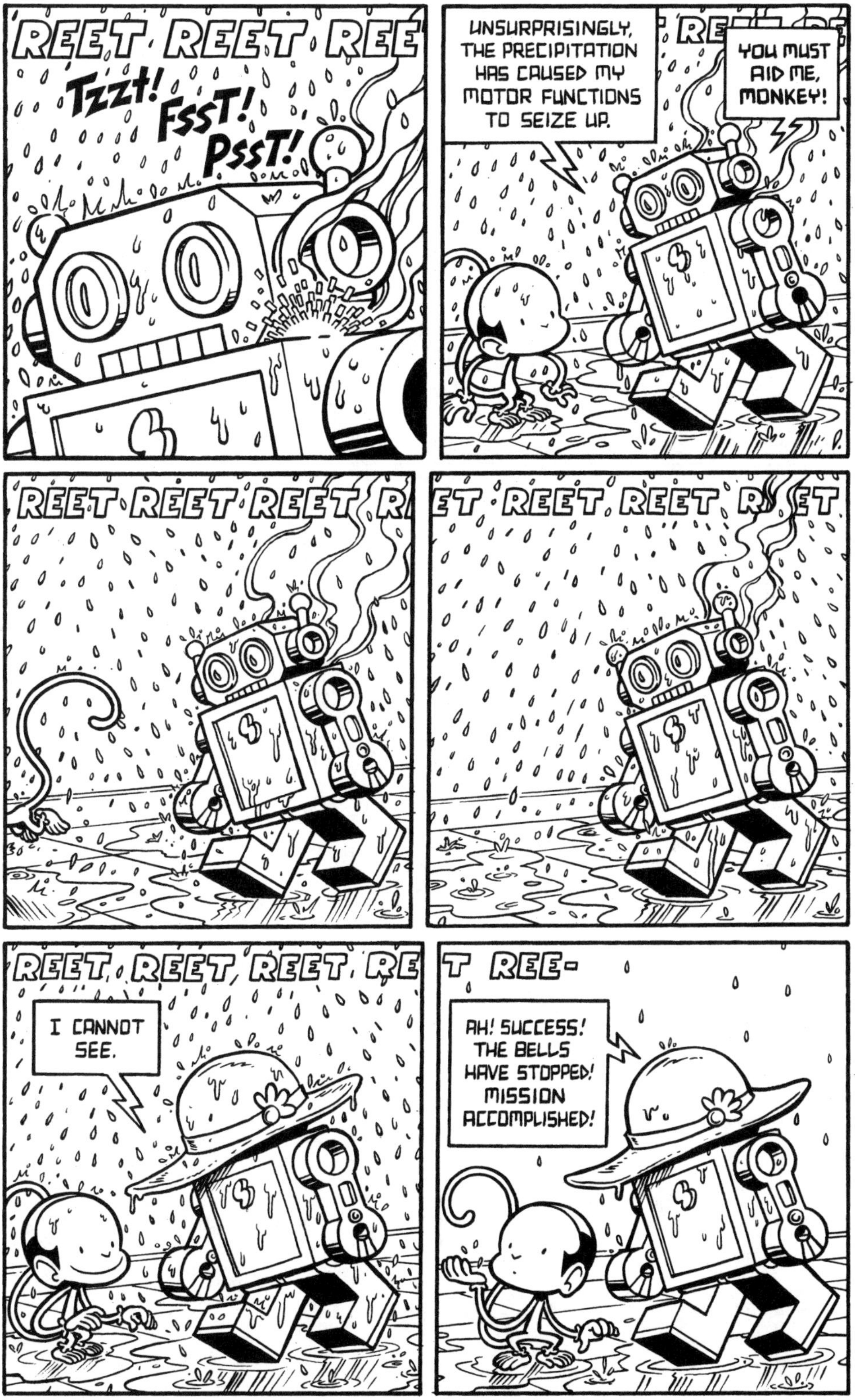
REET REET REE
Tzzt!
FSST!
PSST!
UNSURPRISINGLY, THE PRECIPITATION HAS CAUSED MY MOTOR FUNCTIONS TO SEIZE UP.
YOU MUST AID ME, MONKEY!
REET REET REET R
ET REET REET R ET
REET REET REET RE
T REE-
I CANNOT SEE.
AH! SUCCESS! THE BELLS HAVE STOPPED! MISSION ACCOMPLISHED!

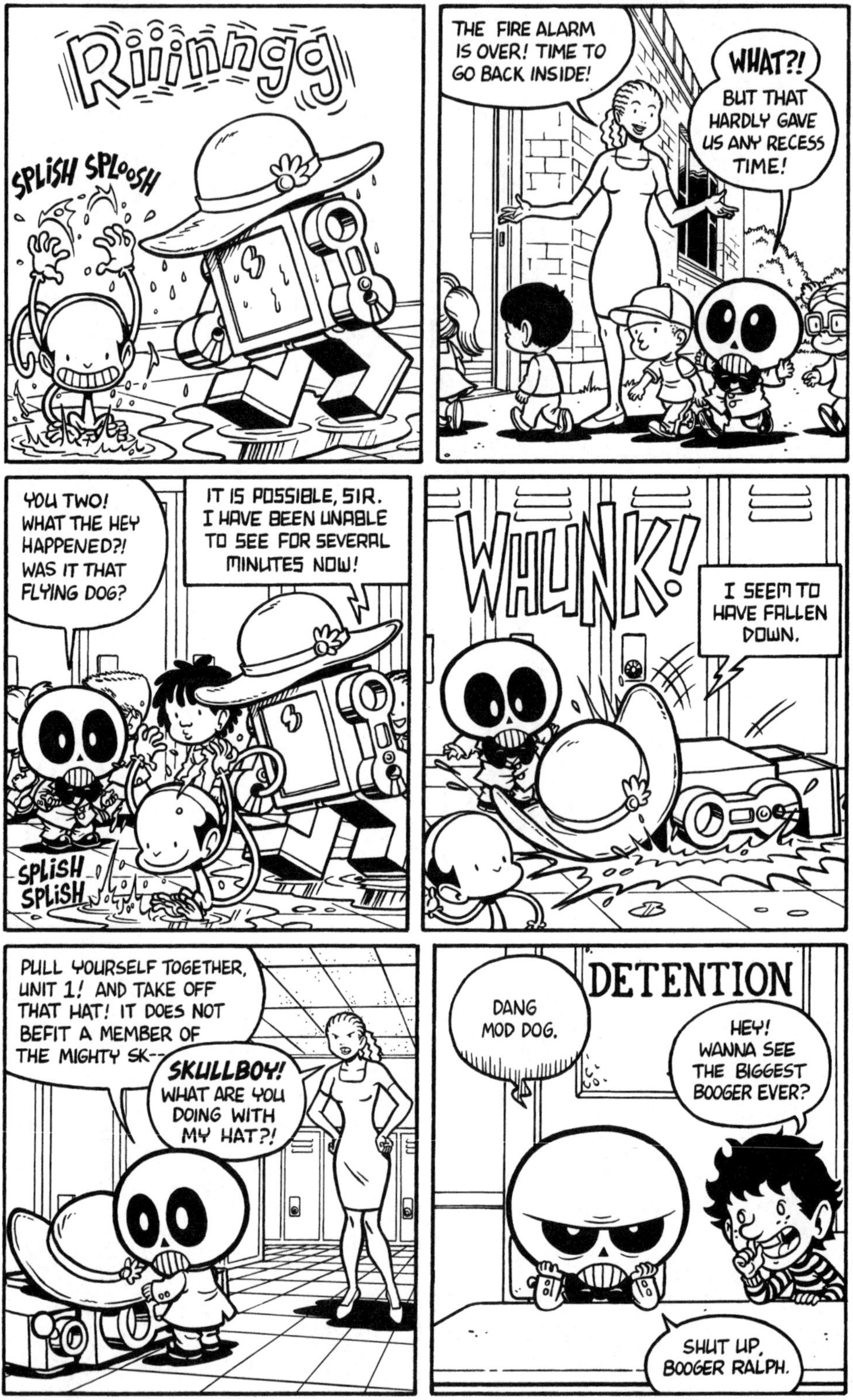
Riiinngg
SPLISH SPLOOSH
THE FIRE ALARM IS OVER! TIME TO GO BACK INSIDE!
WHAT?! BUT THAT HARDLY GAVE US ANY RECESS TIME!
YOU TWO! WHAT THE HEY HAPPENED?! WAS IT THAT FLYING DOG?
IT IS POSSIBLE, SIR. I HAVE BEEN UNABLE TO SEE FOR SEVERAL MINUTES NOW!
SPLISH SPLISH
WHUNK!
I SEEM TO HAVE FALLEN DOWN.
PULL YOURSELF TOGETHER, UNIT 1! AND TAKE OFF THAT HAT! IT DOES NOT BEFIT A MEMBER OF THE MIGHTY SK--
SKULLBOY! WHAT ARE YOU DOING WITH MY HAT?!
DETENTION
DANG MOD DOG.
HEY! WANNA SEE THE BIGGEST BOOGER EVER?
SHUT UP, BOOGER RALPH.

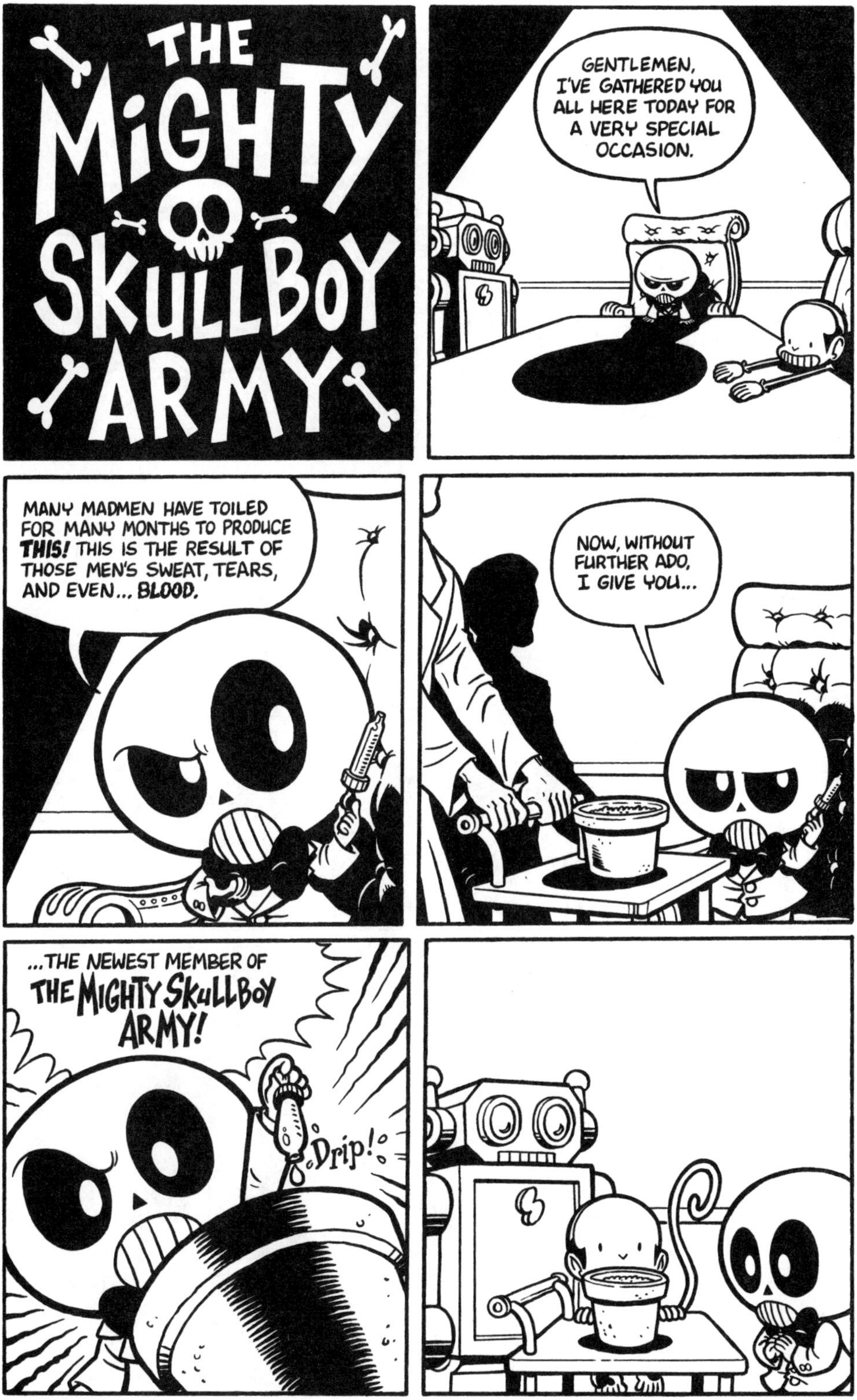
THE MIGHTY SKULLBOY ARMY
GENTLEMEN, I'VE GATHERED YOU ALL HERE TODAY FOR A VERY SPECIAL OCCASION.
MANY MADMEN HAVE TOILED FOR MANY MONTHS TO PRODUCE **THIS!** THIS IS THE RESULT OF THOSE MEN'S SWEAT, TEARS, AND EVEN... **BLOOD.**
NOW, WITHOUT FURTHER ADO, I GIVE YOU...
...THE NEWEST MEMBER OF THE MIGHTY SKULLBOY ARMY!
Drip!

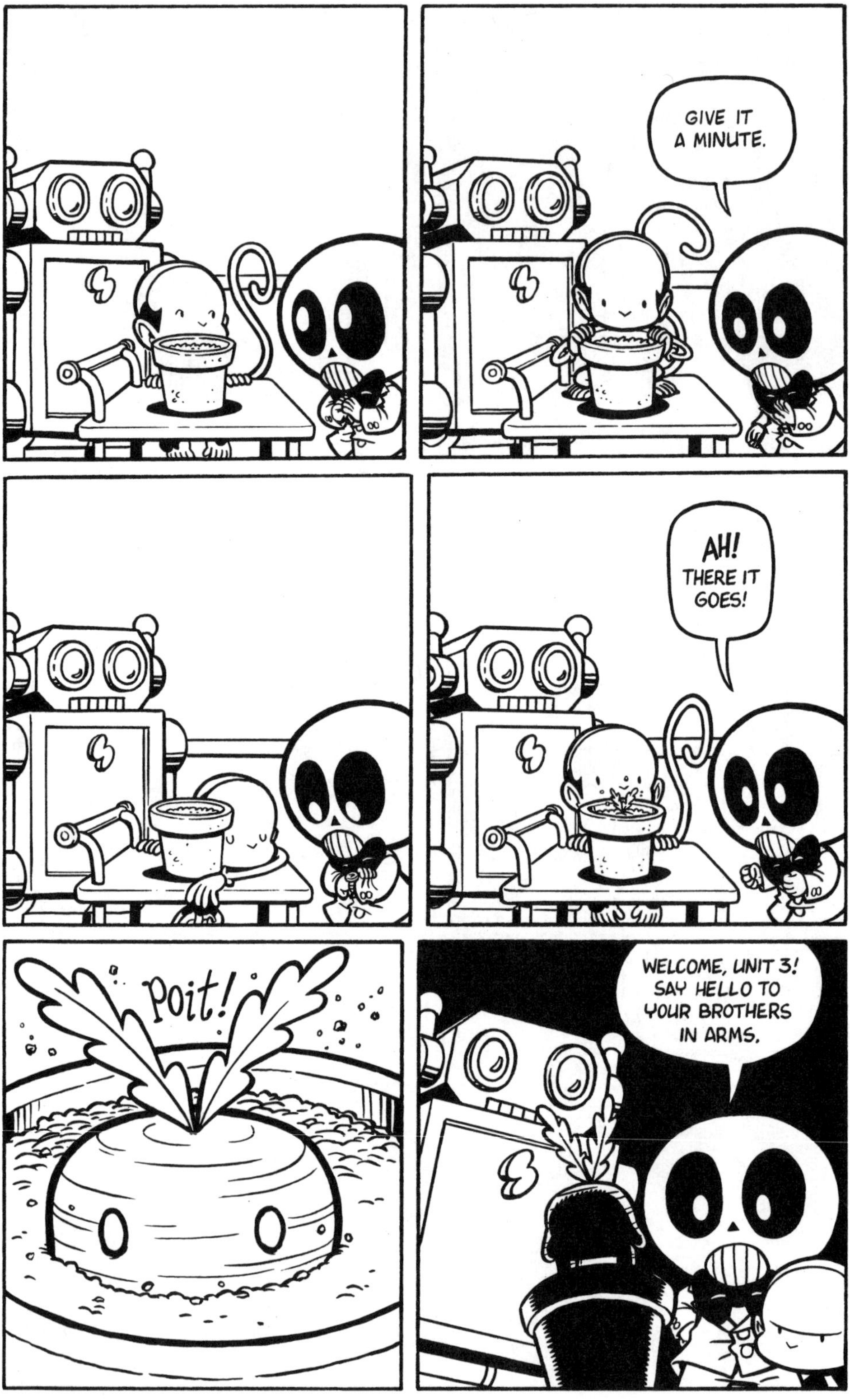
GIVE IT A MINUTE.
AH! THERE IT GOES!
Poit!
WELCOME, UNIT 3! SAY HELLO TO YOUR BROTHERS IN ARMS.

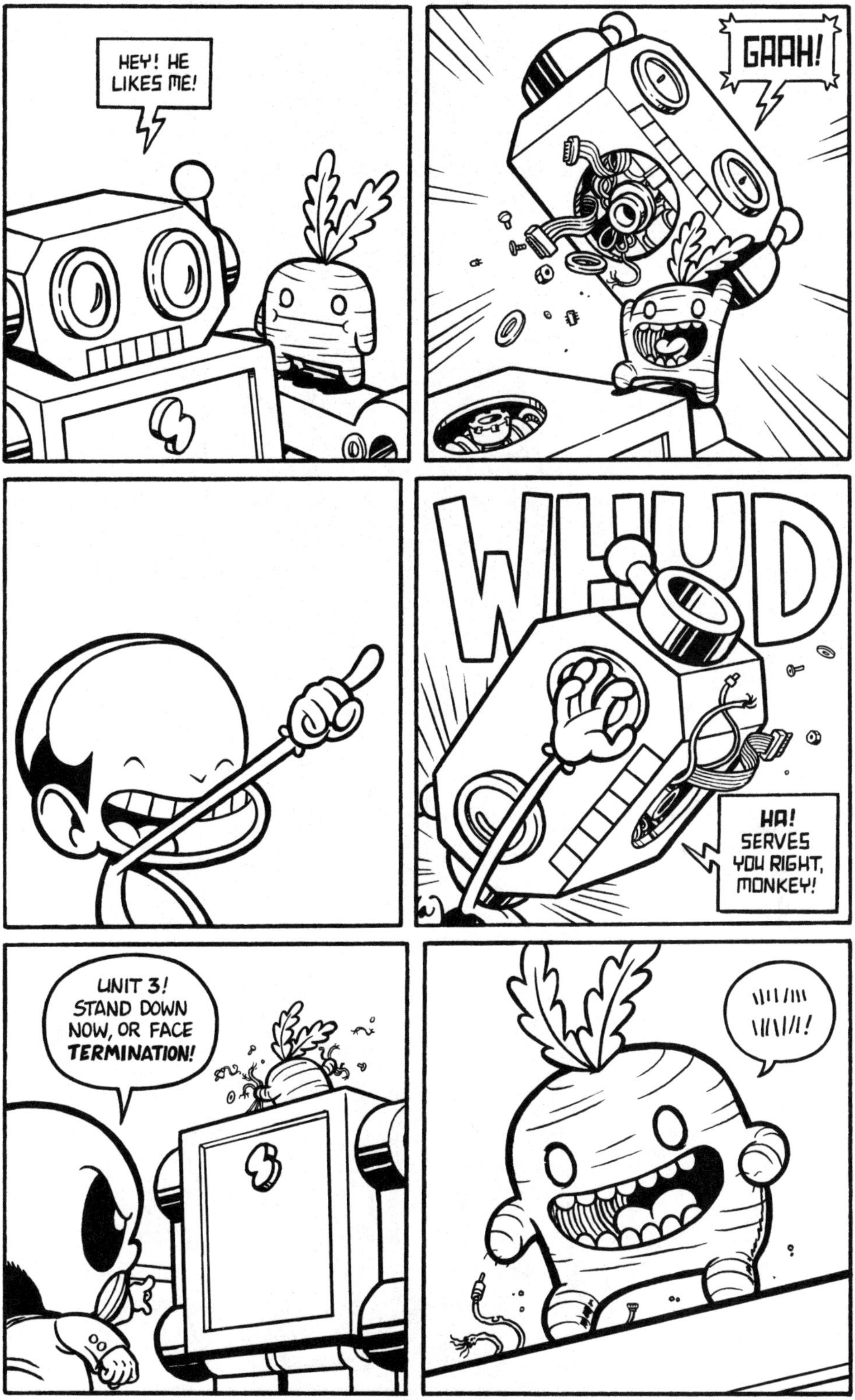
HEY! HE LIKES ME!
GAAH!
WHUD
HA! SERVES YOU RIGHT, MONKEY!
UNIT 3! STAND DOWN NOW, OR FACE **TERMINATION!**
\\\|/|\\ \\|\\|/|!

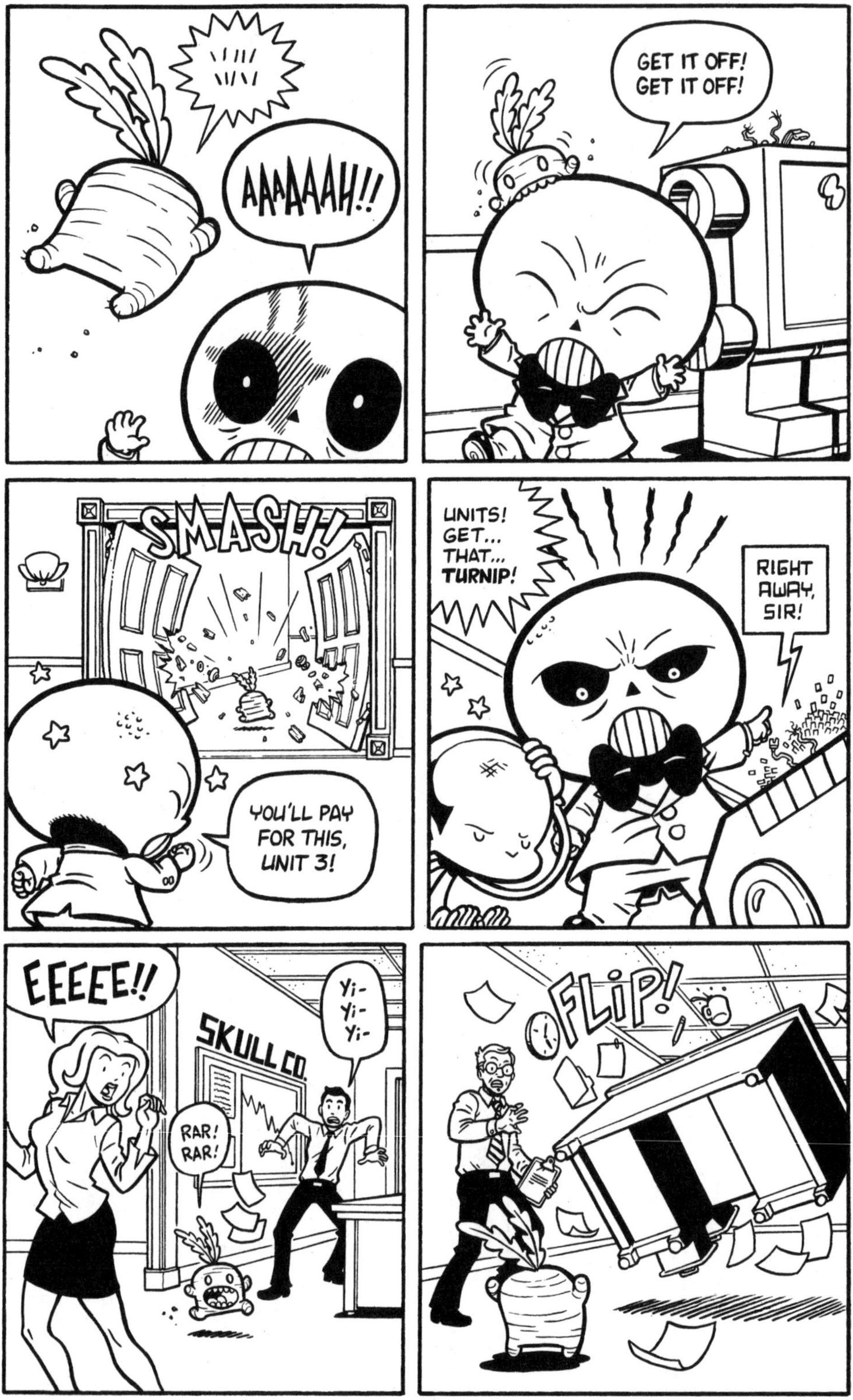
\!/!/
\!/\!
AAAAAAH!!
GET IT OFF!
GET IT OFF!
SMASH!
YOU'LL PAY
FOR THIS,
UNIT 3!
UNITS!
GET...
THAT...
TURNIP!
RIGHT
AWAY,
SIR!
EEEEE!!
SKULL CO.
RAR!
RAR!
Yi-
Yi-
Yi-
FLIP!

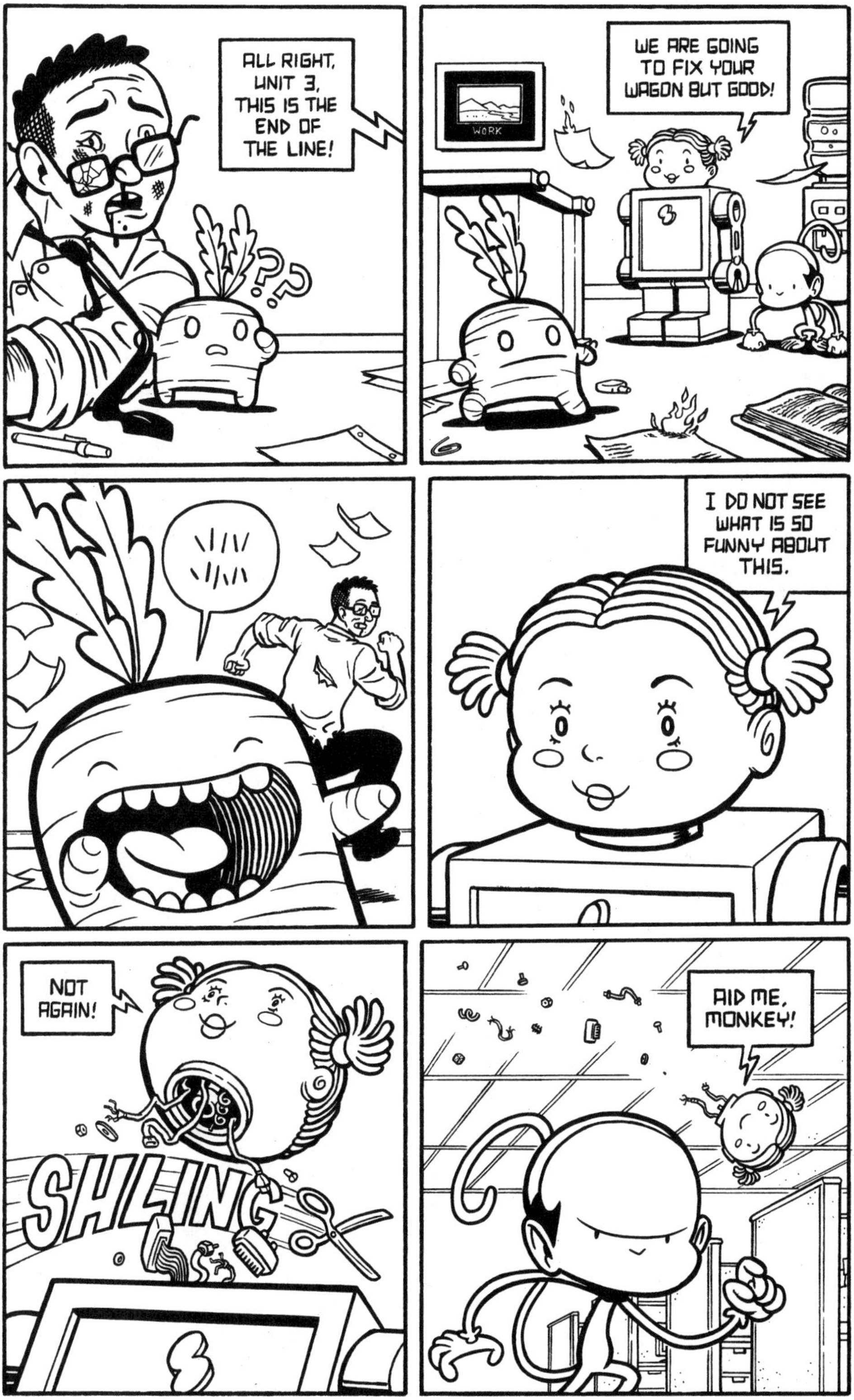
ALL RIGHT, UNIT 3, THIS IS THE END OF THE LINE!
WORK
WE ARE GOING TO FIX YOUR WAGON BUT GOOD!
I DO NOT SEE WHAT IS SO FUNNY ABOUT THIS.
NOT AGAIN!
SHLING
AID ME, MONKEY!

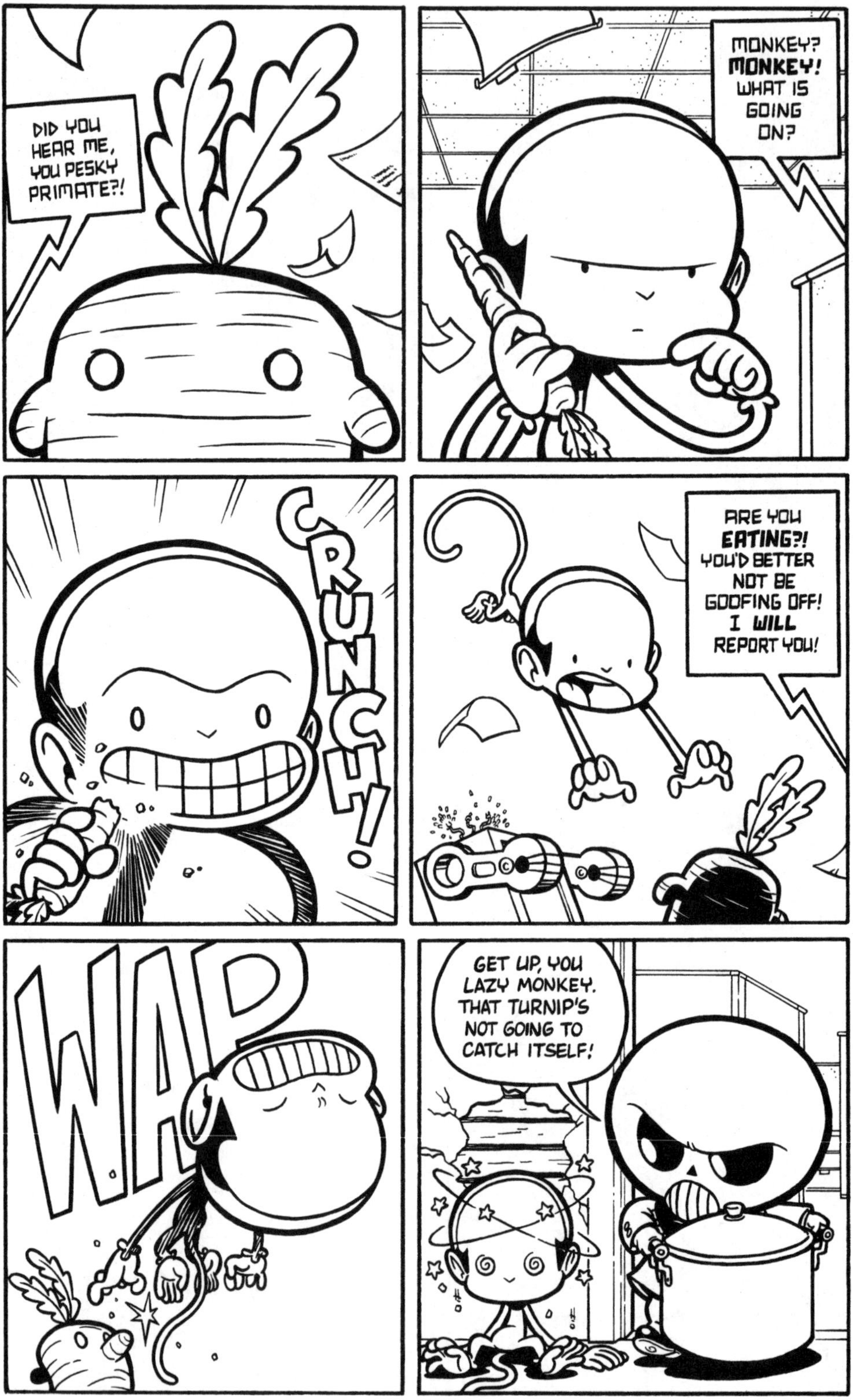
DID YOU HEAR ME, YOU PESKY PRIMATE?!
MONKEY? MONKEY! WHAT IS GOING ON?
CRUNCH!
ARE YOU EATING?! YOU'D BETTER NOT BE GOOFING OFF! I WILL REPORT YOU!
WAP
GET UP, YOU LAZY MONKEY. THAT TURNIP'S NOT GOING TO CATCH ITSELF!

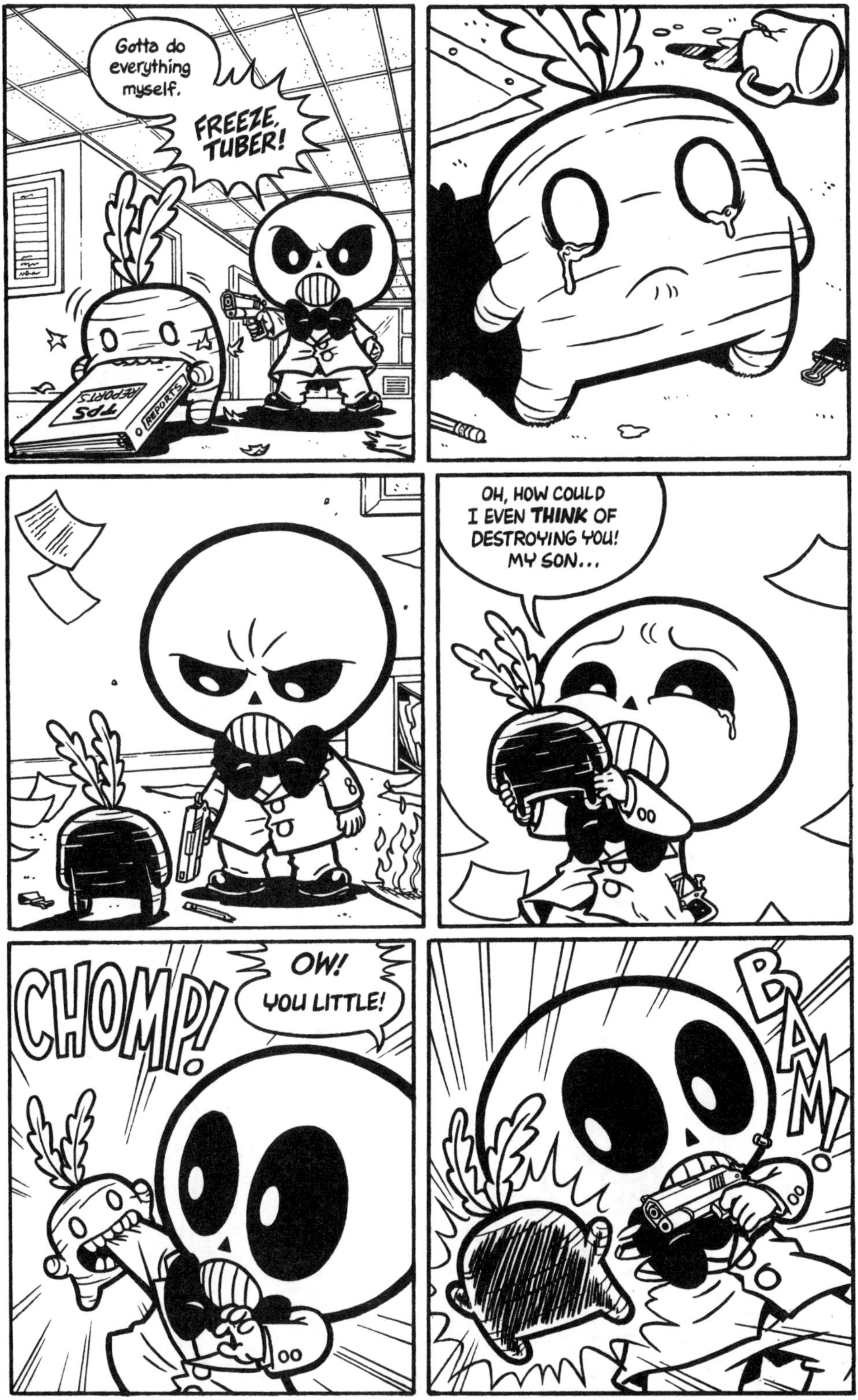
Gotta do everything myself.
FREEZE, TUBER!
TPS REPORTS
REPORTS
OH, HOW COULD I EVEN **THINK** OF DESTROYING YOU! MY SON...
CHOMP!
OW! YOU LITTLE!
BAM!

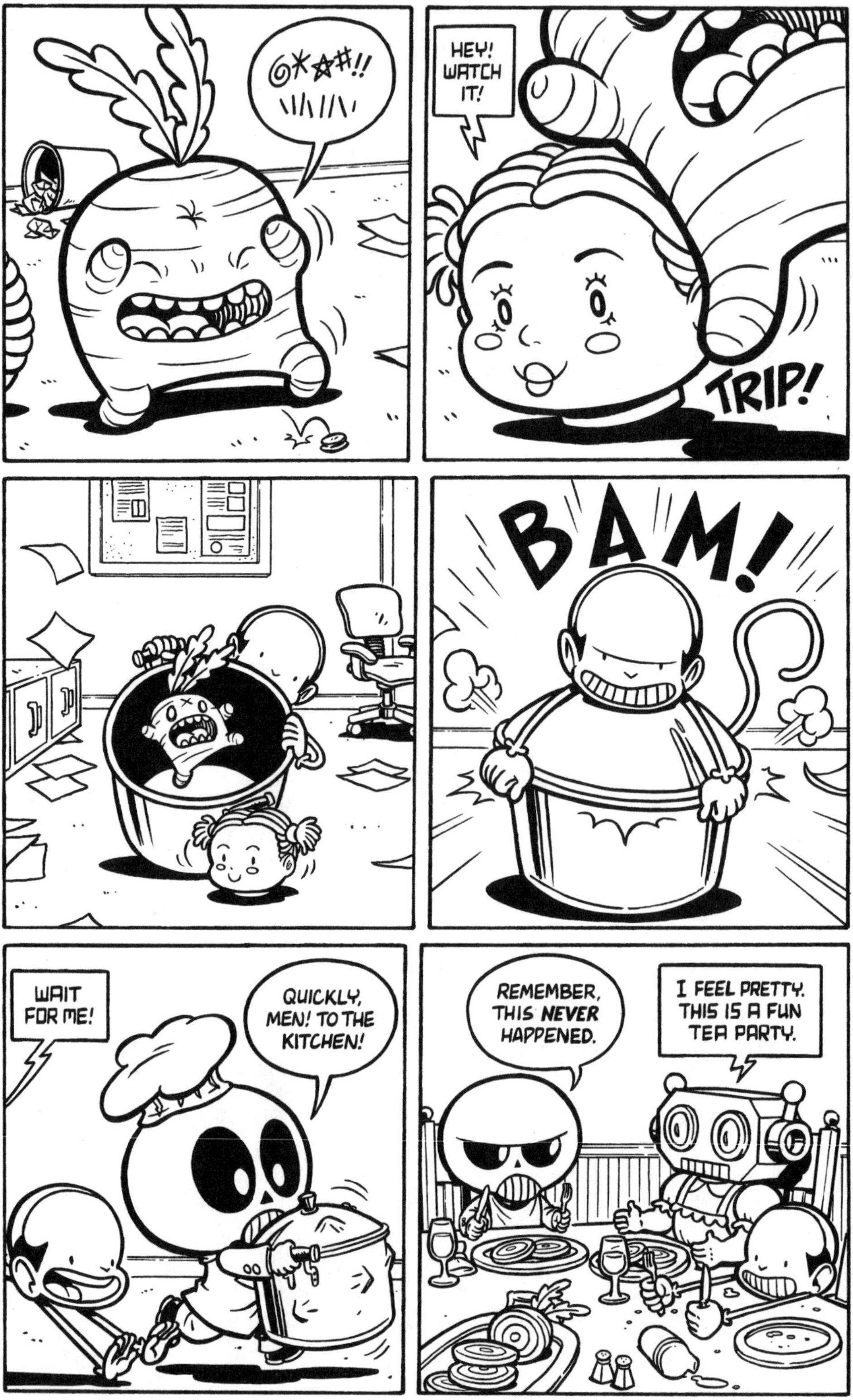

HEY! WATCH IT!
TRIP!
BAM!
WAIT FOR ME!
QUICKLY, MEN! TO THE KITCHEN!
REMEMBER, THIS NEVER HAPPENED.
I FEEL PRETTY. THIS IS A FUN TEA PARTY.

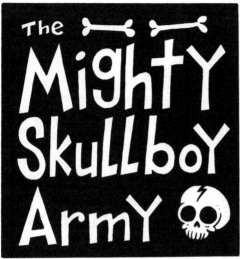

The Mighty Skullboy Army

ALL RIGHT, EVERYONE, TIME TO TURN IN YOUR BOOK REPORTS.

Books RIGHT?

THANK YOU, STACY.

THANK YOU, DWAYNE.

THANK YOU, uhhh...

KEVIN SCHUBERT, MA'AM. I'M SKULLBOY'S NEW INTERN. IT'S NICE TO MEET YOU.

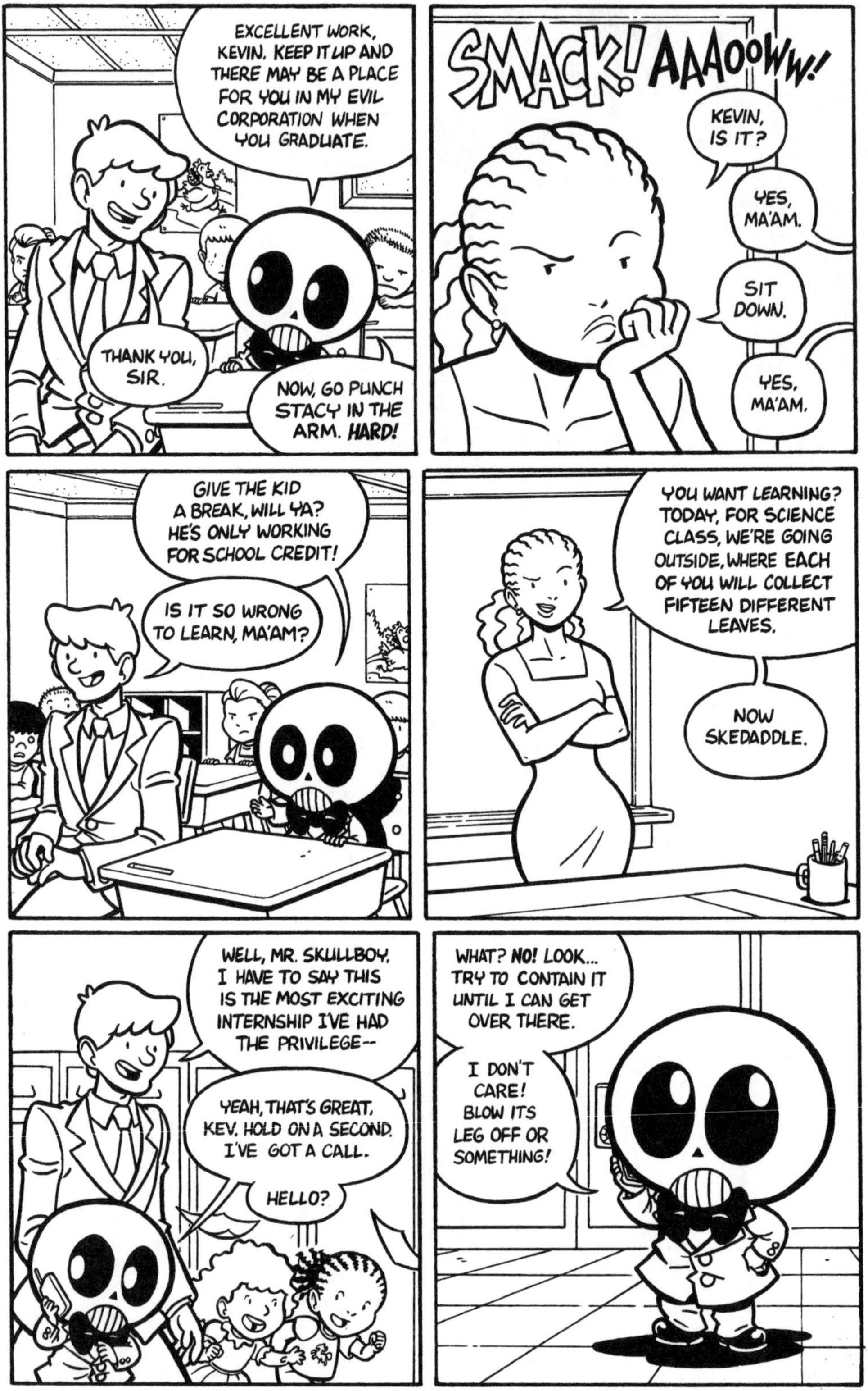
EXCELLENT WORK, KEVIN. KEEP IT UP AND THERE MAY BE A PLACE FOR YOU IN MY EVIL CORPORATION WHEN YOU GRADUATE.
THANK YOU, SIR.
NOW, GO PUNCH STACY IN THE ARM. **HARD!**
SMACK! AAAOOWW!
KEVIN, IS IT?
YES, MA'AM.
SIT DOWN.
YES, MA'AM.
GIVE THE KID A BREAK, WILL YA? HE'S ONLY WORKING FOR SCHOOL CREDIT!
IS IT SO WRONG TO LEARN, MA'AM?
YOU WANT LEARNING? TODAY, FOR SCIENCE CLASS, WE'RE GOING OUTSIDE, WHERE EACH OF YOU WILL COLLECT FIFTEEN DIFFERENT LEAVES.
NOW SKEDADDLE.
WELL, MR. SKULLBOY, I HAVE TO SAY THIS IS THE MOST EXCITING INTERNSHIP I'VE HAD THE PRIVILEGE--
YEAH, THAT'S GREAT, KEV. HOLD ON A SECOND. I'VE GOT A CALL.
HELLO?
WHAT? **NO!** LOOK... TRY TO CONTAIN IT UNTIL I CAN GET OVER THERE.
I DON'T CARE! BLOW ITS LEG OFF OR SOMETHING!

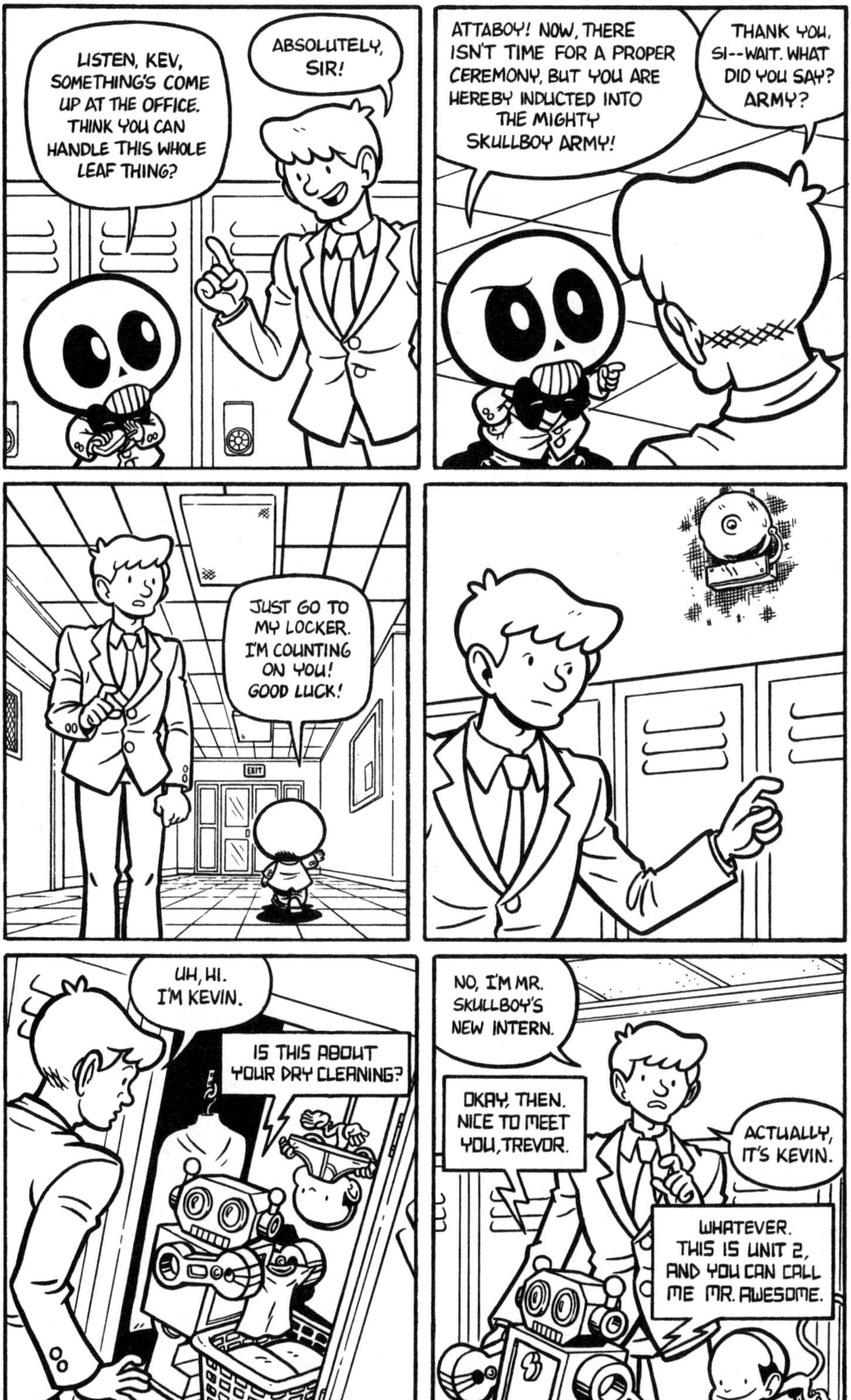
LISTEN, KEV, SOMETHING'S COME UP AT THE OFFICE. THINK YOU CAN HANDLE THIS WHOLE LEAF THING?
ABSOLUTELY, SIR!
ATTABOY! NOW, THERE ISN'T TIME FOR A PROPER CEREMONY, BUT YOU ARE HEREBY INDUCTED INTO THE MIGHTY SKULLBOY ARMY!
THANK YOU, SI--WAIT. WHAT DID YOU SAY? ARMY?
JUST GO TO MY LOCKER. I'M COUNTING ON YOU! GOOD LUCK!
EXIT
UH, HI. I'M KEVIN.
IS THIS ABOUT YOUR DRY CLEANING?
NO, I'M MR. SKULLBOY'S NEW INTERN.
OKAY, THEN. NICE TO MEET YOU, TREVOR.
ACTUALLY, IT'S KEVIN.
WHATEVER. THIS IS UNIT 2, AND YOU CAN CALL ME MR. AWESOME.

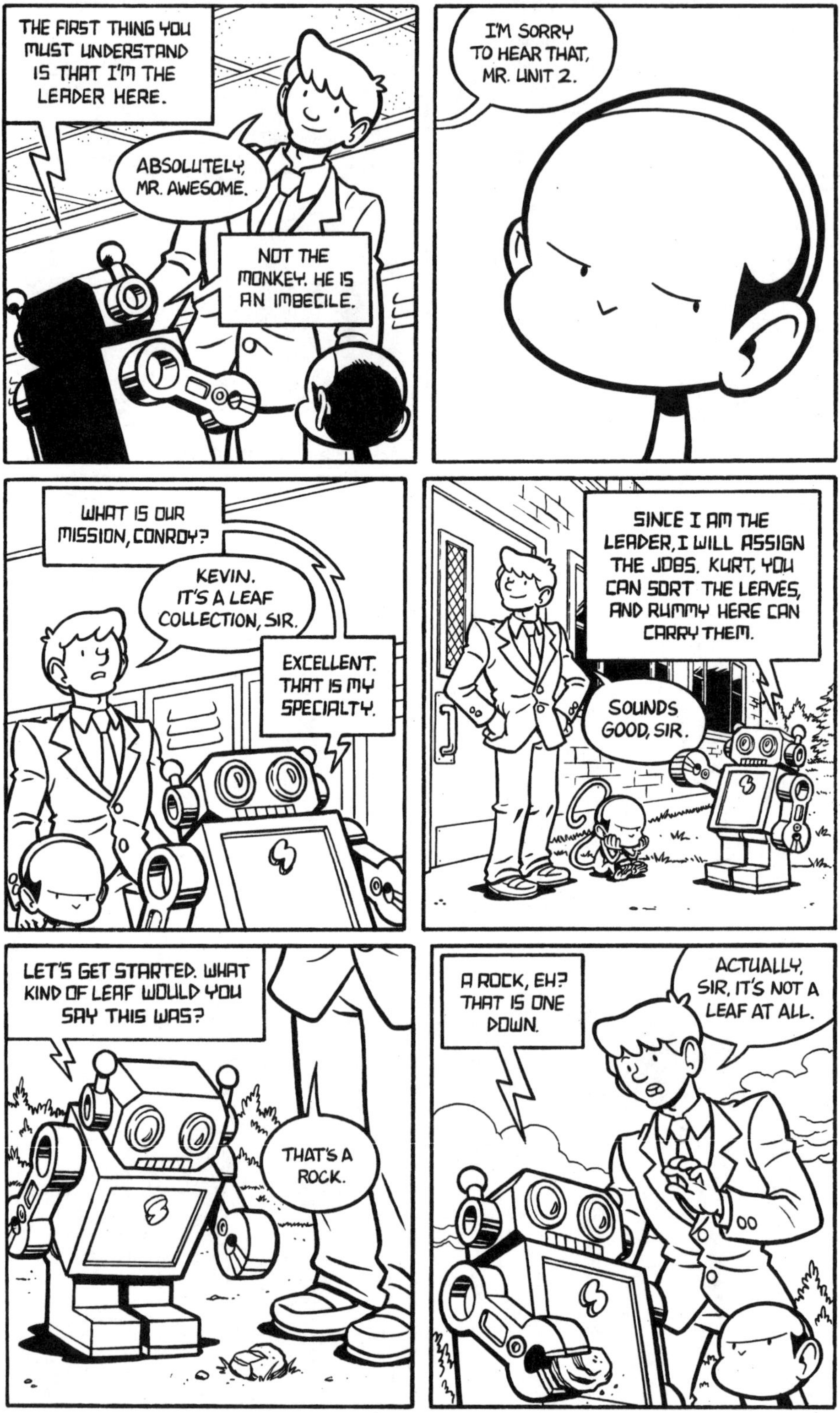
THE FIRST THING YOU MUST UNDERSTAND IS THAT I'M THE LEADER HERE.
ABSOLUTELY, MR. AWESOME.
NOT THE MONKEY. HE IS AN IMBECILE.
I'M SORRY TO HEAR THAT, MR. UNIT 2.
WHAT IS OUR MISSION, CONROY?
KEVIN. IT'S A LEAF COLLECTION, SIR.
EXCELLENT. THAT IS MY SPECIALTY.
SINCE I AM THE LEADER, I WILL ASSIGN THE JOBS. KURT, YOU CAN SORT THE LEAVES, AND RUMMY HERE CAN CARRY THEM.
SOUNDS GOOD, SIR.
LET'S GET STARTED. WHAT KIND OF LEAF WOULD YOU SAY THIS WAS?
THAT'S A ROCK.
A ROCK, EH? THAT IS ONE DOWN.
ACTUALLY, SIR, IT'S NOT A LEAF AT ALL.

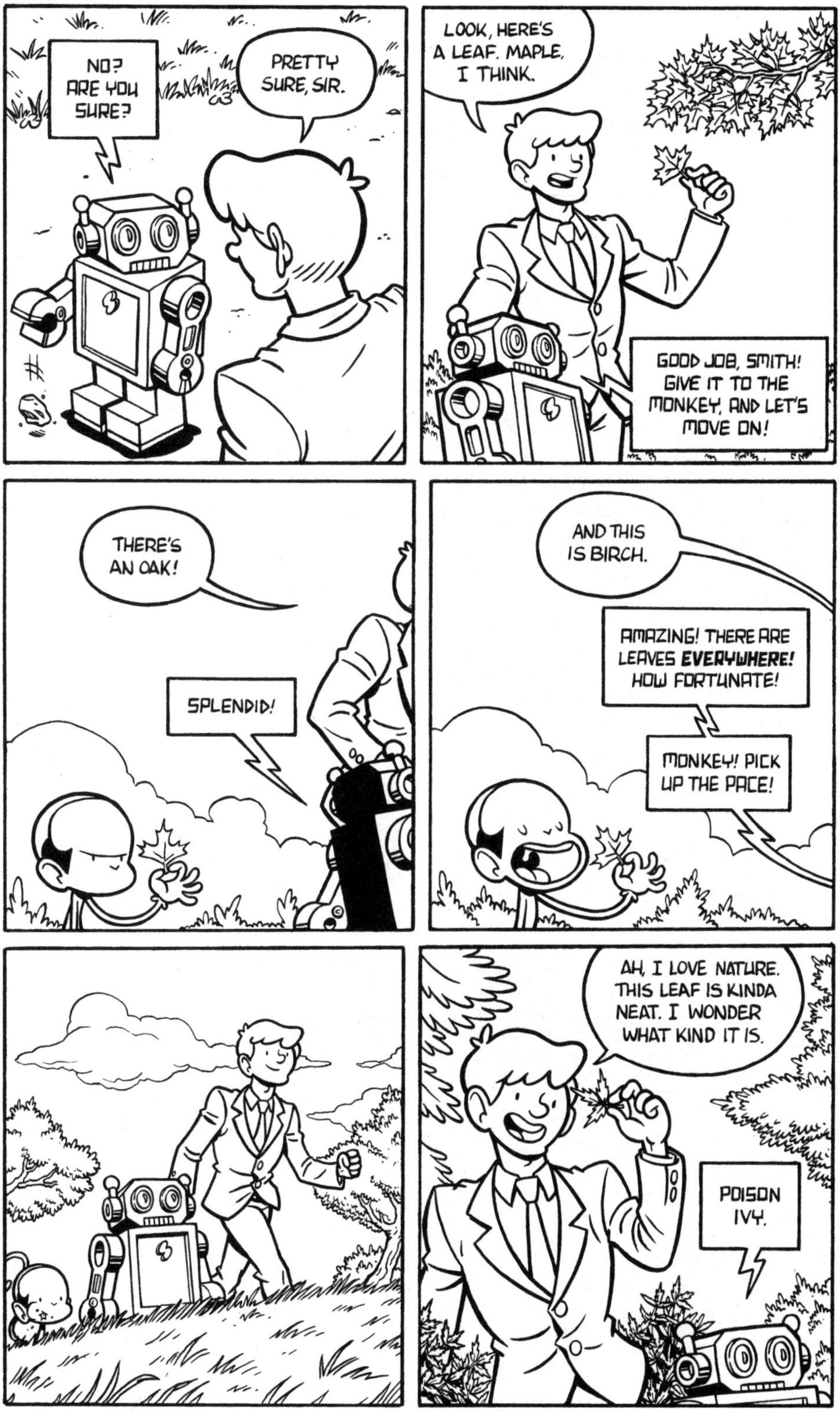
NO? ARE YOU SURE?
PRETTY SURE, SIR.
LOOK, HERE'S A LEAF. MAPLE, I THINK.
GOOD JOB, SMITH! GIVE IT TO THE MONKEY, AND LET'S MOVE ON!
THERE'S AN OAK!
SPLENDID!
AND THIS IS BIRCH.
AMAZING! THERE ARE LEAVES **EVERYWHERE!** HOW FORTUNATE!
MONKEY! PICK UP THE PACE!
AH, I LOVE NATURE. THIS LEAF IS KINDA NEAT. I WONDER WHAT KIND IT IS.
POISON IVY.

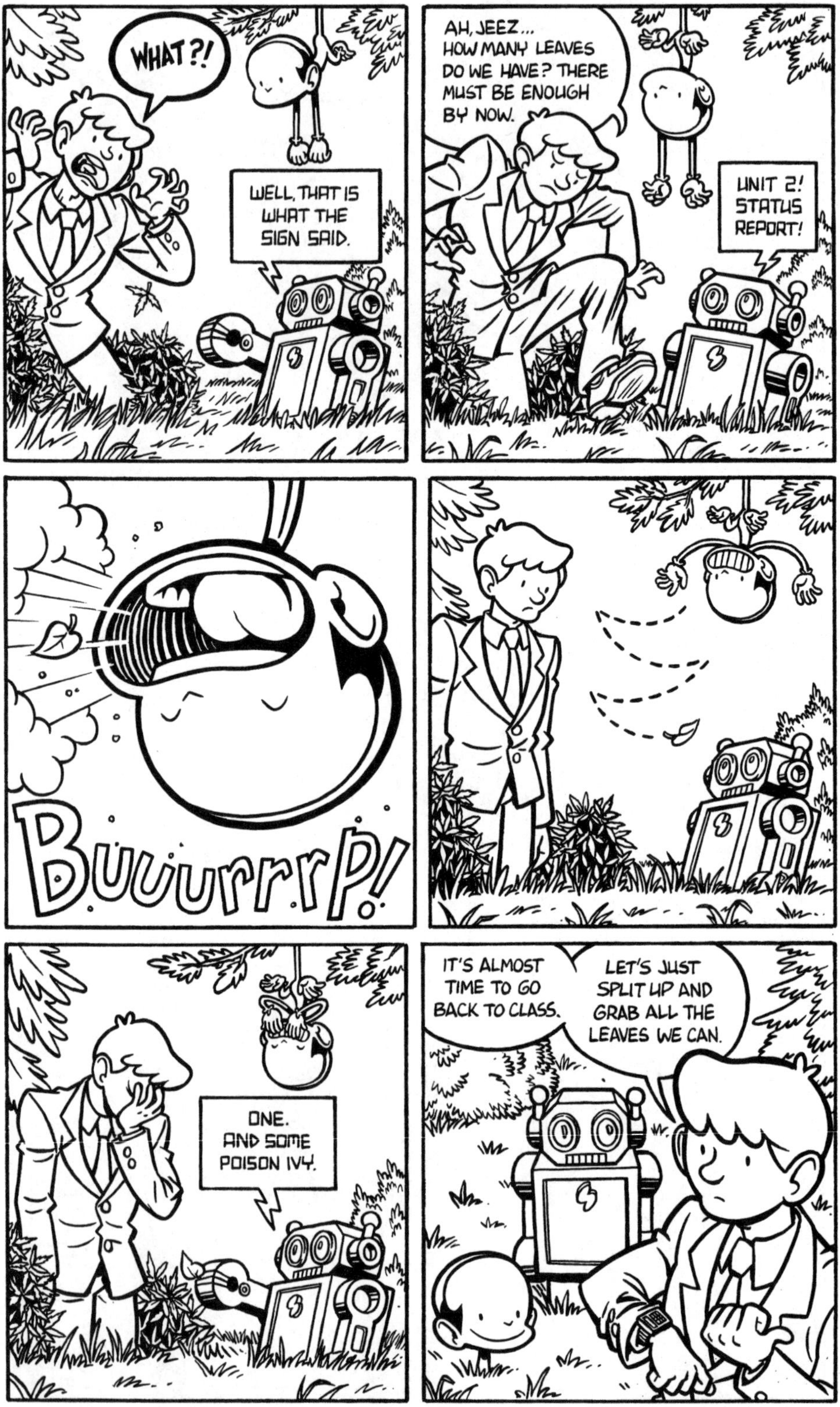
WHAT?!
WELL, THAT IS WHAT THE SIGN SAID.
AH, JEEZ... HOW MANY LEAVES DO WE HAVE? THERE MUST BE ENOUGH BY NOW.
UNIT 2! STATUS REPORT!
Buuurrrp!
ONE. AND SOME POISON IVY.
IT'S ALMOST TIME TO GO BACK TO CLASS.
LET'S JUST SPLIT UP AND GRAB ALL THE LEAVES WE CAN.

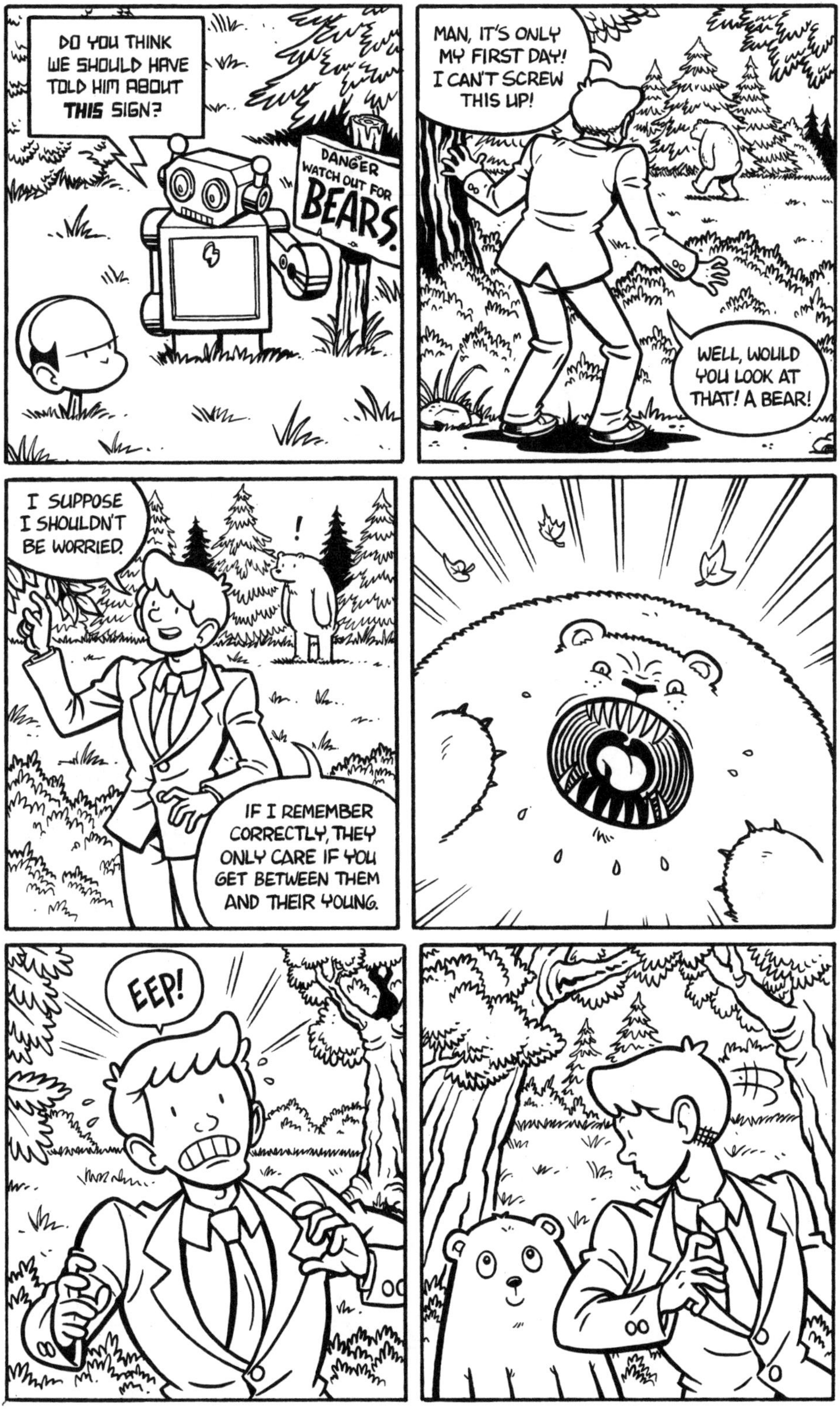
DO YOU THINK WE SHOULD HAVE TOLD HIM ABOUT **THIS** SIGN?
DANGER WATCH OUT FOR BEARS.
MAN, IT'S ONLY MY FIRST DAY! I CAN'T SCREW THIS UP!
WELL, WOULD YOU LOOK AT THAT! A BEAR!
I SUPPOSE I SHOULDN'T BE WORRIED.
!
IF I REMEMBER CORRECTLY, THEY ONLY CARE IF YOU GET BETWEEN THEM AND THEIR YOUNG.
EEP!

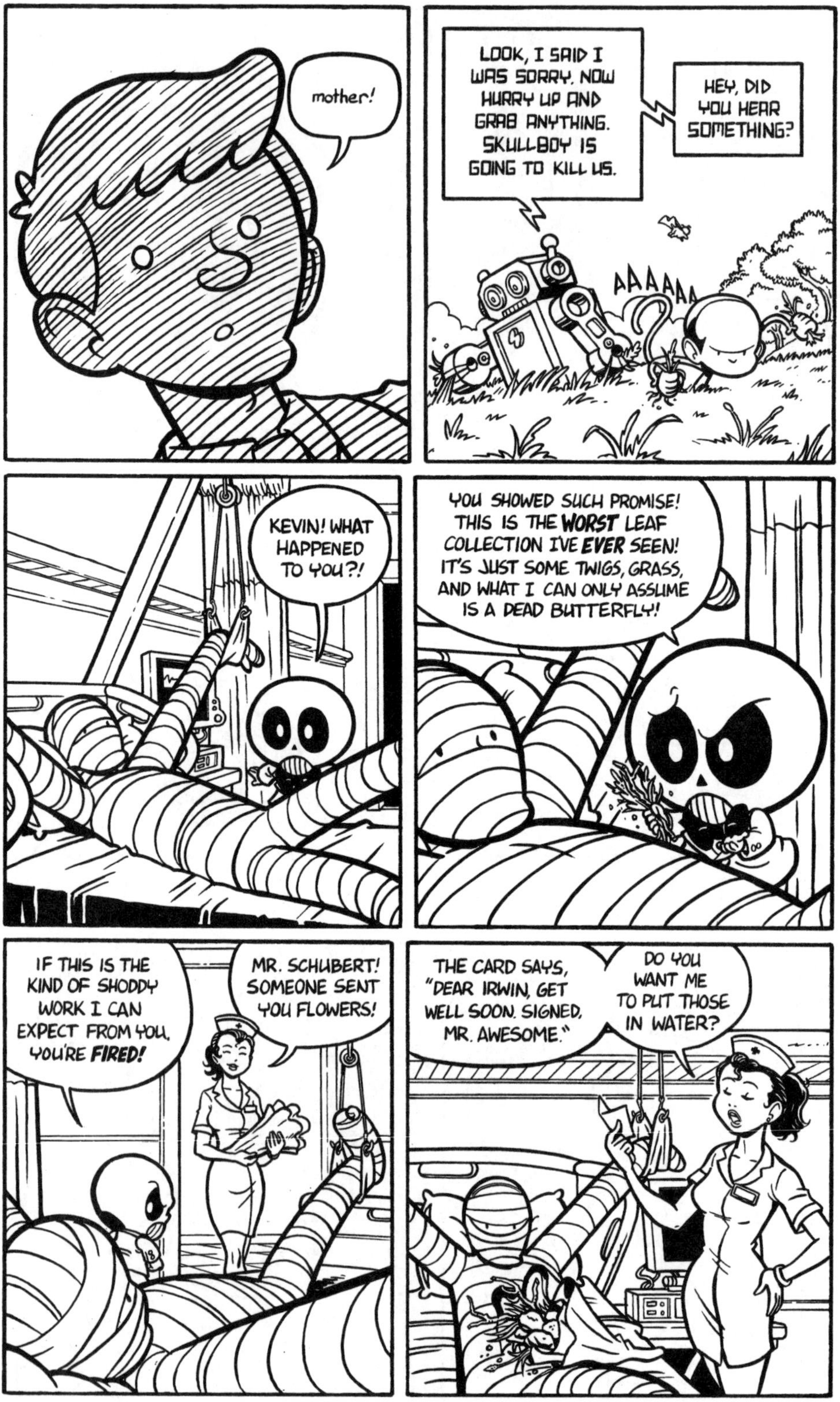
mother!
LOOK, I SAID I WAS SORRY. NOW HURRY UP AND GRAB ANYTHING. SKULLBOY IS GOING TO KILL US.
HEY, DID YOU HEAR SOMETHING?
AAAAAA
KEVIN! WHAT HAPPENED TO YOU?!
YOU SHOWED SUCH PROMISE! THIS IS THE WORST LEAF COLLECTION I'VE EVER SEEN! IT'S JUST SOME TWIGS, GRASS, AND WHAT I CAN ONLY ASSUME IS A DEAD BUTTERFLY!
IF THIS IS THE KIND OF SHODDY WORK I CAN EXPECT FROM YOU, YOU'RE FIRED!
MR. SCHUBERT! SOMEONE SENT YOU FLOWERS!
THE CARD SAYS, "DEAR IRWIN, GET WELL SOON. SIGNED, MR. AWESOME."
DO YOU WANT ME TO PUT THOSE IN WATER?

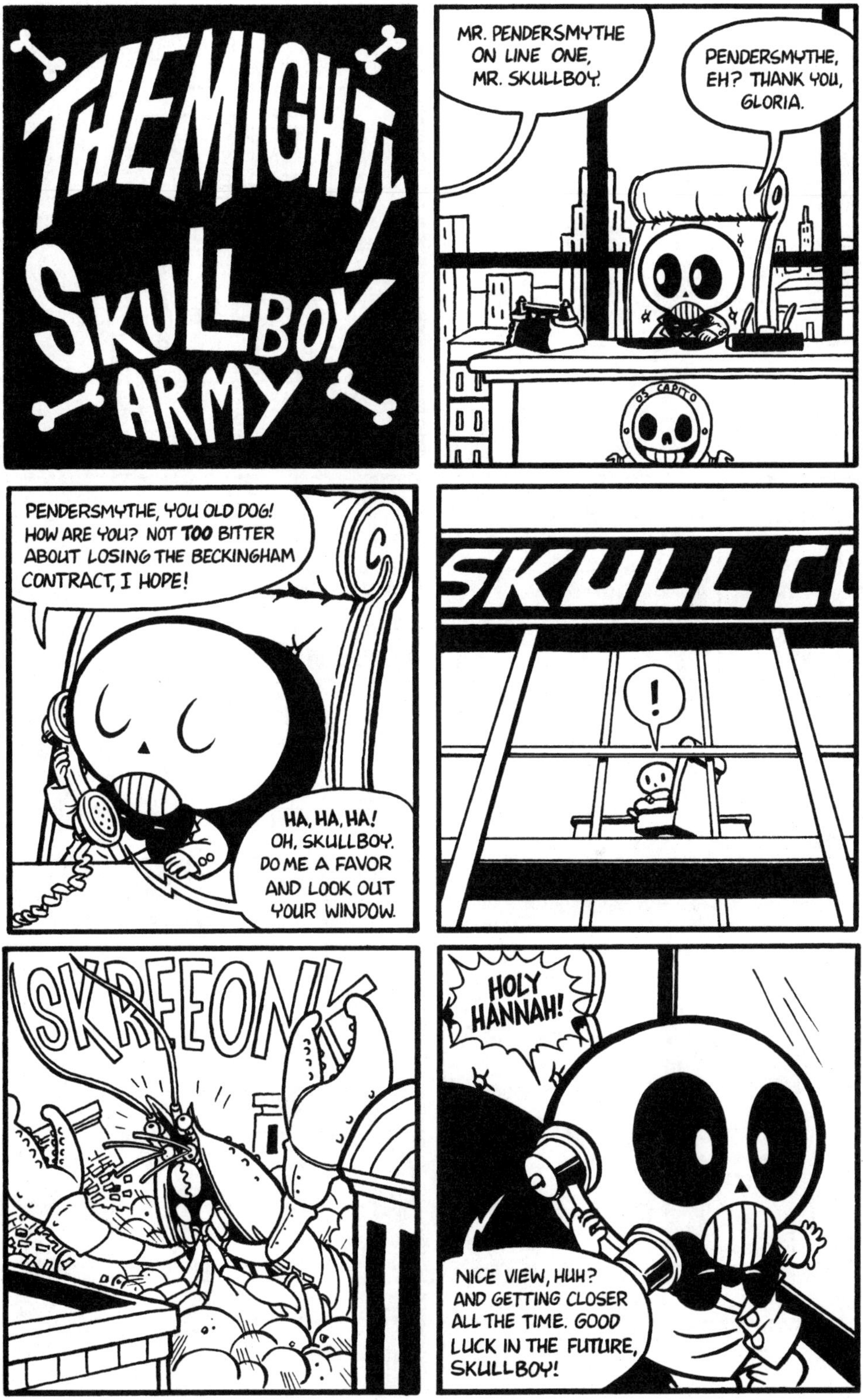
THE MIGHTY SKULLBOY ARMY
MR. PENDERSMYTHE ON LINE ONE, MR. SKULLBOY.
PENDERSMYTHE, EH? THANK YOU, GLORIA.
OS CAPITO
PENDERSMYTHE, YOU OLD DOG! HOW ARE YOU? NOT **TOO** BITTER ABOUT LOSING THE BECKINGHAM CONTRACT, I HOPE!
HA, HA, HA! OH, SKULLBOY. DO ME A FAVOR AND LOOK OUT YOUR WINDOW.
SKULL CO
!
SKREEONK
HOLY HANNAH!
NICE VIEW, HUH? AND GETTING CLOSER ALL THE TIME. GOOD LUCK IN THE FUTURE, SKULLBOY!

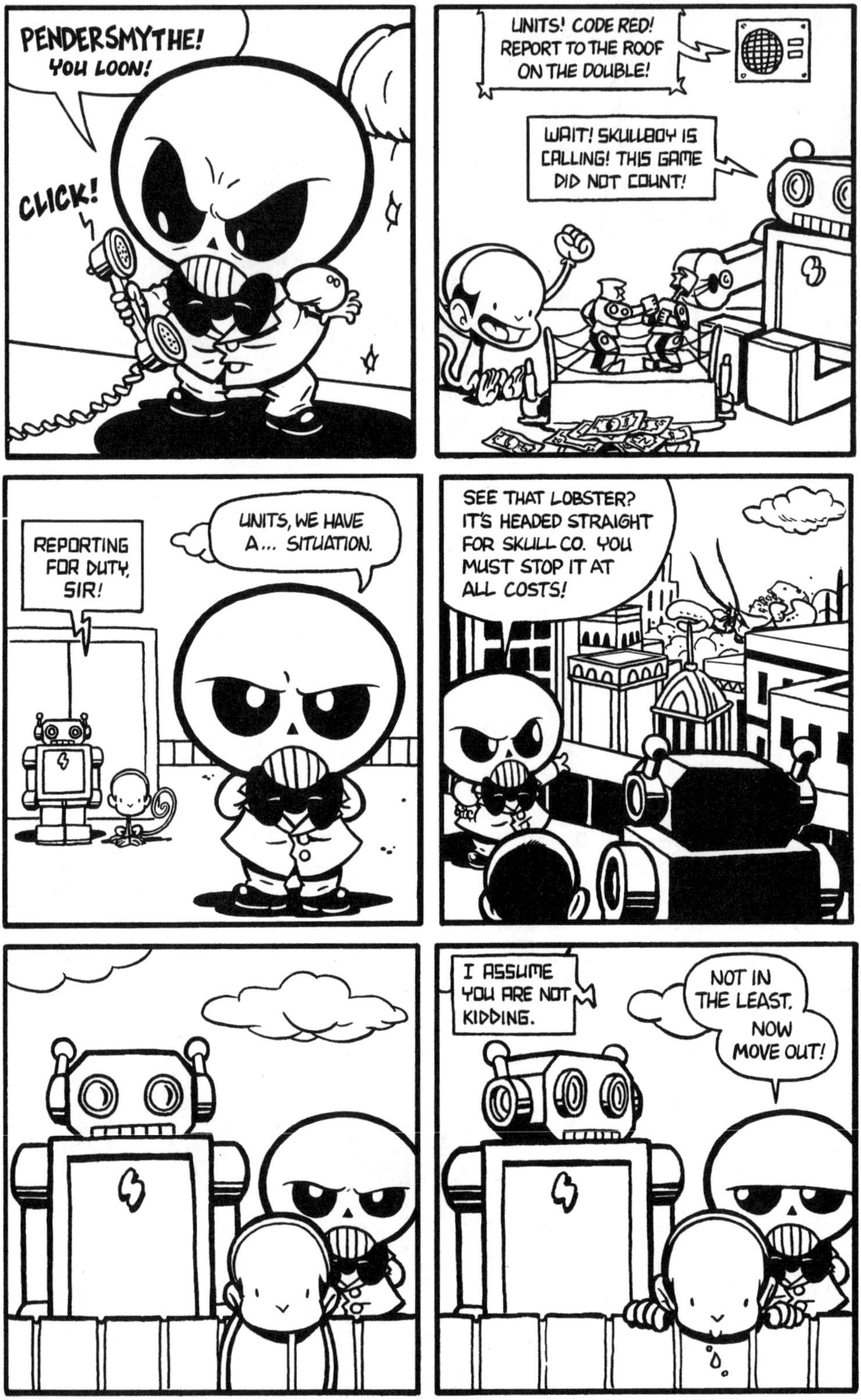
PENDERSMYTHE! YOU LOON!
CLICK!
UNITS! CODE RED! REPORT TO THE ROOF ON THE DOUBLE!
WAIT! SKULLBOY IS CALLING! THIS GAME DID NOT COUNT!
REPORTING FOR DUTY, SIR!
UNITS, WE HAVE A... SITUATION.
SEE THAT LOBSTER? IT'S HEADED STRAIGHT FOR SKULL CO. YOU MUST STOP IT AT ALL COSTS!
I ASSUME YOU ARE NOT KIDDING.
NOT IN THE LEAST. NOW MOVE OUT!

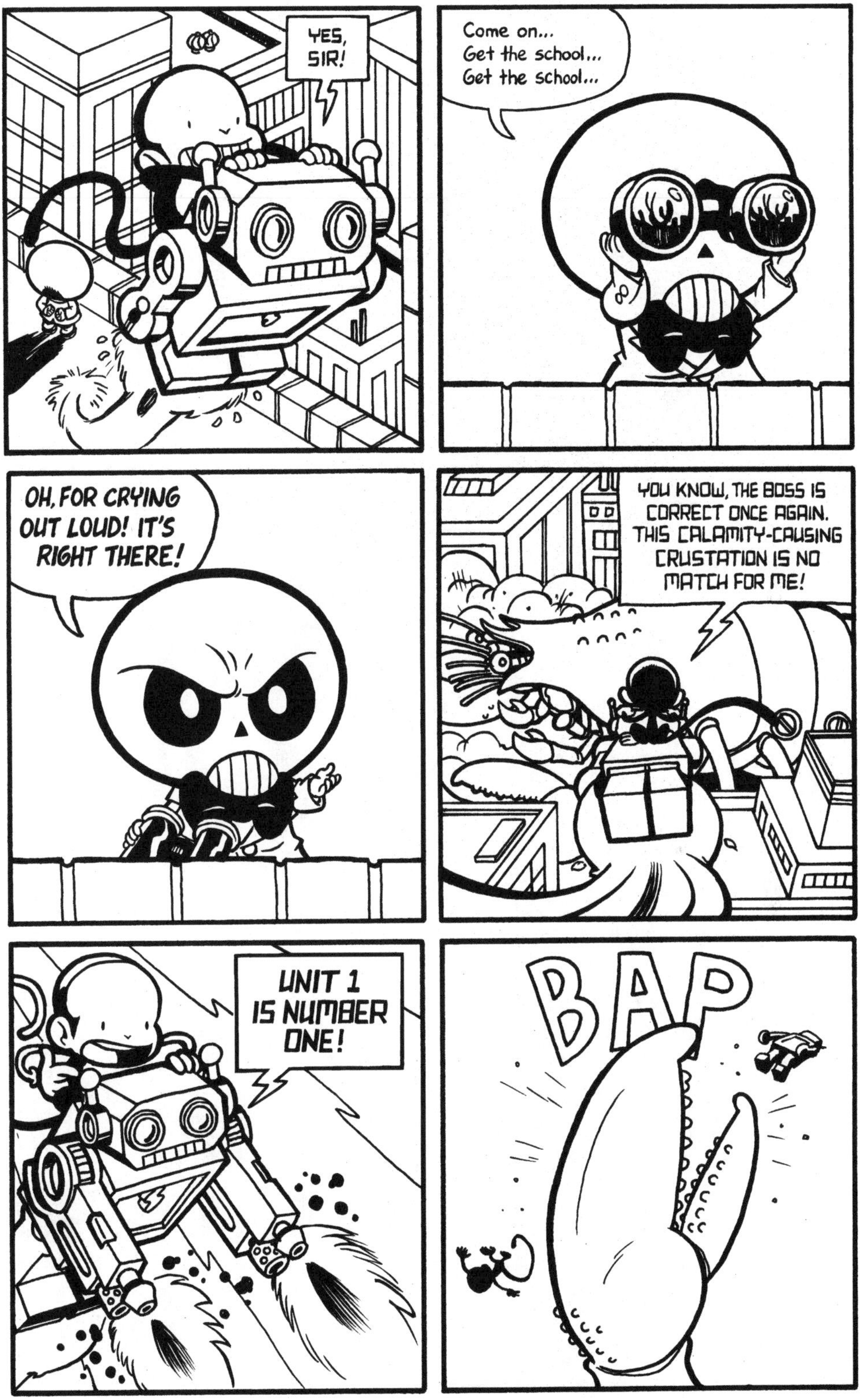
YES, SIR!
Come on...
Get the school...
Get the school...
OH, FOR CRYING OUT LOUD! IT'S RIGHT THERE!
YOU KNOW, THE BOSS IS CORRECT ONCE AGAIN. THIS CALAMITY-CAUSING CRUSTATION IS NO MATCH FOR ME!
UNIT 1 IS NUMBER ONE!
BAP

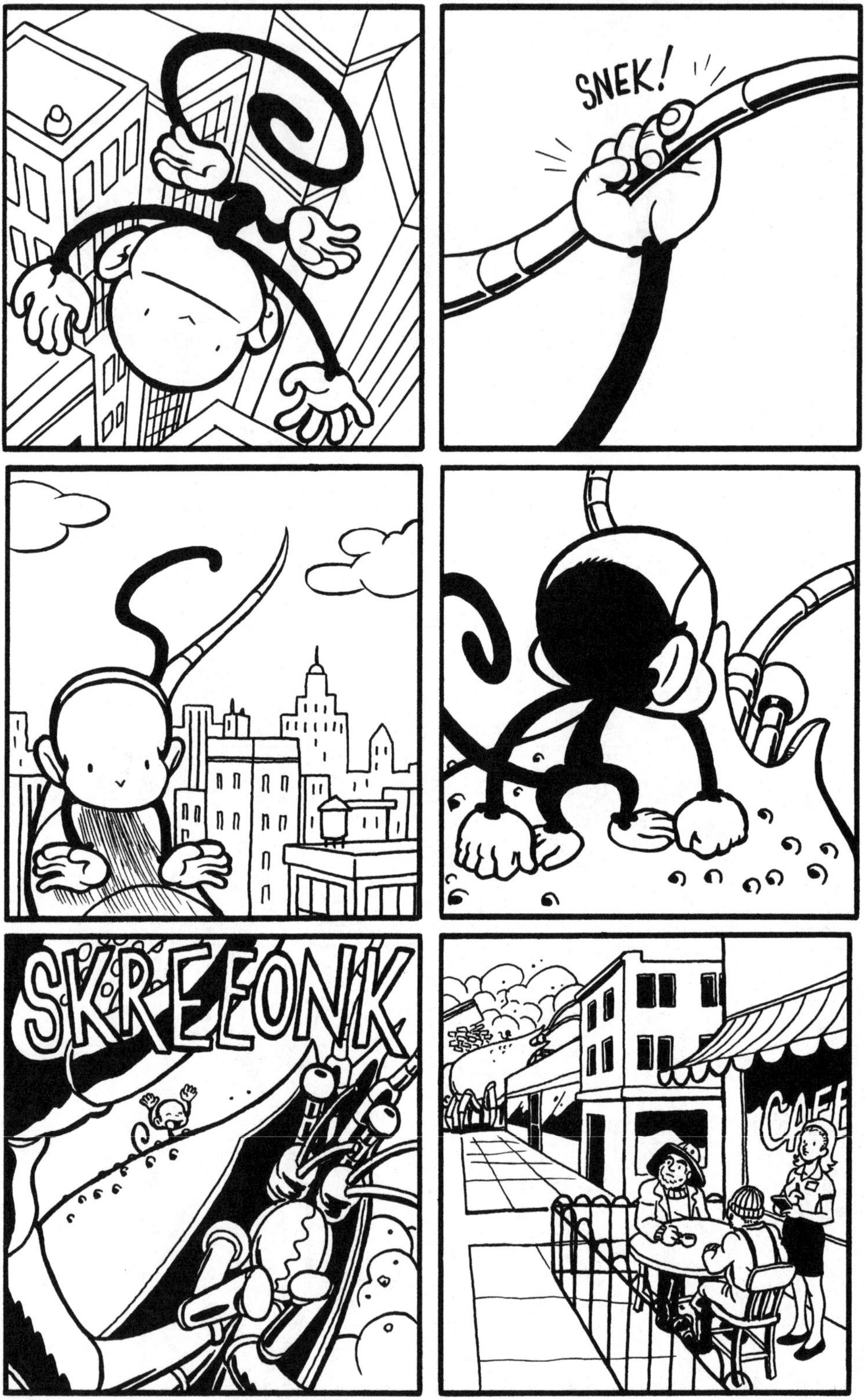
SNEK!
SKREEONK
CAFE

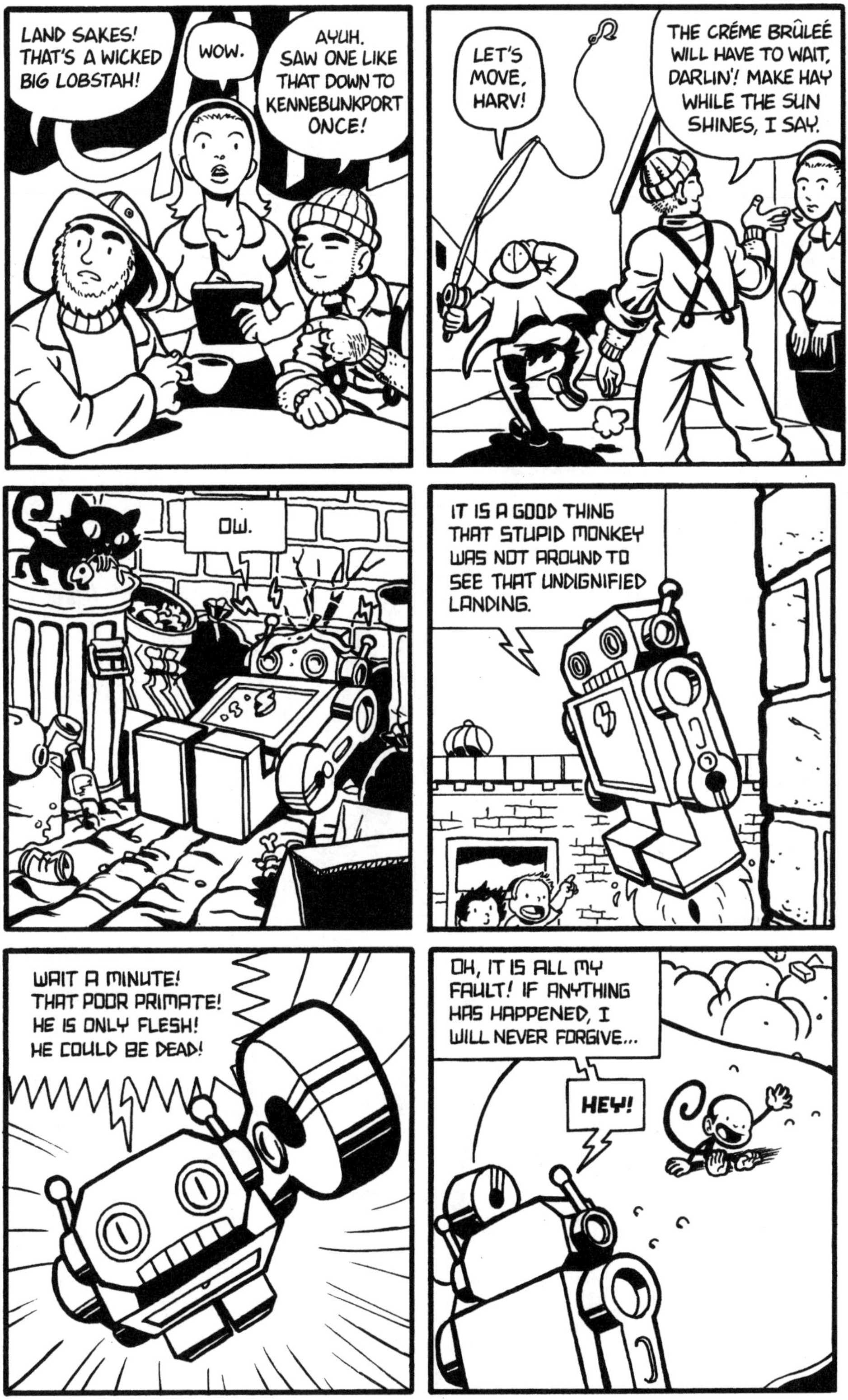
LAND SAKES! THAT'S A WICKED BIG LOBSTAH!
WOW.
AYUH. SAW ONE LIKE THAT DOWN TO KENNEBUNKPORT ONCE!
LET'S MOVE, HARV!
THE CRÉME BRÛLEÉ WILL HAVE TO WAIT, DARLIN'! MAKE HAY WHILE THE SUN SHINES, I SAY.
OW.
IT IS A GOOD THING THAT STUPID MONKEY WAS NOT AROUND TO SEE THAT UNDIGNIFIED LANDING.
WAIT A MINUTE! THAT POOR PRIMATE! HE IS ONLY FLESH! HE COULD BE DEAD!
OH, IT IS ALL MY FAULT! IF ANYTHING HAS HAPPENED, I WILL NEVER FORGIVE...
HEY!

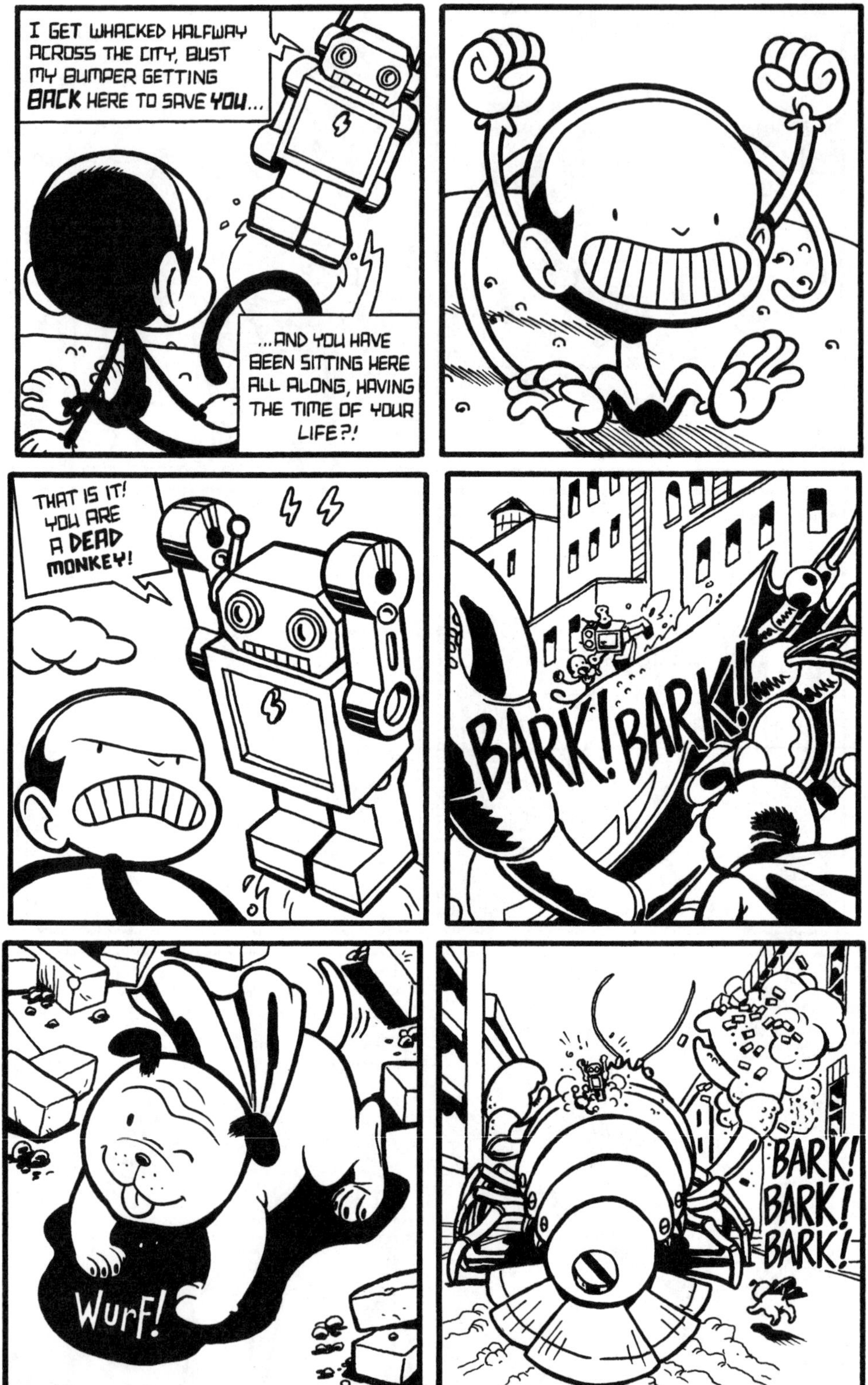
I GET WHACKED HALFWAY ACROSS THE CITY, BUST MY BUMPER GETTING BACK HERE TO SAVE YOU...
...AND YOU HAVE BEEN SITTING HERE ALL ALONG, HAVING THE TIME OF YOUR LIFE?!
THAT IS IT! YOU ARE A DEAD MONKEY!
BARK! BARK!
WURF!
BARK! BARK! BARK!

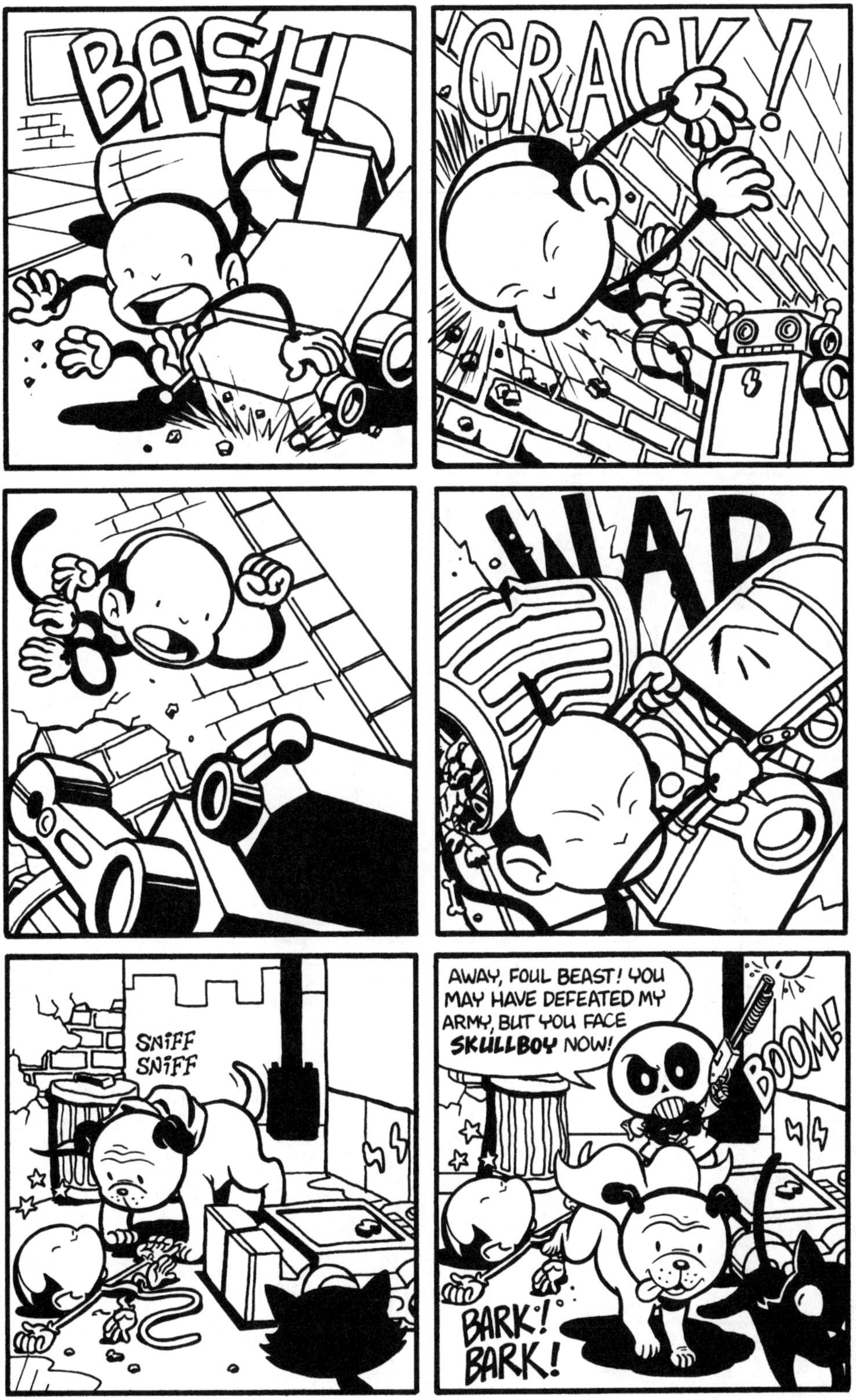
BASH
CRACK!
WAP
SNIFF SNIFF
AWAY, FOUL BEAST! YOU MAY HAVE DEFEATED MY ARMY, BUT YOU FACE SKULLBOY NOW!
BOOM!
BARK! BARK!

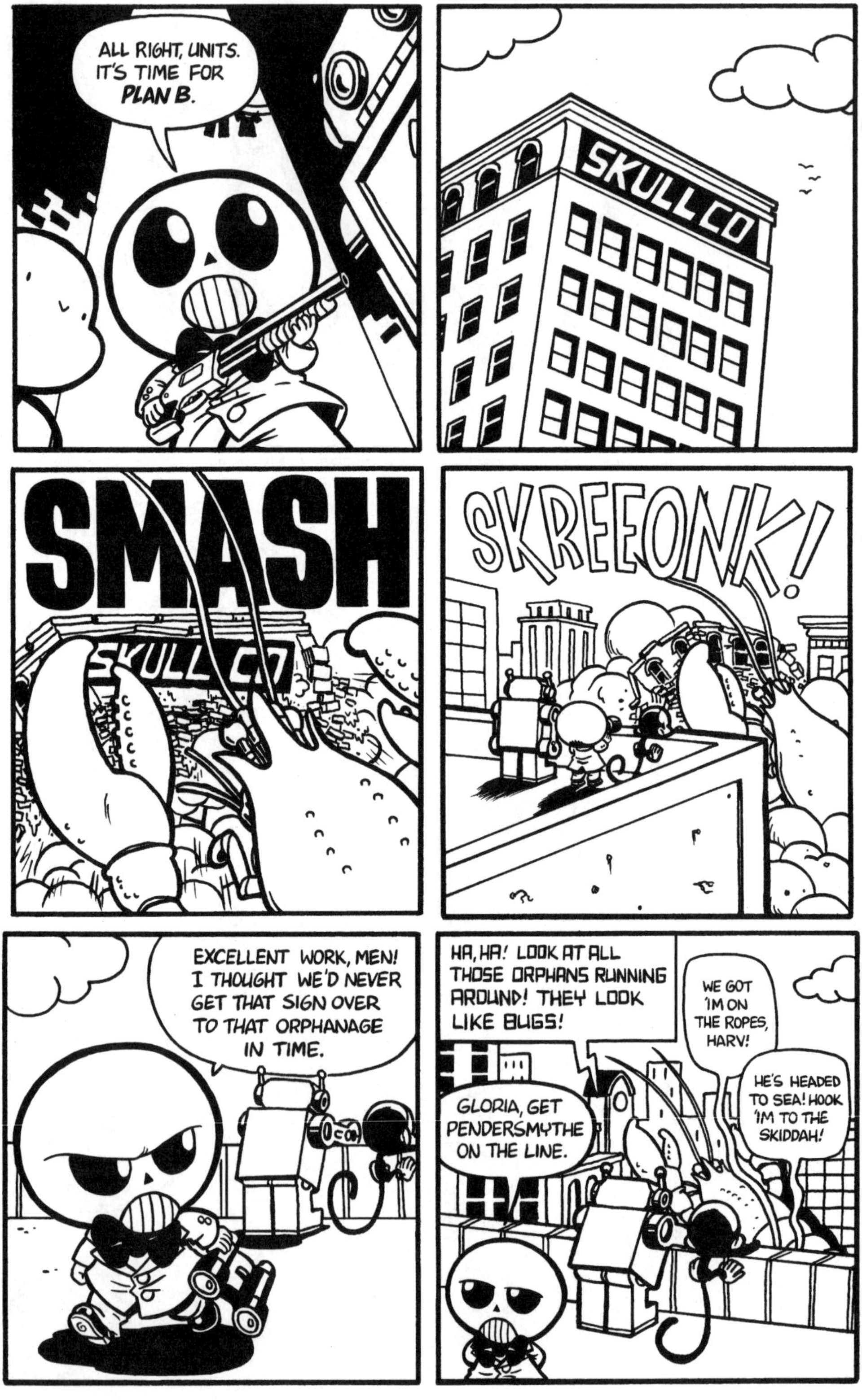
ALL RIGHT, UNITS. IT'S TIME FOR PLAN B.
SKULL CO
SMASH
SKULL CO
SKREEONK!
EXCELLENT WORK, MEN! I THOUGHT WE'D NEVER GET THAT SIGN OVER TO THAT ORPHANAGE IN TIME.
HA, HA! LOOK AT ALL THOSE ORPHANS RUNNING AROUND! THEY LOOK LIKE BUGS!
WE GOT 'IM ON THE ROPES, HARV!
HE'S HEADED TO SEA! HOOK 'IM TO THE SKIDDAH!
GLORIA, GET PENDERSMYTHE ON THE LINE.

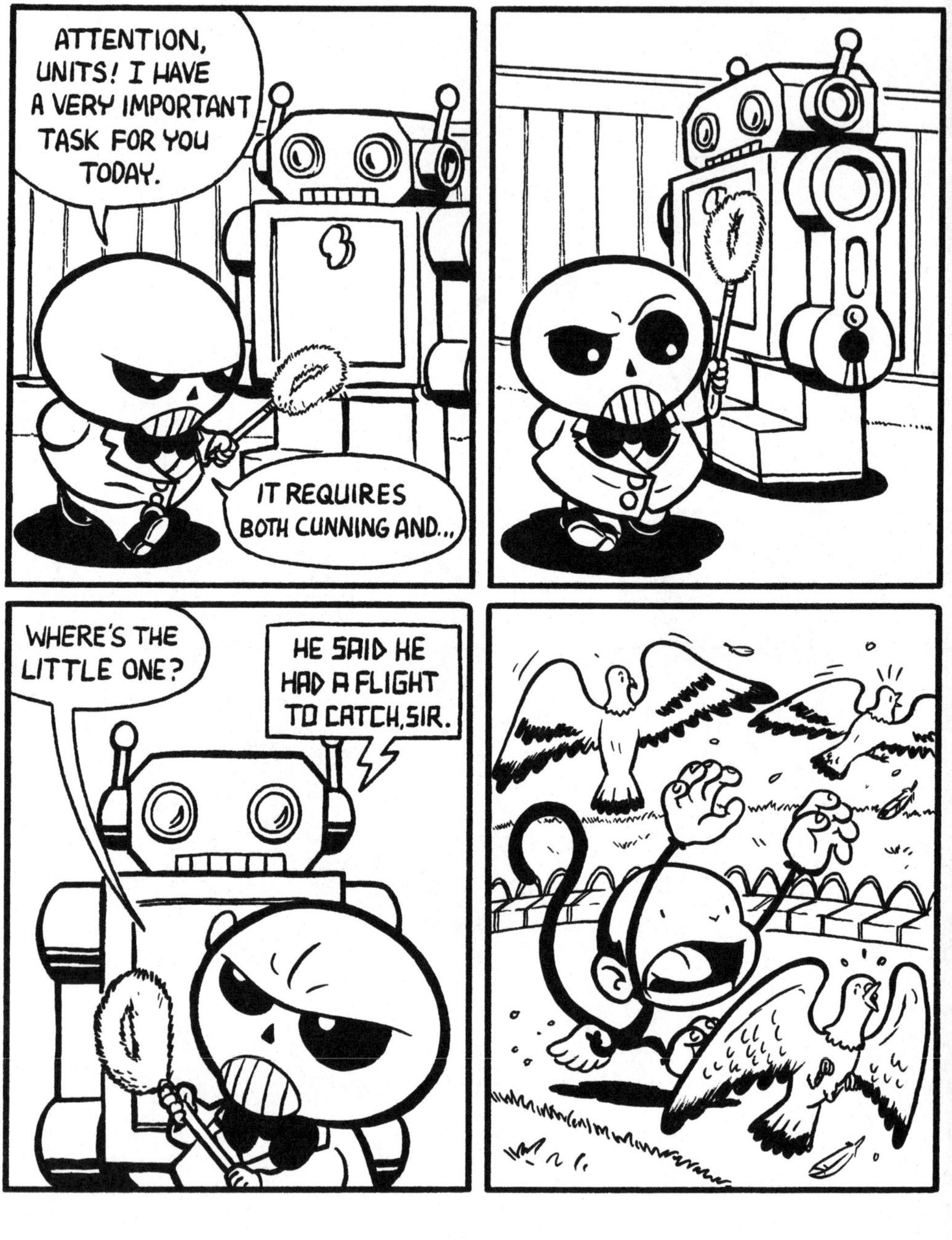
ATTENTION, UNITS! I HAVE A VERY IMPORTANT TASK FOR YOU TODAY.
IT REQUIRES BOTH CUNNING AND...
WHERE'S THE LITTLE ONE?
HE SAID HE HAD A FLIGHT TO CATCH, SIR.

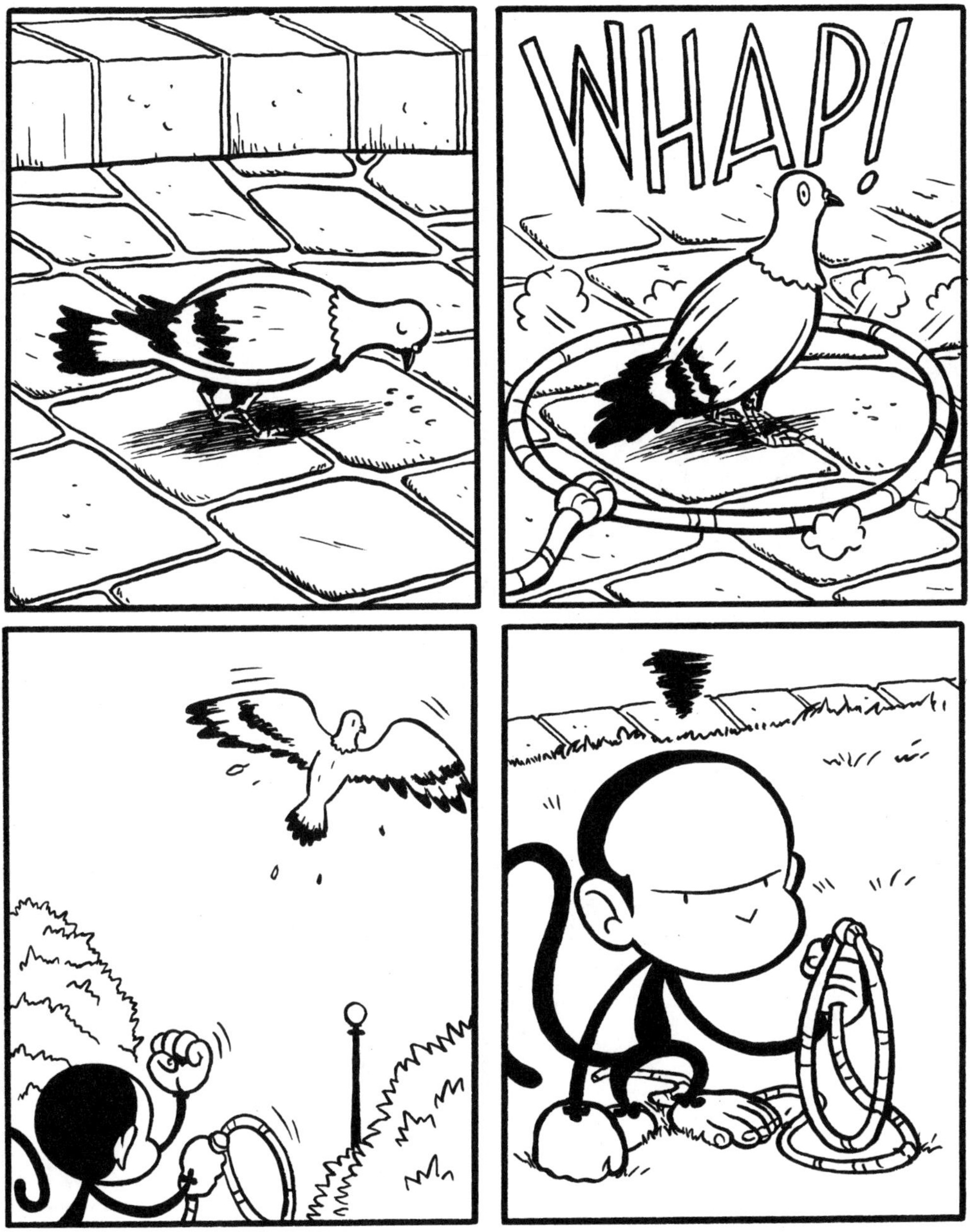
WHAP!

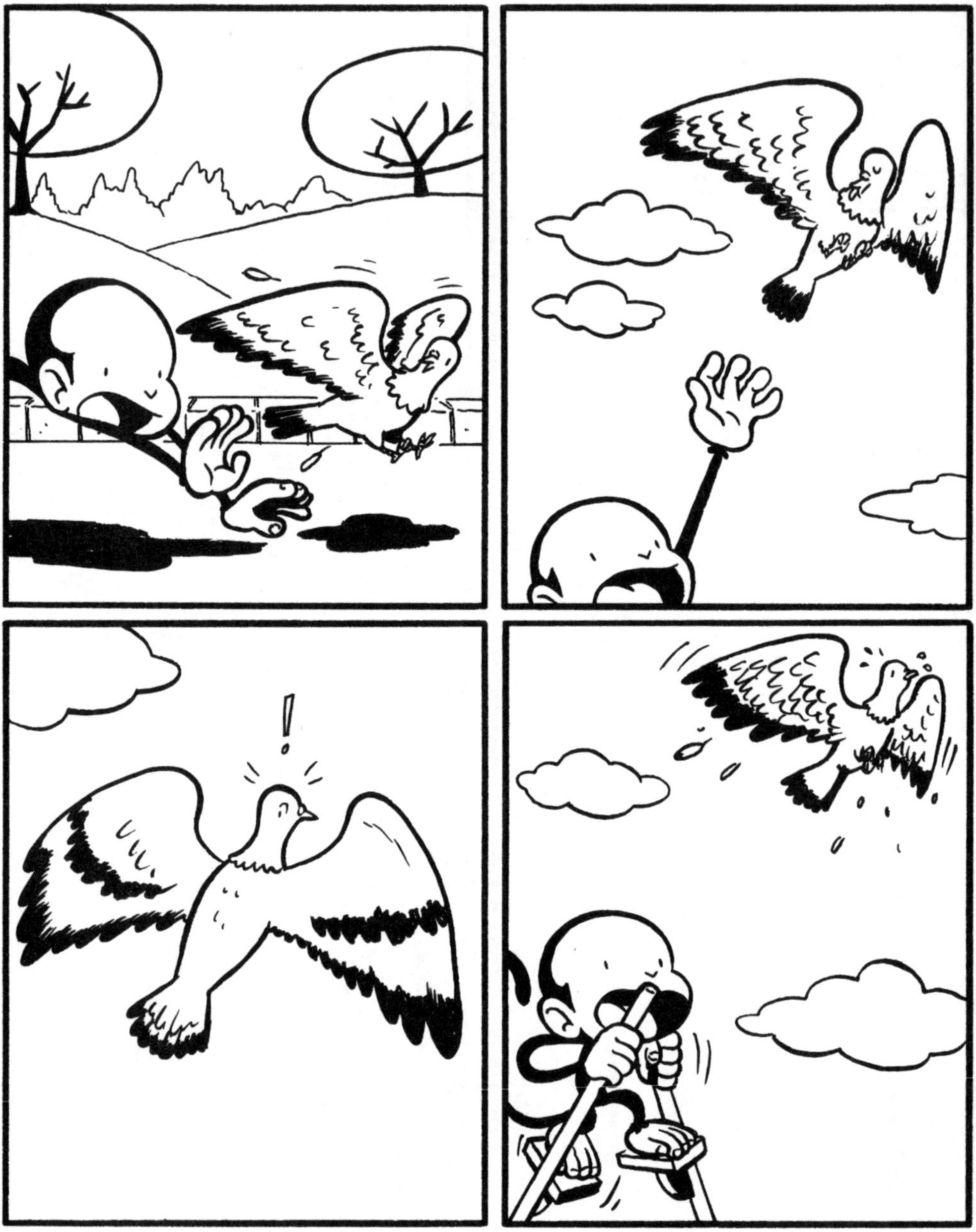
!

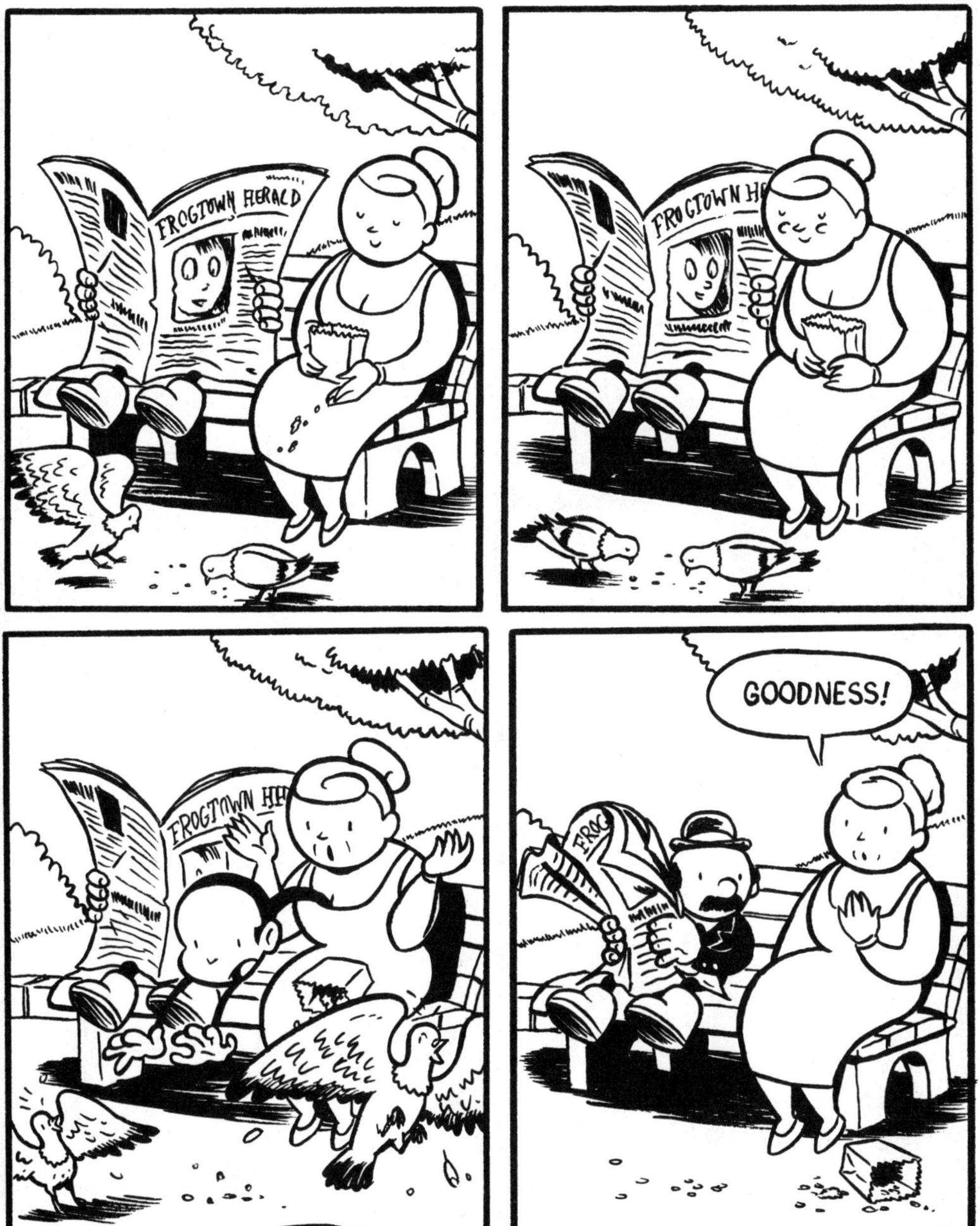
FROGTOWN HERALD
FROGTOWN H
FROGTOWN H
GOODNESS!

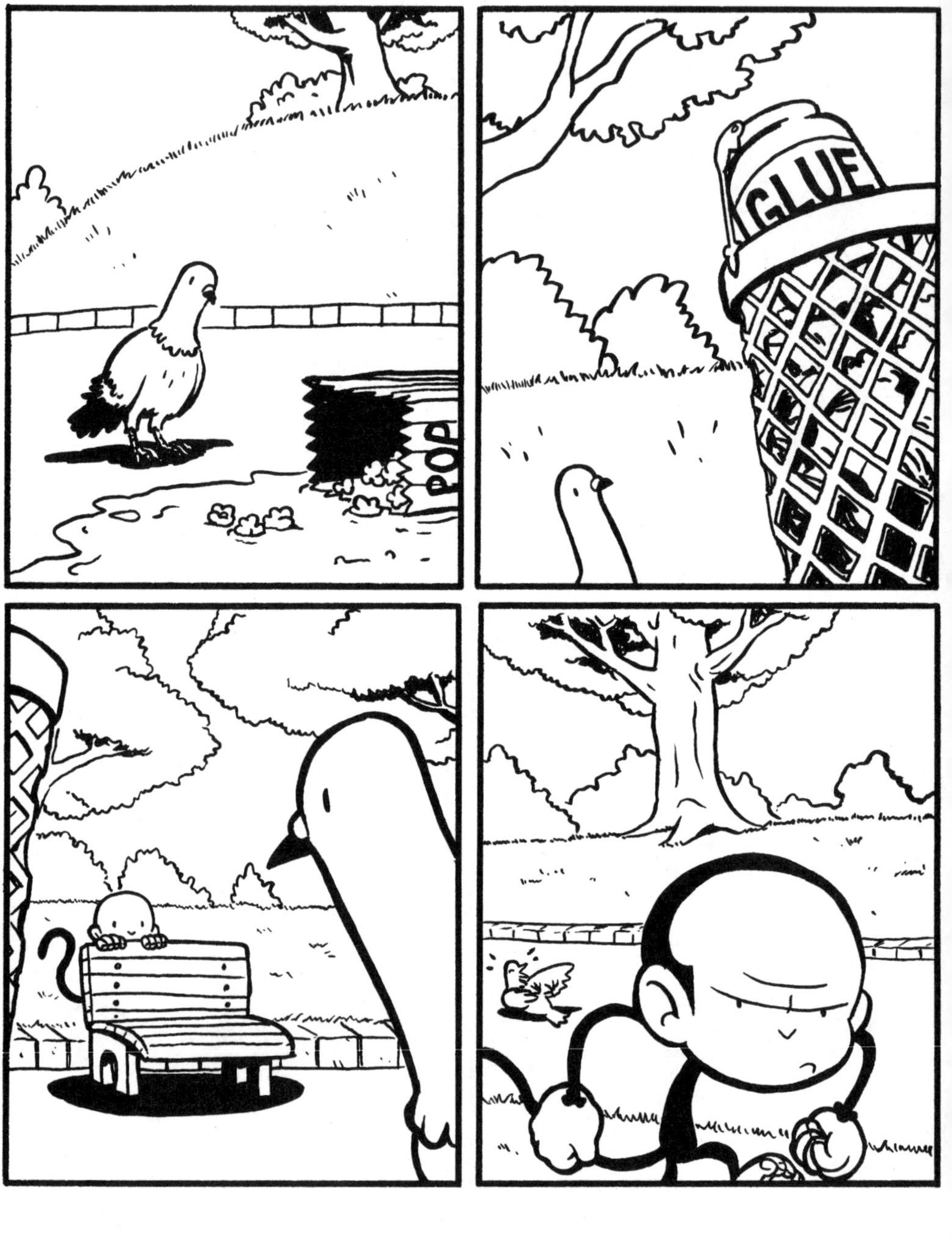
POP
GLUE

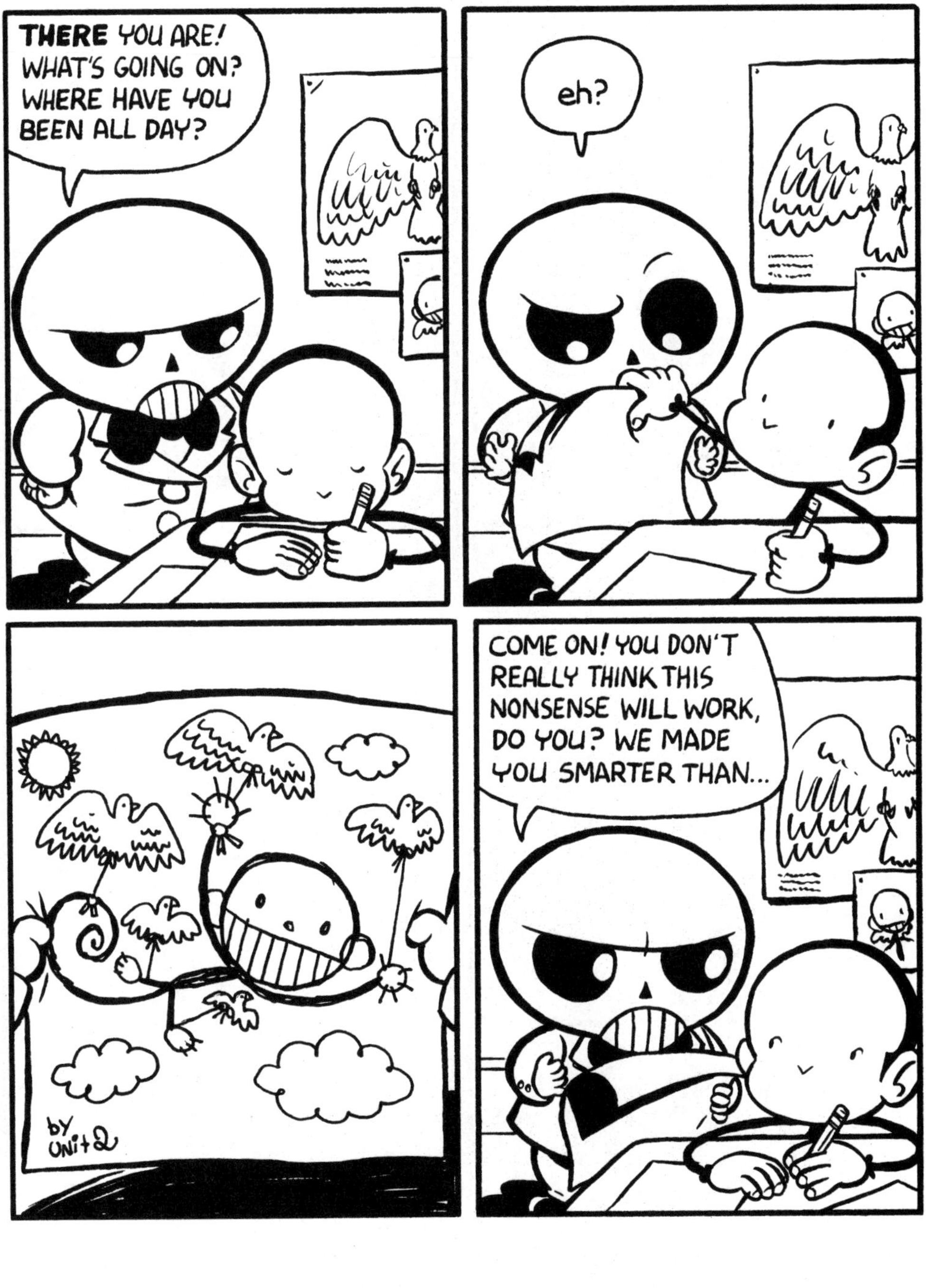
THERE YOU ARE! WHAT'S GOING ON? WHERE HAVE YOU BEEN ALL DAY?
eh?
COME ON! YOU DON'T REALLY THINK THIS NONSENSE WILL WORK, DO YOU? WE MADE YOU SMARTER THAN...
by Unit 2

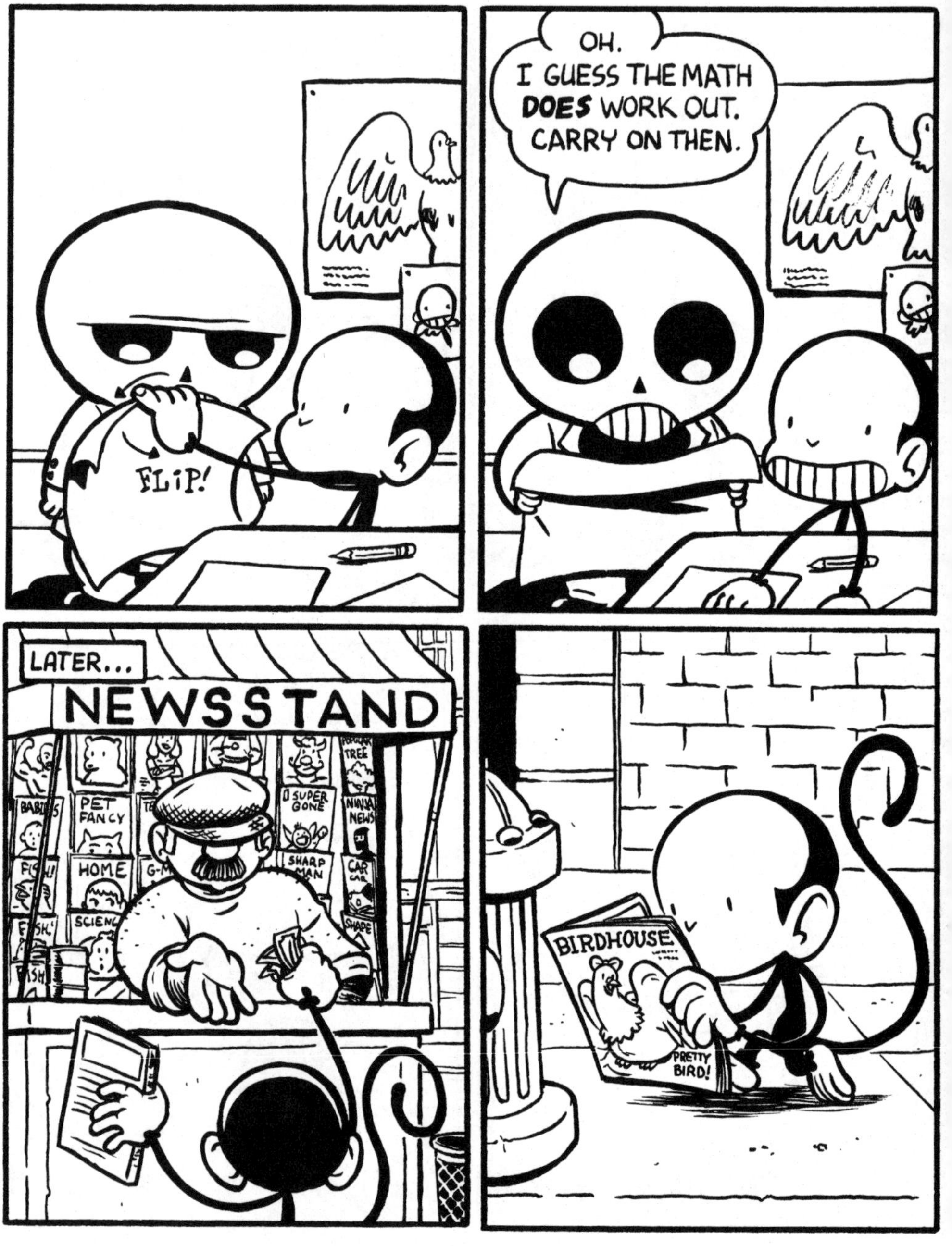
FLIP!
OH. I GUESS THE MATH **DOES** WORK OUT. CARRY ON THEN.
LATER...
NEWSSTAND
PET FANCY
SUPER GONE
NINJA NEWS
HOME
SHARP MAN
SHAPE
BIRDHOUSE
PRETTY BIRD!

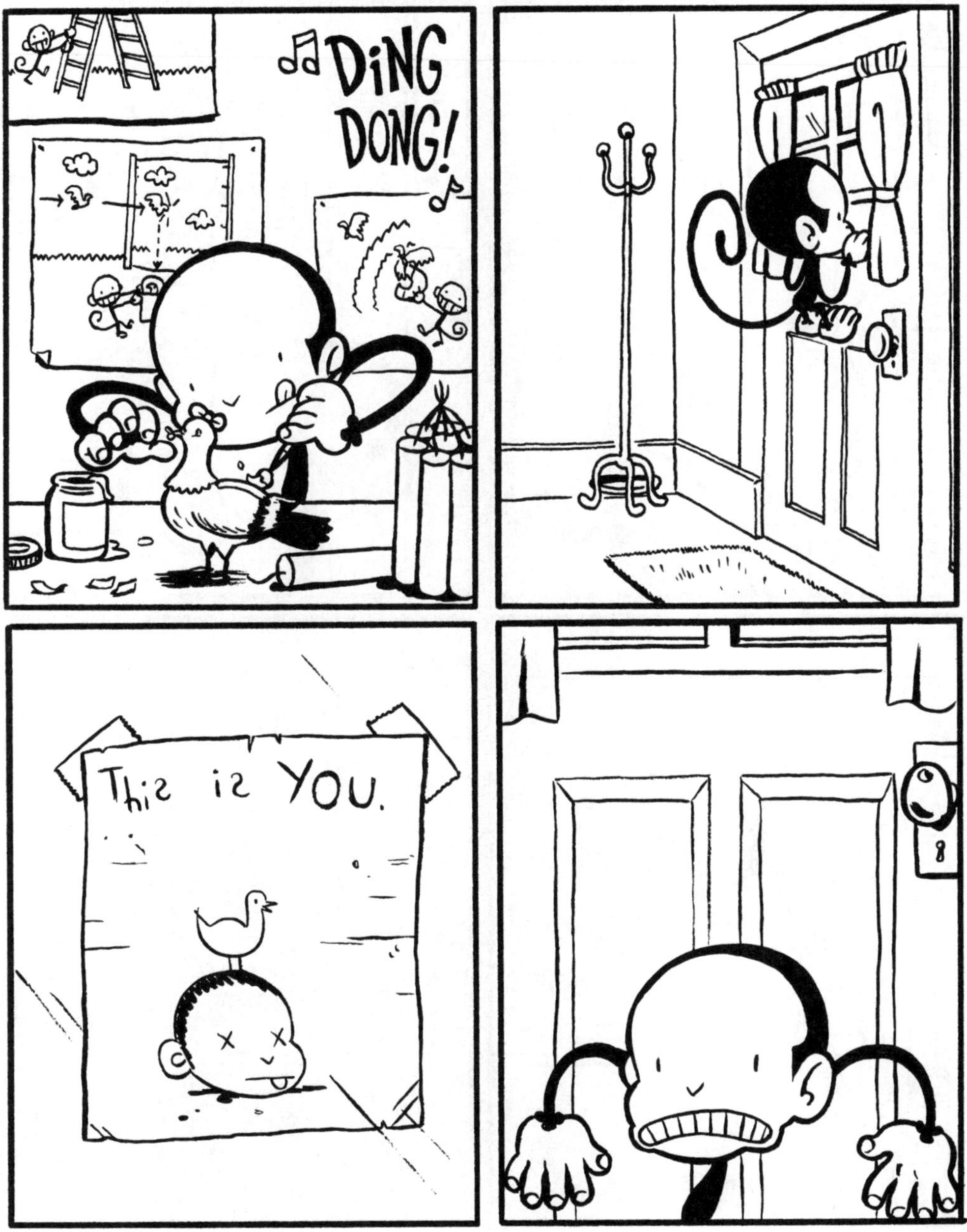
DiNG DONG!
This is YOU.

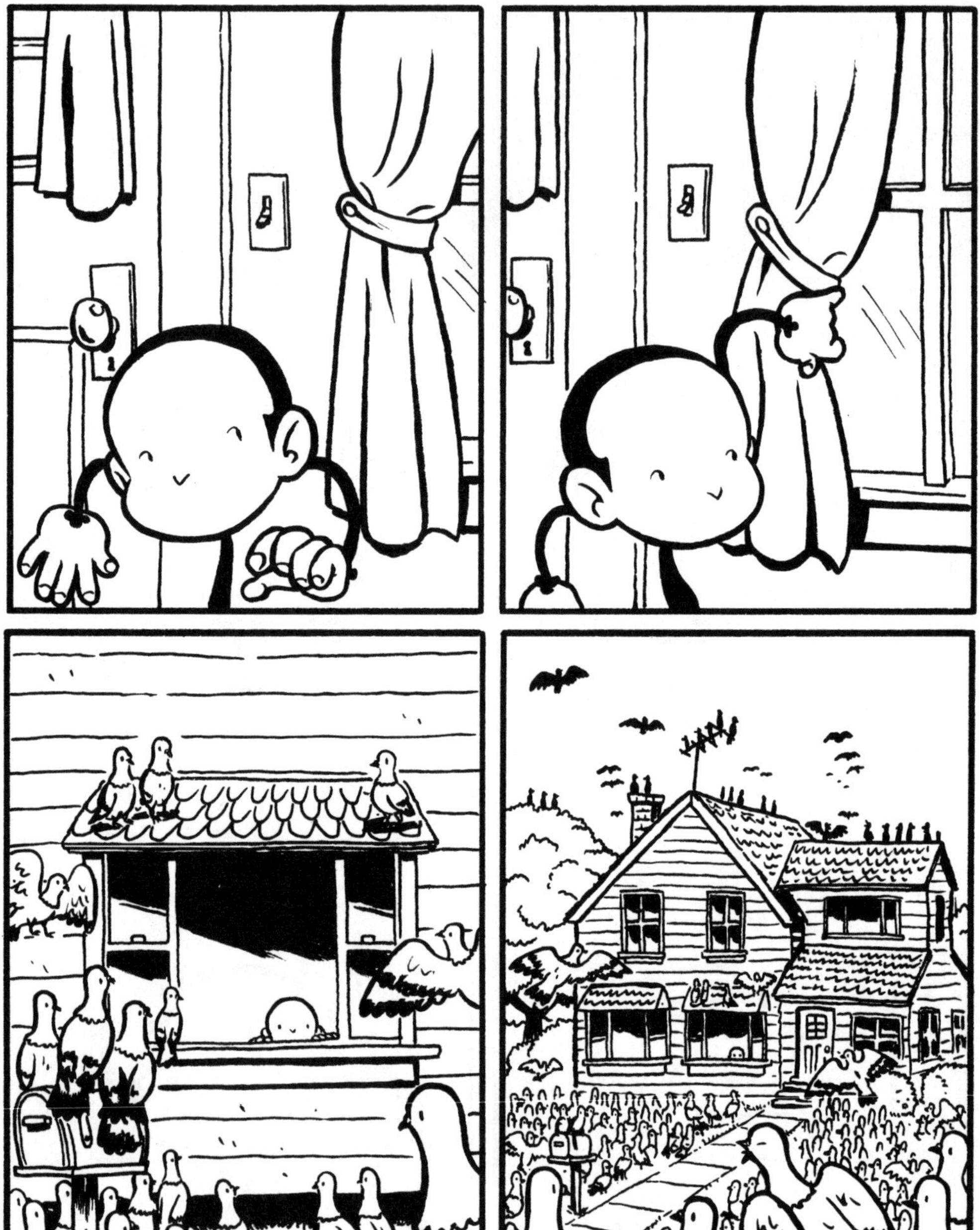

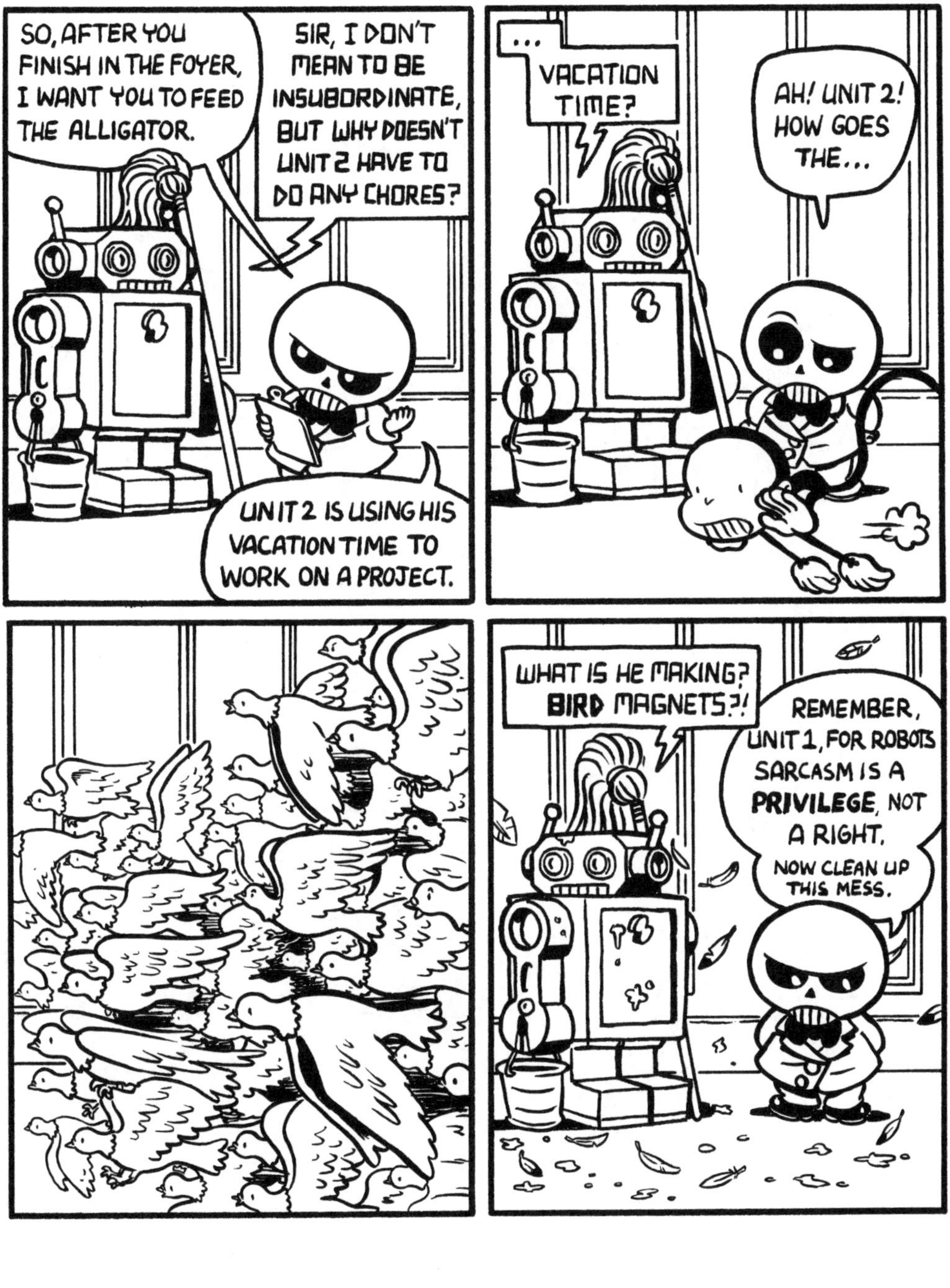
SO, AFTER YOU FINISH IN THE FOYER, I WANT YOU TO FEED THE ALLIGATOR.
SIR, I DON'T MEAN TO BE INSUBORDINATE, BUT WHY DOESN'T UNIT 2 HAVE TO DO ANY CHORES?
UNIT 2 IS USING HIS VACATION TIME TO WORK ON A PROJECT.
...
VACATION TIME?
AH! UNIT 2! HOW GOES THE...
WHAT IS HE MAKING? BIRD MAGNETS?!
REMEMBER, UNIT 1, FOR ROBOTS SARCASM IS A PRIVILEGE, NOT A RIGHT.
NOW CLEAN UP THIS MESS.

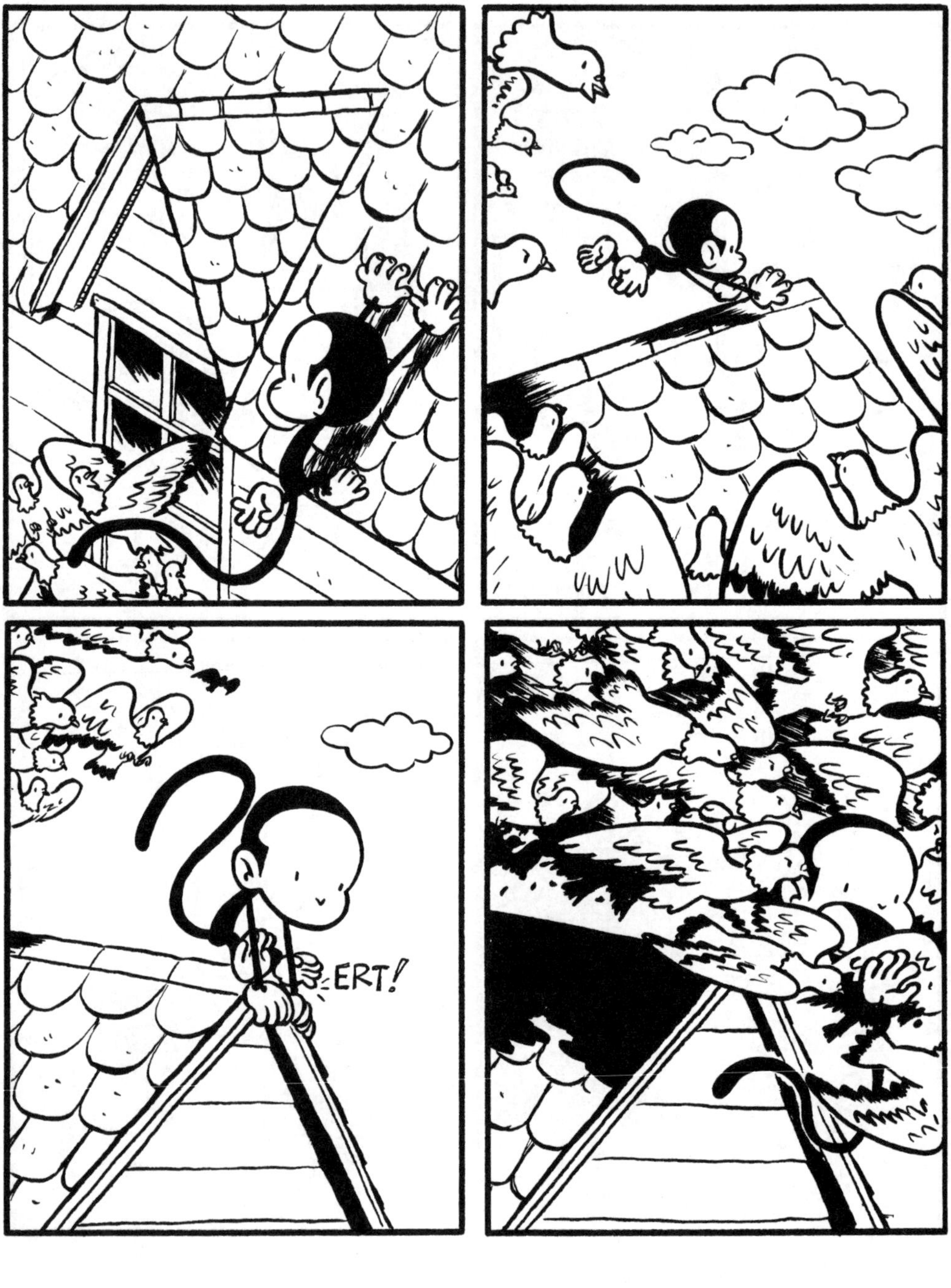
ERT!

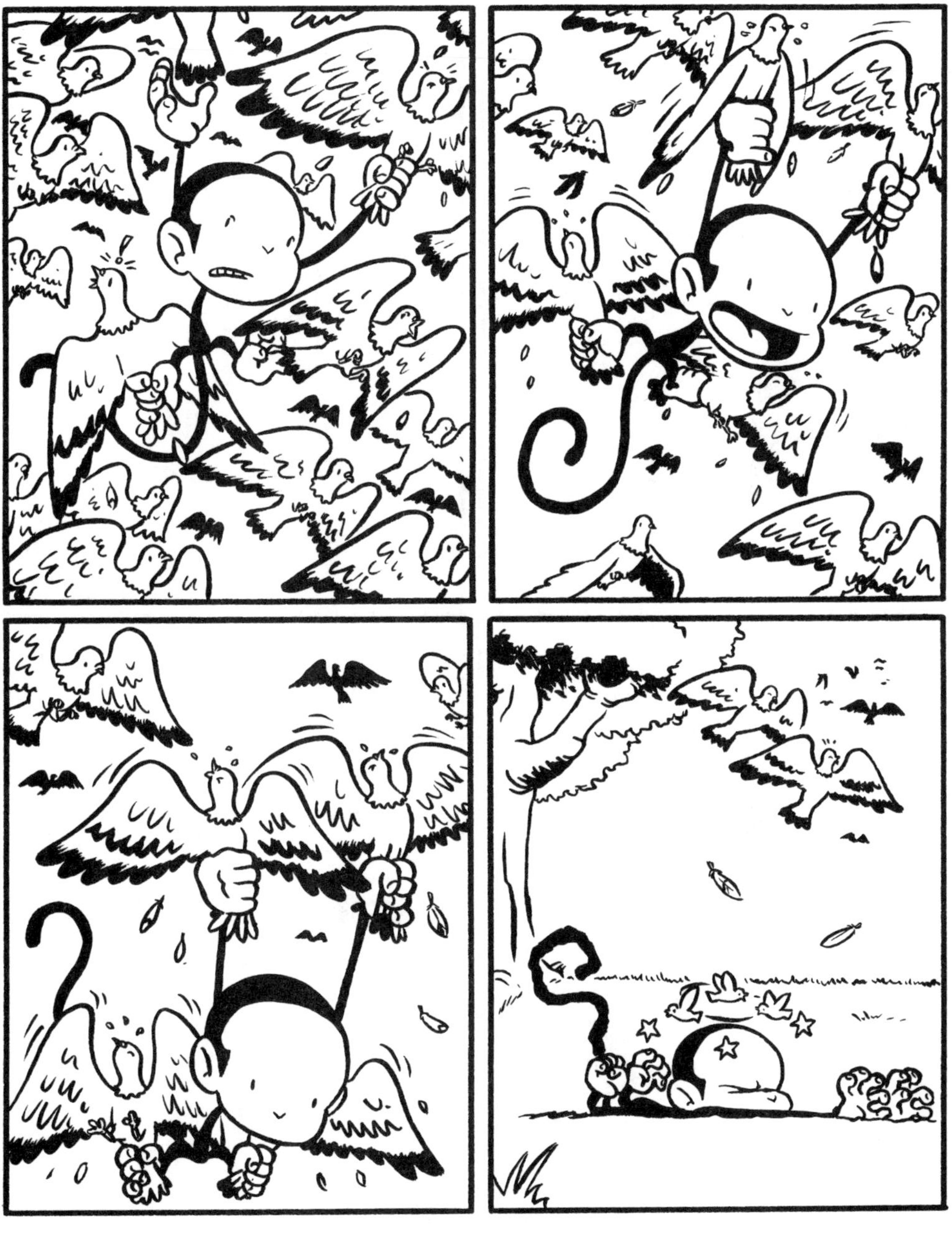

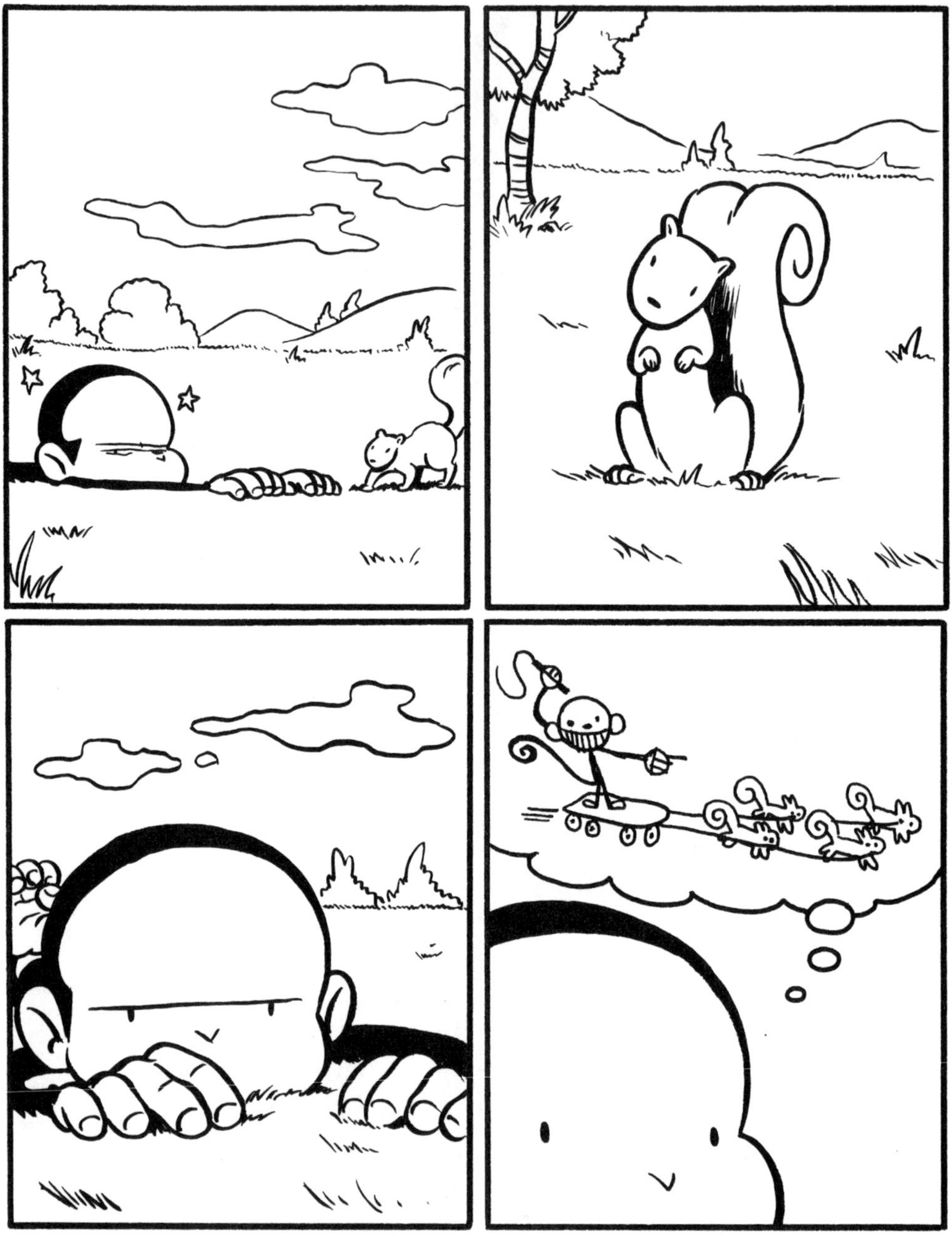

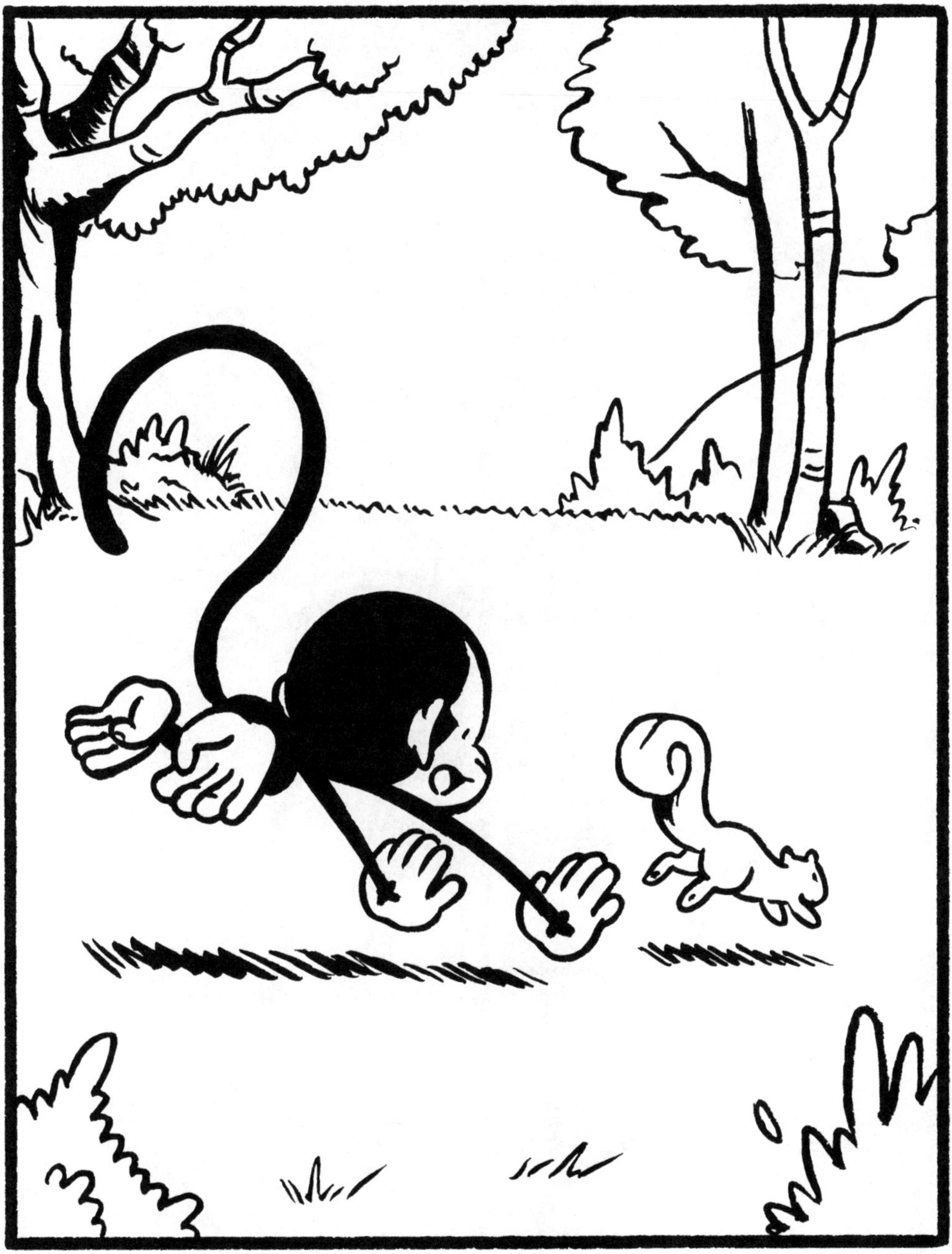

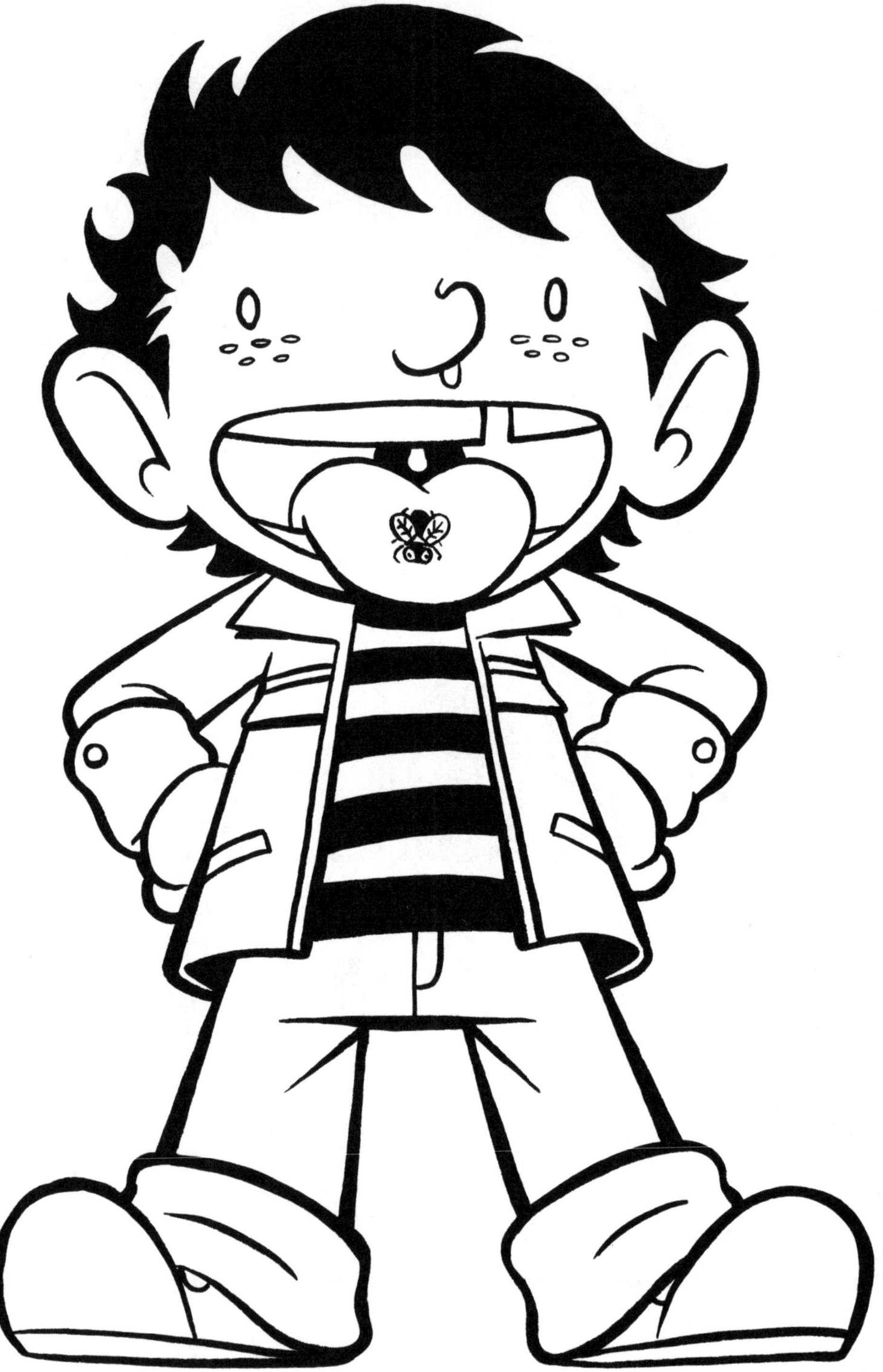
JC · 04

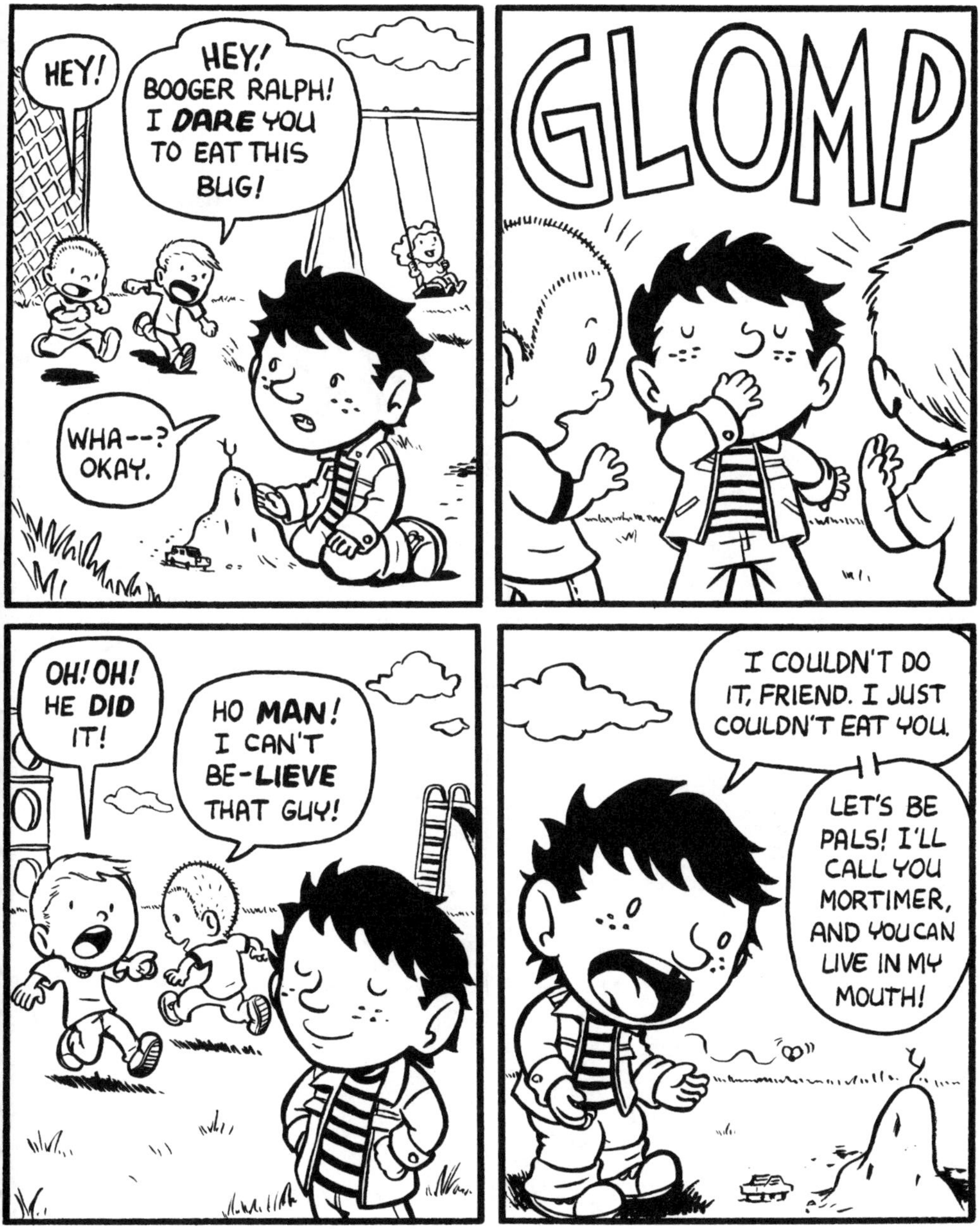
HEY!
HEY! BOOGER RALPH! I DARE YOU TO EAT THIS BUG!
WHA--? OKAY.
GLOMP
OH! OH! HE DID IT!
HO MAN! I CAN'T BE-LIEVE THAT GUY!
I COULDN'T DO IT, FRIEND. I JUST COULDN'T EAT YOU.
LET'S BE PALS! I'LL CALL YOU MORTIMER, AND YOU CAN LIVE IN MY MOUTH!

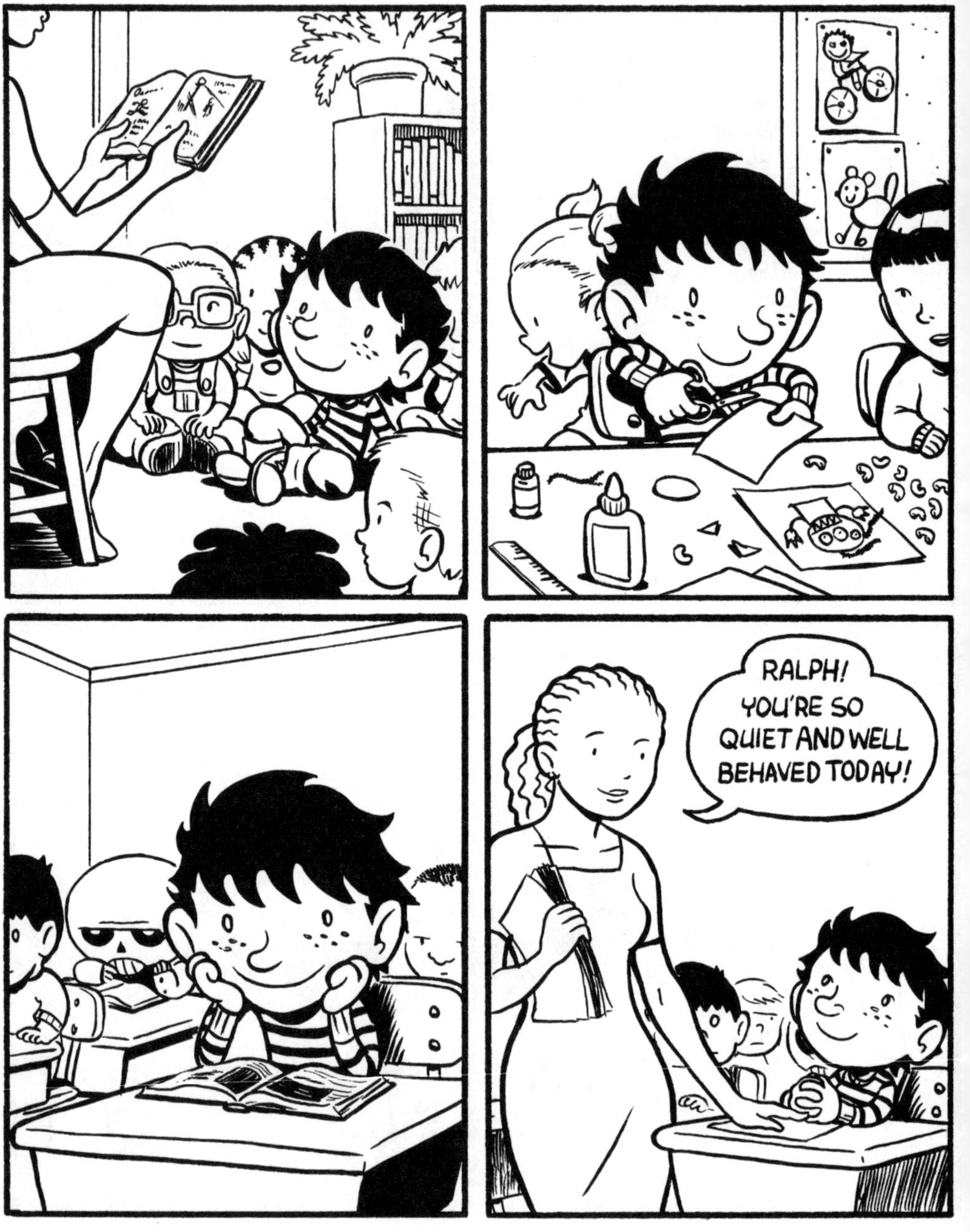
RALPH!
YOU'RE SO
QUIET AND WELL
BEHAVED TODAY!

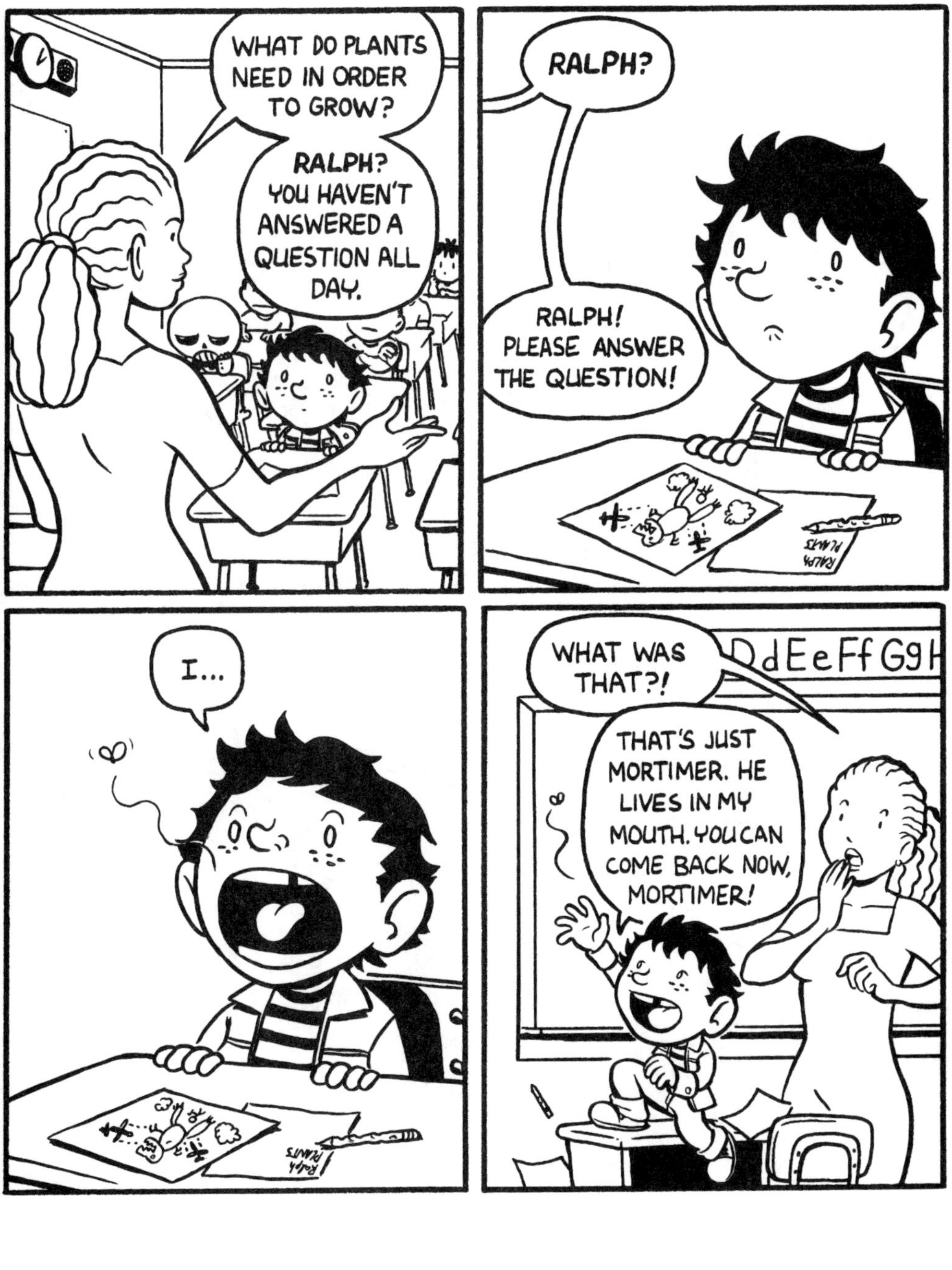
WHAT DO PLANTS NEED IN ORDER TO GROW?
RALPH? YOU HAVEN'T ANSWERED A QUESTION ALL DAY.
RALPH?
RALPH! PLEASE ANSWER THE QUESTION!
RALPH PLANTS
I...
Ralph PLANTS
WHAT WAS THAT?!
DdEeFfGgH
THAT'S JUST MORTIMER. HE LIVES IN MY MOUTH. YOU CAN COME BACK NOW, MORTIMER!

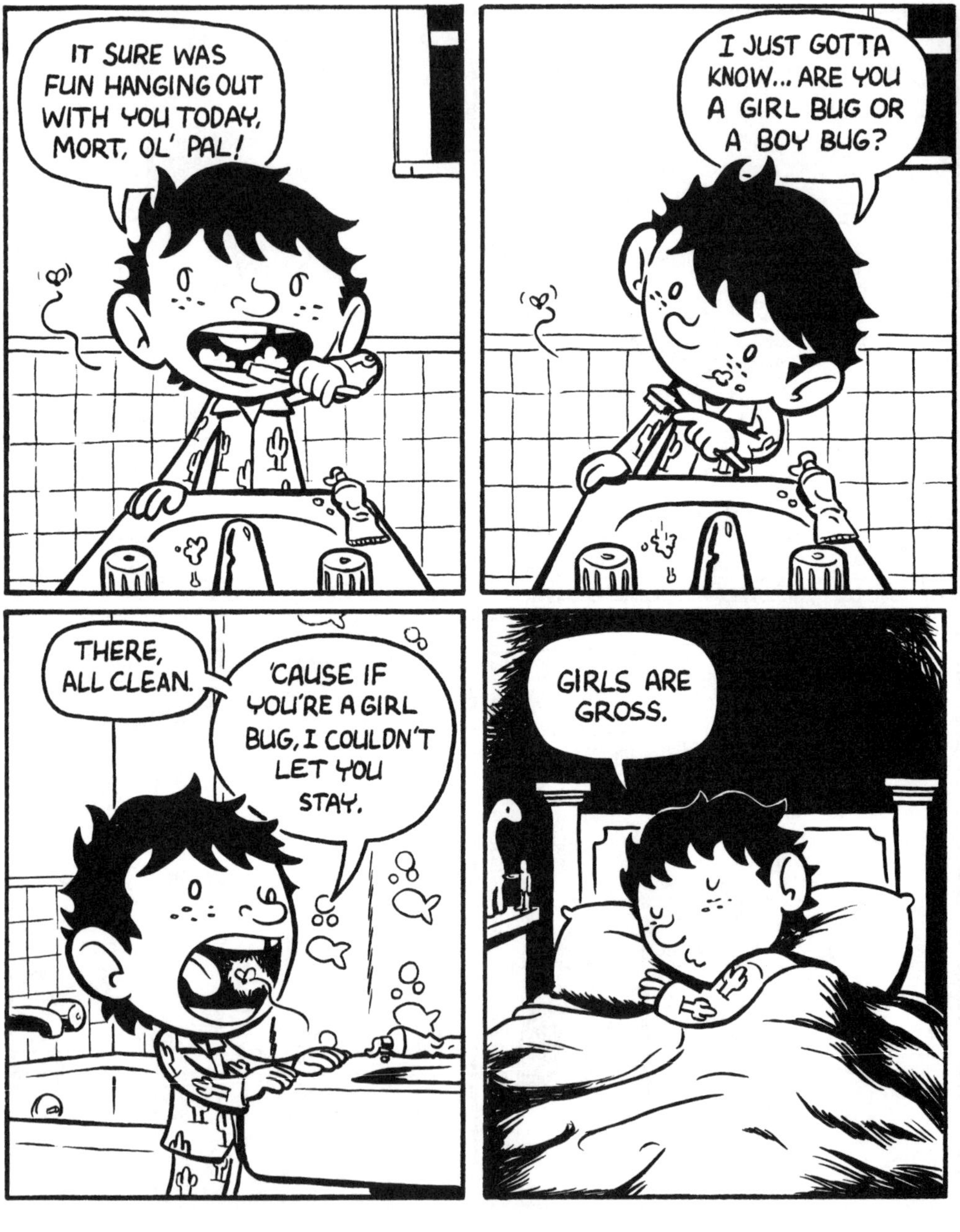
IT SURE WAS FUN HANGING OUT WITH YOU TODAY, MORT, OL' PAL!
I JUST GOTTA KNOW... ARE YOU A GIRL BUG OR A BOY BUG?
THERE, ALL CLEAN.
'CAUSE IF YOU'RE A GIRL BUG, I COULDN'T LET YOU STAY.
GIRLS ARE GROSS.

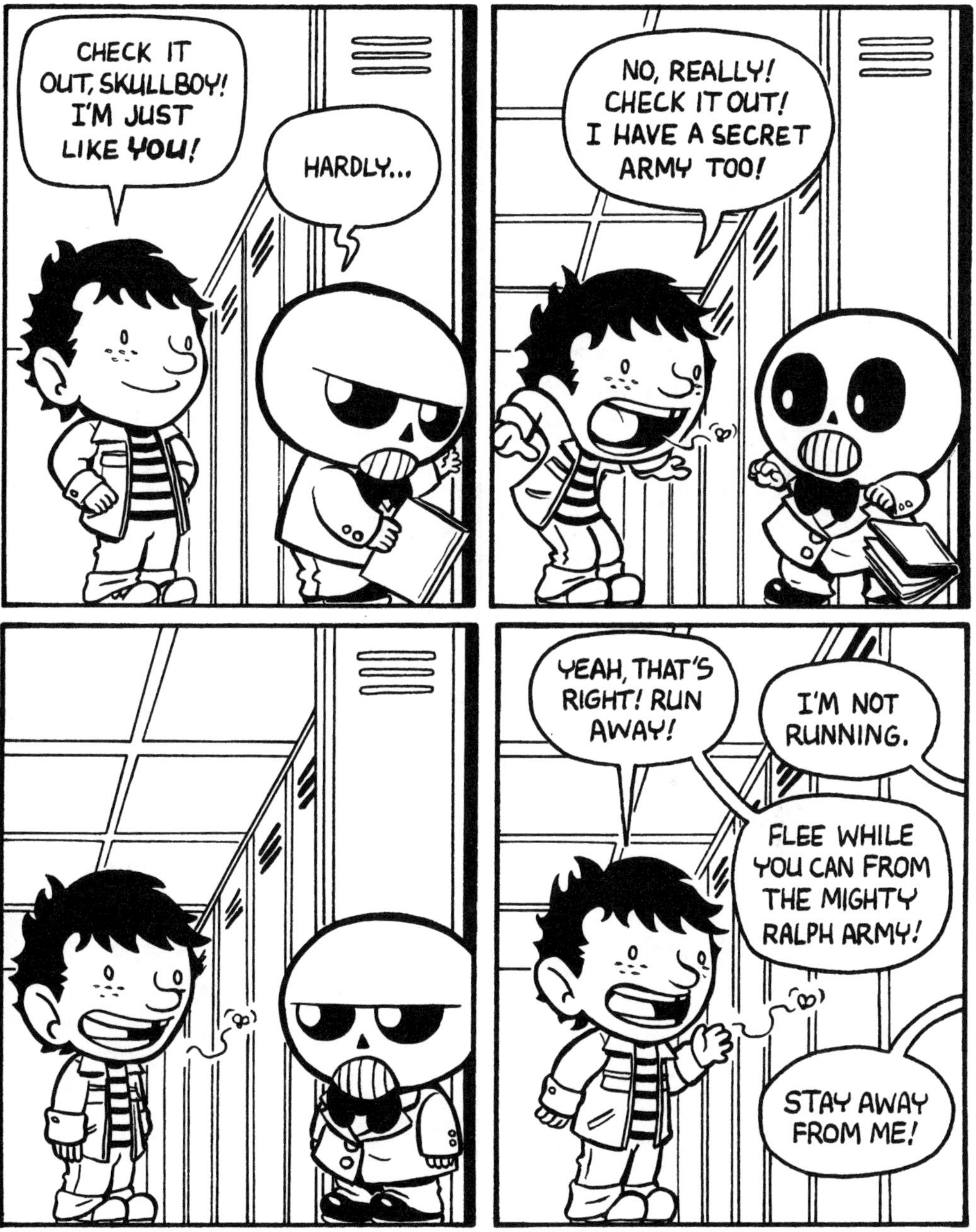
CHECK IT OUT, SKULLBOY! I'M JUST LIKE YOU!
HARDLY...
NO, REALLY! CHECK IT OUT! I HAVE A SECRET ARMY TOO!
YEAH, THAT'S RIGHT! RUN AWAY!
I'M NOT RUNNING.
FLEE WHILE YOU CAN FROM THE MIGHTY RALPH ARMY!
STAY AWAY FROM ME!

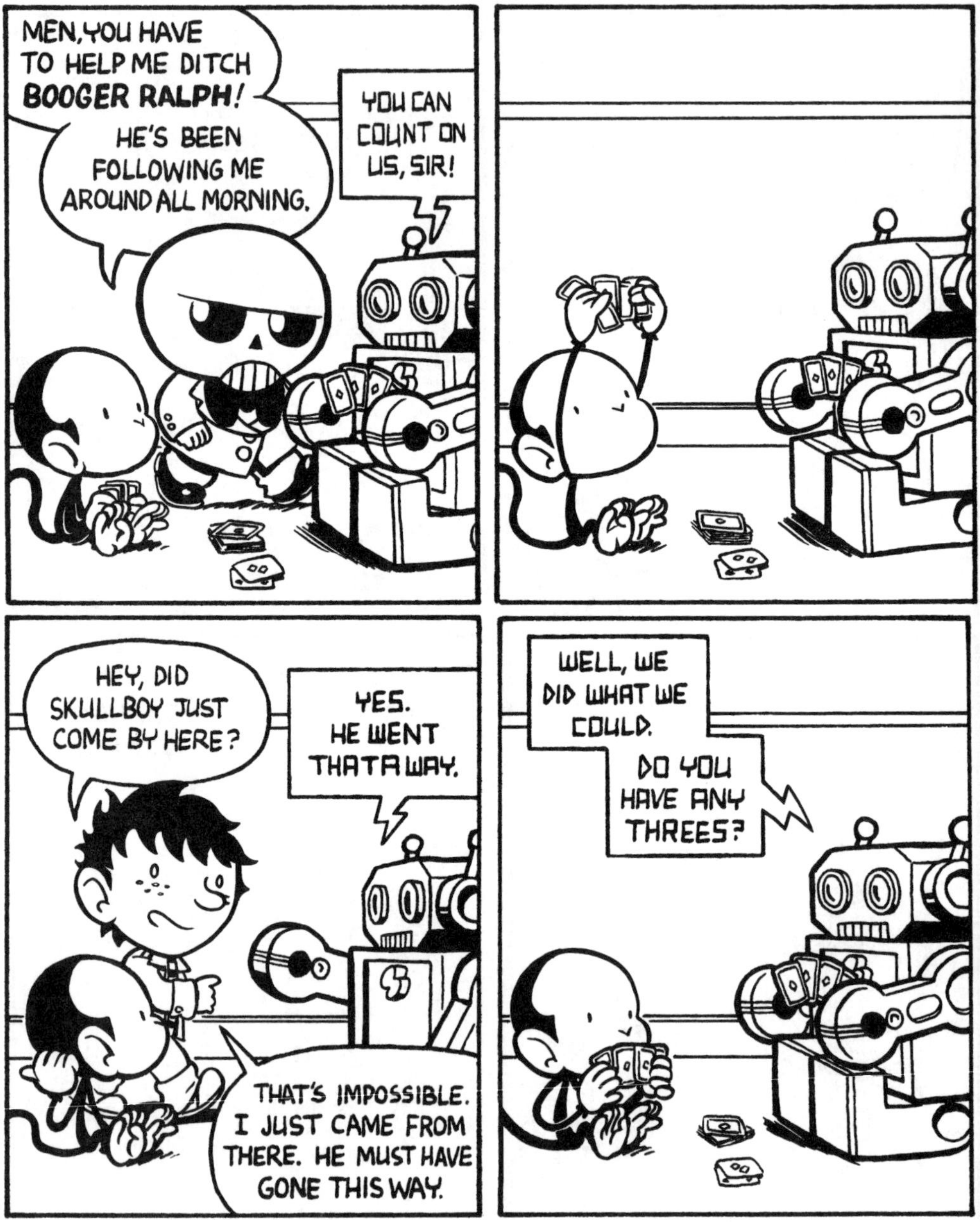
MEN, YOU HAVE TO HELP ME DITCH BOOGER RALPH!
HE'S BEEN FOLLOWING ME AROUND ALL MORNING.
YOU CAN COUNT ON US, SIR!
HEY, DID SKULLBOY JUST COME BY HERE?
YES. HE WENT THATA WAY.
THAT'S IMPOSSIBLE. I JUST CAME FROM THERE. HE MUST HAVE GONE THIS WAY.
WELL, WE DID WHAT WE COULD.
DO YOU HAVE ANY THREES?

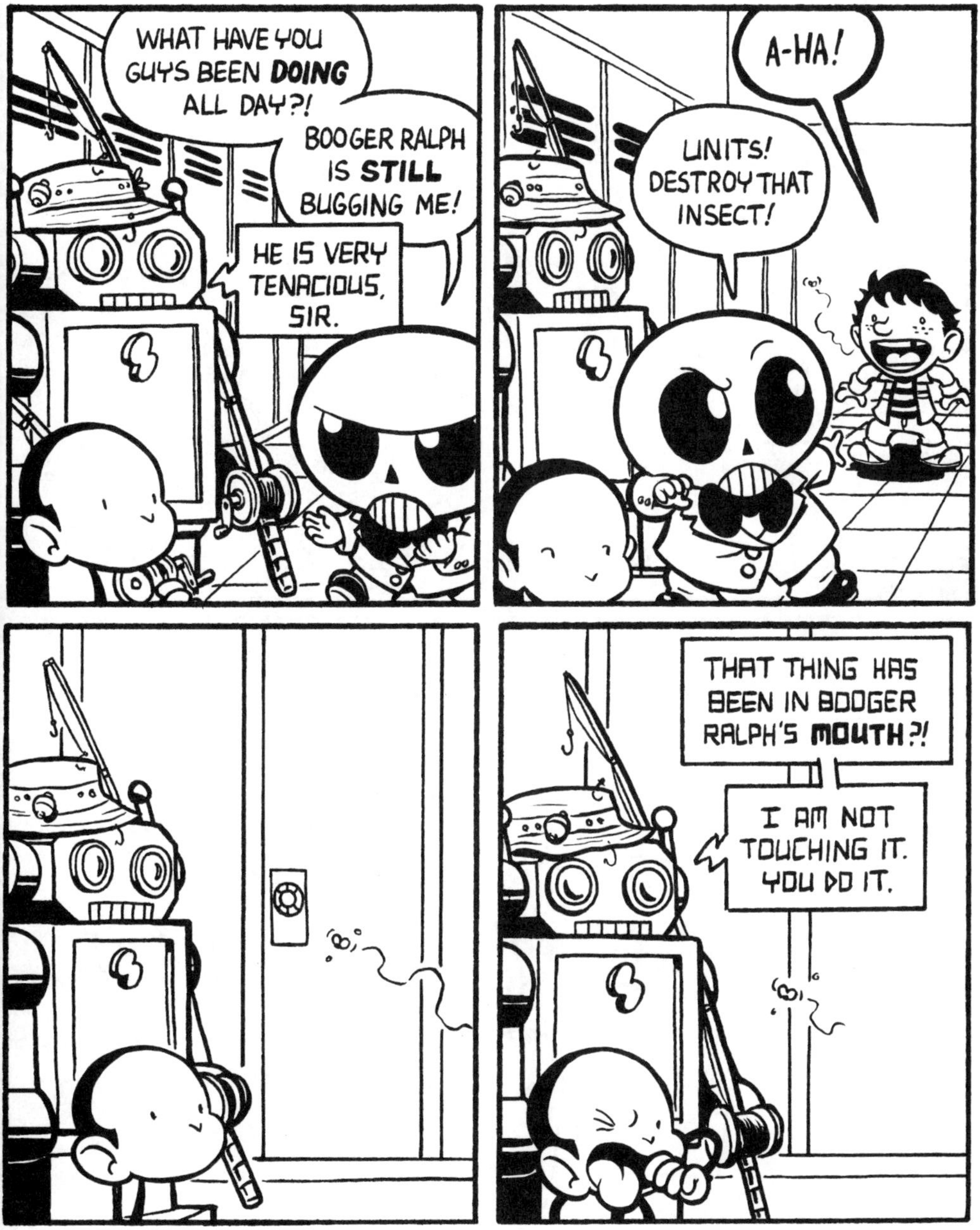
WHAT HAVE YOU GUYS BEEN **DOING** ALL DAY?!
BOOGER RALPH IS **STILL** BUGGING ME!
HE IS VERY TENACIOUS, SIR.
A-HA!
UNITS! DESTROY THAT INSECT!
THAT THING HAS BEEN IN BOOGER RALPH'S **MOUTH**?!
I AM NOT TOUCHING IT. YOU DO IT.

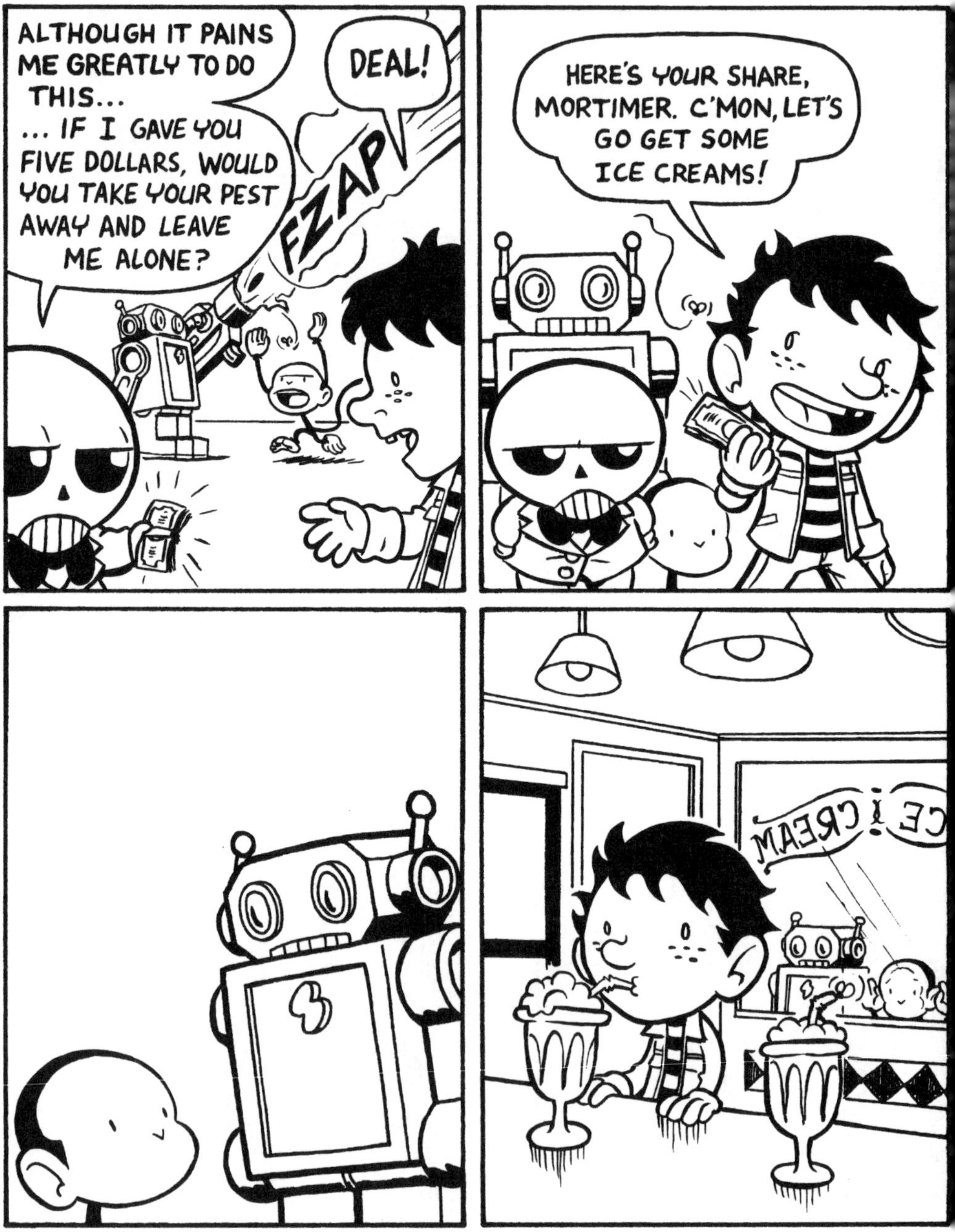
ALTHOUGH IT PAINS ME GREATLY TO DO THIS... ... IF I GAVE YOU FIVE DOLLARS, WOULD YOU TAKE YOUR PEST AWAY AND LEAVE ME ALONE?
DEAL!
FZAP
HERE'S YOUR SHARE, MORTIMER. C'MON, LET'S GO GET SOME ICE CREAMS!

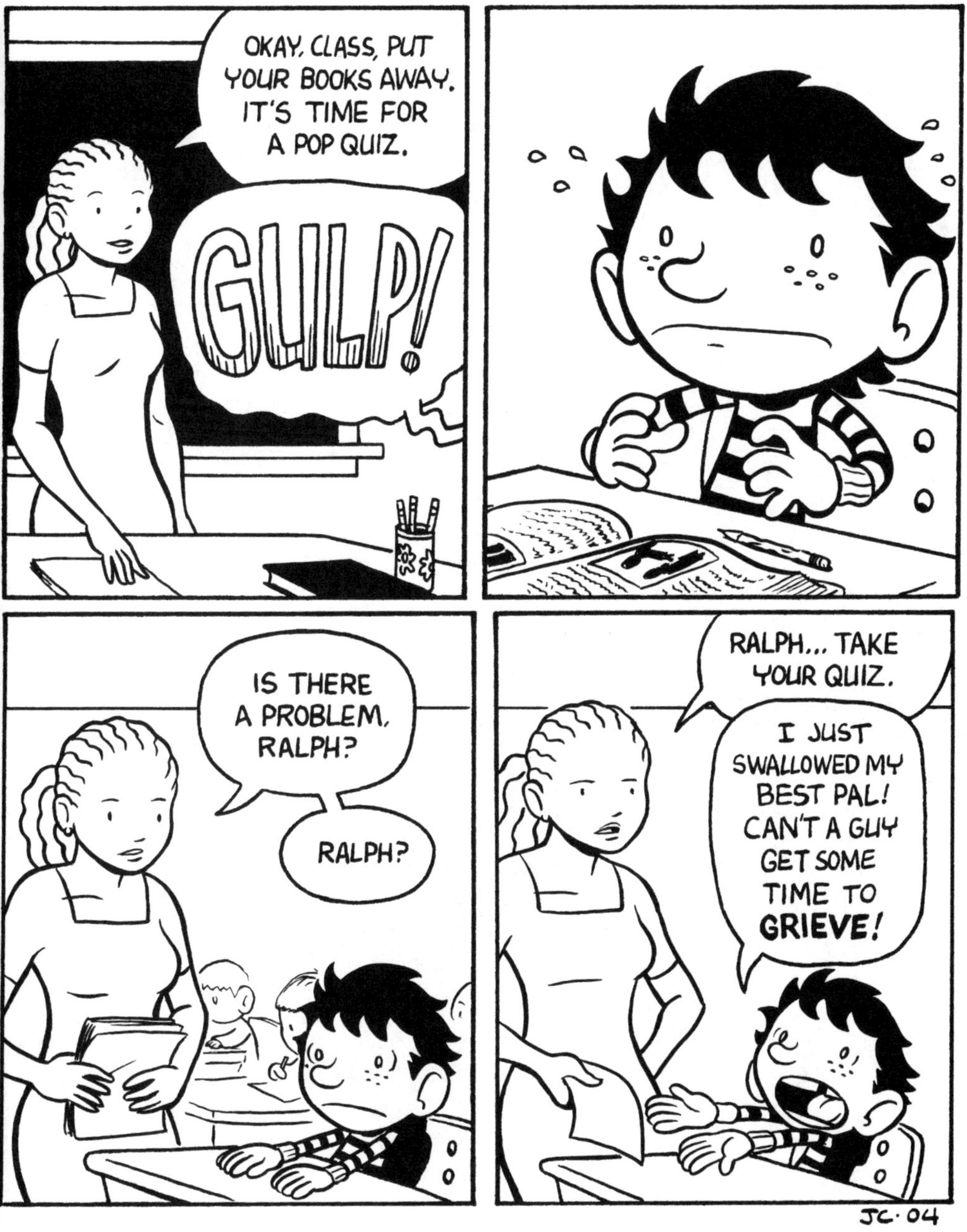
OKAY, CLASS, PUT YOUR BOOKS AWAY. IT'S TIME FOR A POP QUIZ.
GULP!
IS THERE A PROBLEM, RALPH?
RALPH?
RALPH... TAKE YOUR QUIZ.
I JUST SWALLOWED MY BEST PAL! CAN'T A GUY GET SOME TIME TO **GRIEVE**!
JC·04

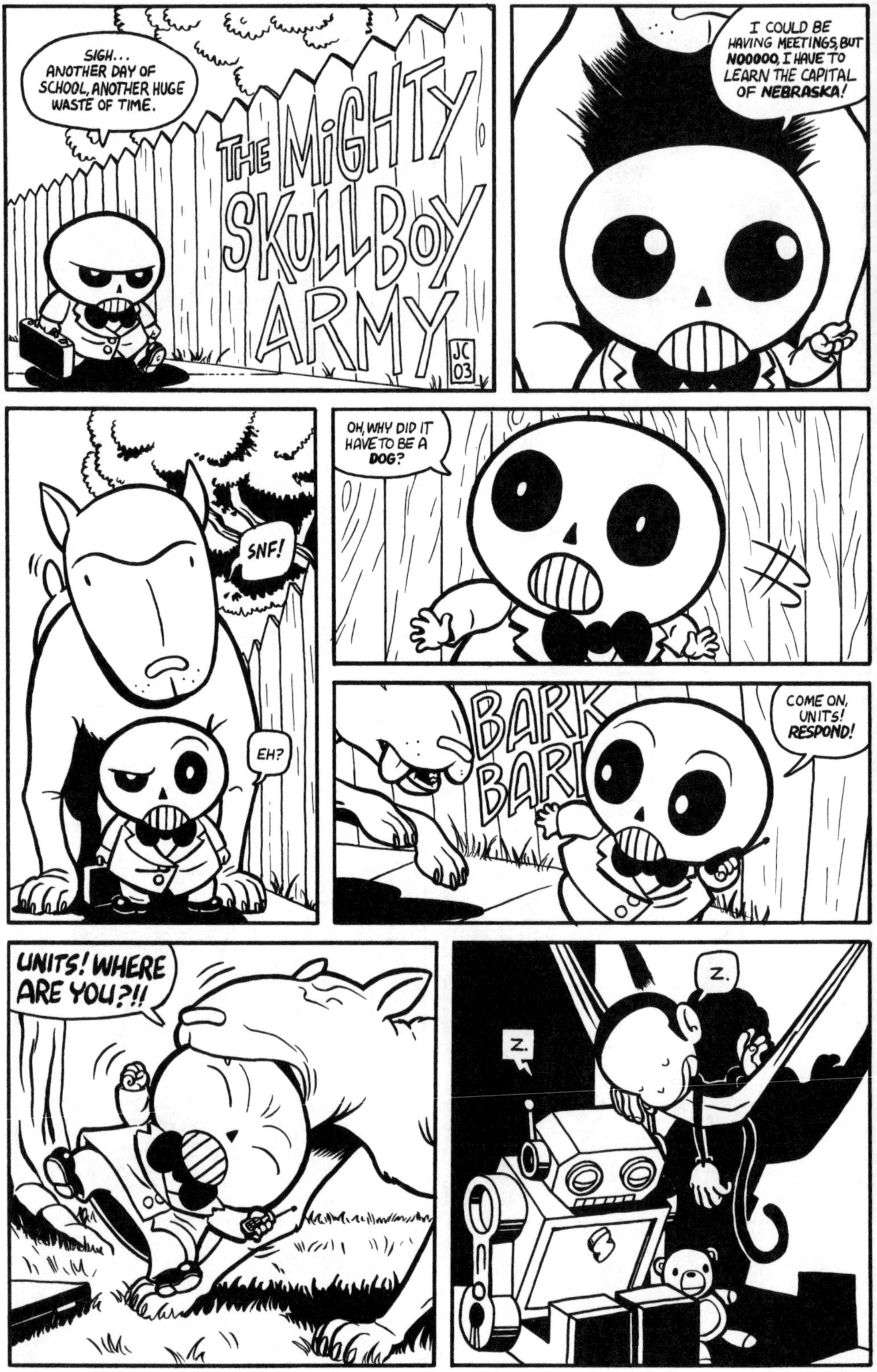

SIGH... ANOTHER DAY OF SCHOOL, ANOTHER HUGE WASTE OF TIME.
THE MIGHTY SKULLBOY ARMY
JC 03
I COULD BE HAVING MEETINGS, BUT NOOOOO, I HAVE TO LEARN THE CAPITAL OF NEBRASKA!
SNF!
EH?
OH, WHY DID IT HAVE TO BE A DOG?
BARK BARK
COME ON, UNITS! RESPOND!
UNITS! WHERE ARE YOU?!!
Z.
Z.

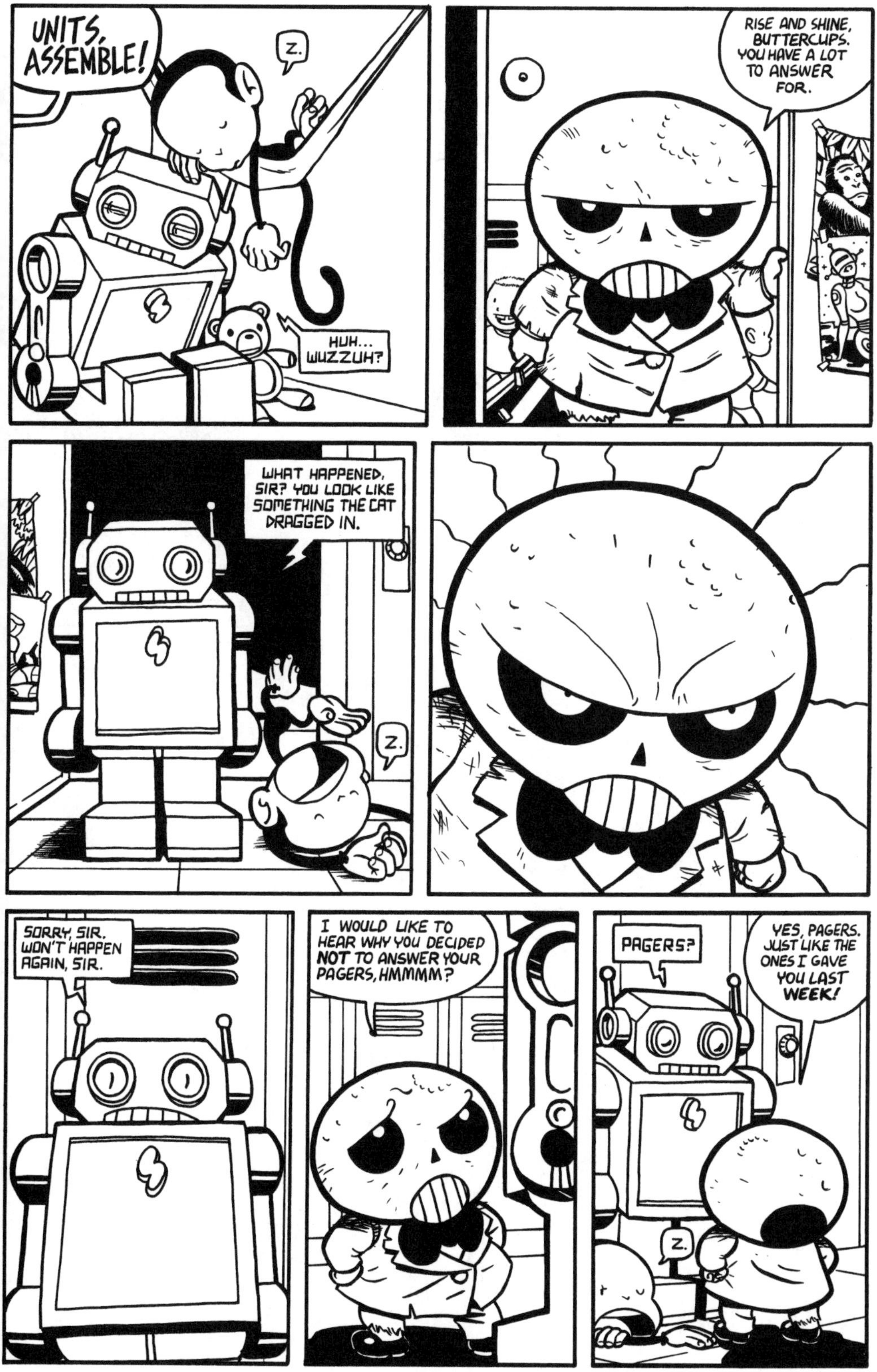
UNITS, ASSEMBLE!
Z.
HUH... WUZZUH?
RISE AND SHINE, BUTTERCUPS. YOU HAVE A LOT TO ANSWER FOR.
WHAT HAPPENED, SIR? YOU LOOK LIKE SOMETHING THE CAT DRAGGED IN.
Z.
SORRY, SIR. WON'T HAPPEN AGAIN, SIR.
I WOULD LIKE TO HEAR WHY YOU DECIDED NOT TO ANSWER YOUR PAGERS, HMMMM?
PAGERS?
YES, PAGERS. JUST LIKE THE ONES I GAVE YOU LAST WEEK!
Z.

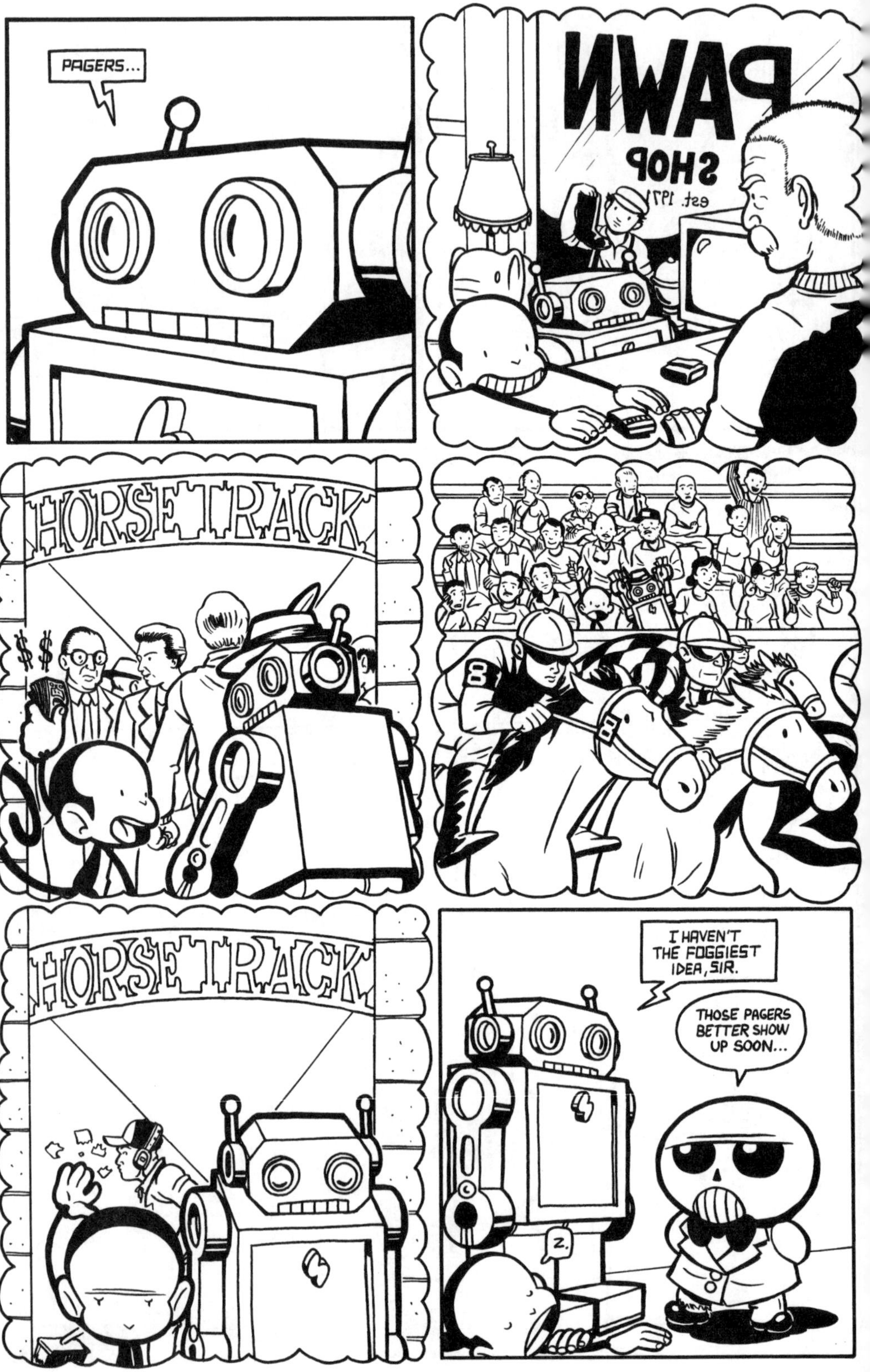
PAGERS...
PAWN
SHOP
est. 1971
HORSE TRACK
$ $
HORSE TRACK
I HAVEN'T THE FOGGIEST IDEA, SIR.
THOSE PAGERS BETTER SHOW UP SOON...
Z.

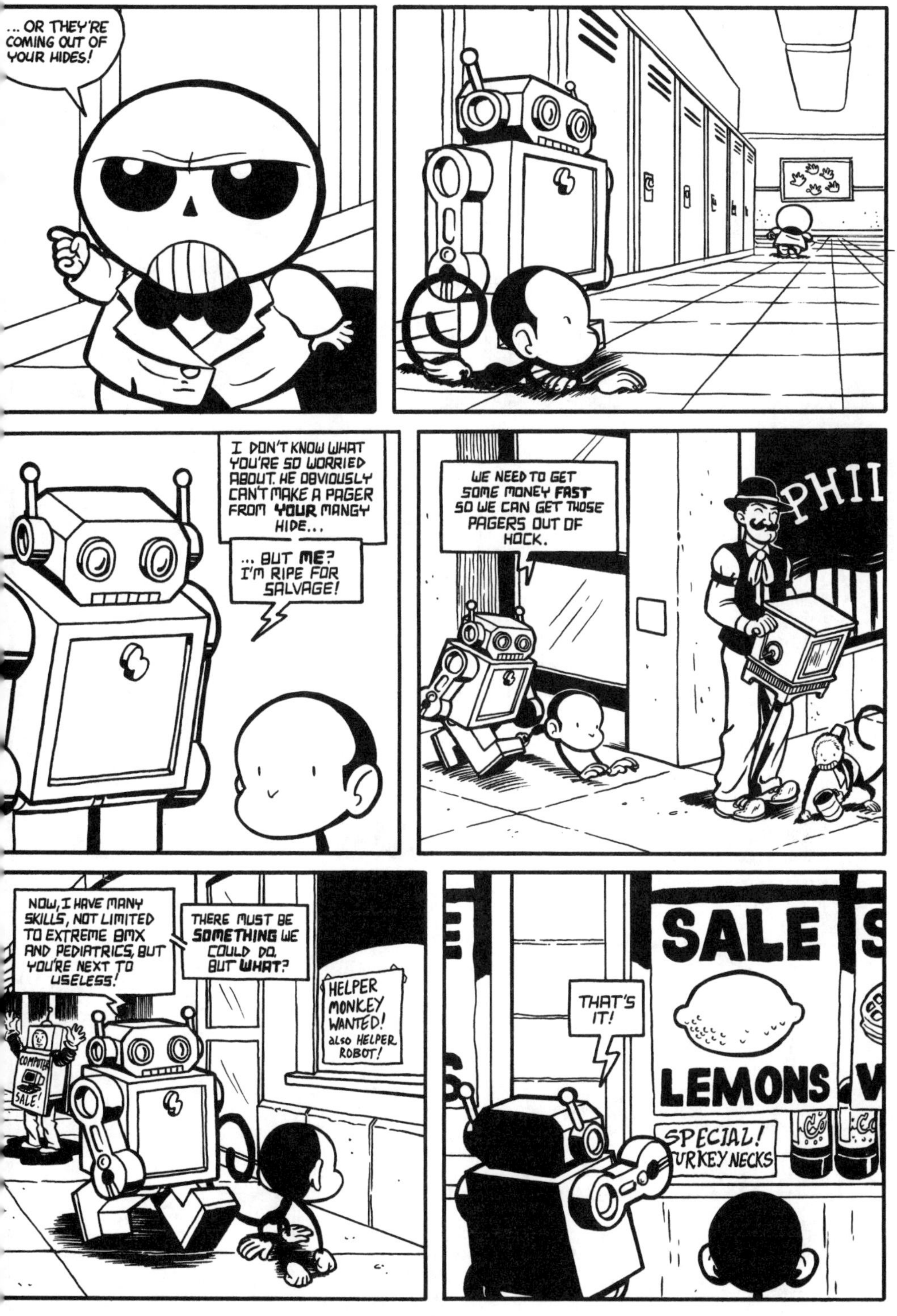

... OR THEY'RE COMING OUT OF YOUR HIDES!
I DON'T KNOW WHAT YOU'RE SO WORRIED ABOUT. HE OBVIOUSLY CAN'T MAKE A PAGER FROM **YOUR** MANGY HIDE...
... BUT **ME**? I'M RIPE FOR SALVAGE!
WE NEED TO GET SOME MONEY **FAST** SO WE CAN GET THOSE PAGERS OUT OF HOCK.
PHII
NOW, I HAVE MANY SKILLS, NOT LIMITED TO EXTREME BMX AND PEDIATRICS, BUT YOU'RE NEXT TO USELESS!
THERE MUST BE **SOMETHING** WE COULD DO. BUT **WHAT**?
HELPER MONKEY WANTED! also HELPER ROBOT!
COMPUTER SALE!
SALE
LEMONS
SPECIAL! TURKEY NECKS
THAT'S IT!

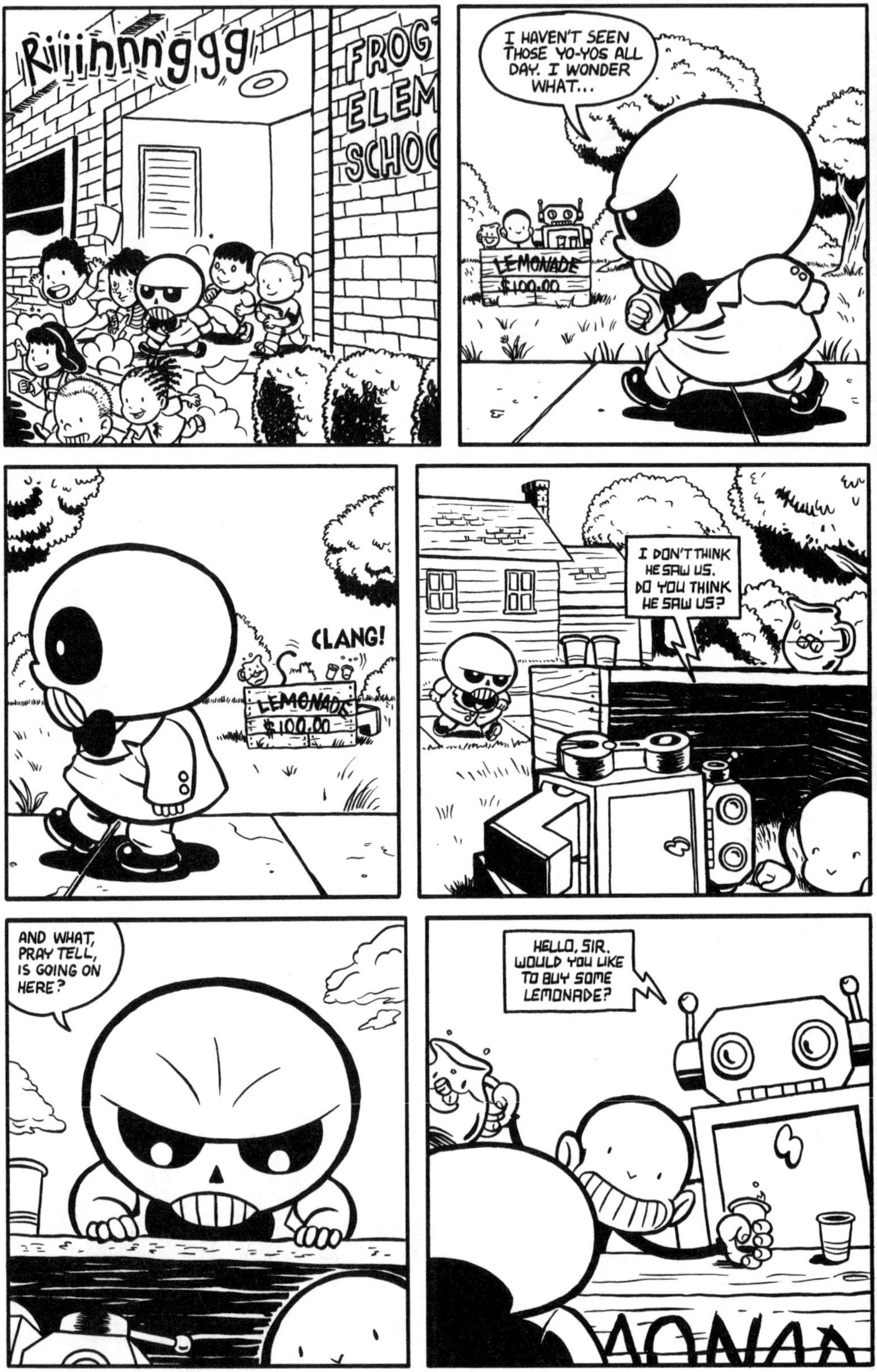

Riiinnnggg
FROG
ELEM
SCHOO
I HAVEN'T SEEN THOSE YO-YOS ALL DAY. I WONDER WHAT...
LEMONADE
$100.00
CLANG!
LEMONADE
$100.00
I DON'T THINK HE SAW US. DO YOU THINK HE SAW US?
AND WHAT, PRAY TELL, IS GOING ON HERE?
HELLO, SIR. WOULD YOU LIKE TO BUY SOME LEMONADE?

HEH. YOU THINK THAT YOU CAN SELL LEMONADE? HOW MUCH MONEY HAVE YOU MADE SO FAR?

FIFTY-TWO CENTS.

BUT THAT'S JUST WHAT WE HAVE LEFT OF YOUR LUNCH MONEY AFTER BUYING SUPPLIES.

SAY WHAT?

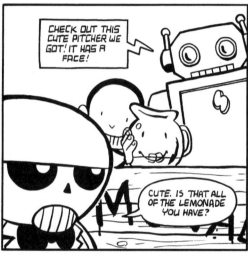

CHECK OUT THIS CUTE PITCHER WE GOT! IT HAS A FACE!

CUTE. IS THAT ALL OF THE LEMONADE YOU HAVE?

IT SHOULDN'T BE. WE HAVEN'T ACTUALLY SOLD ANY.

SLURP

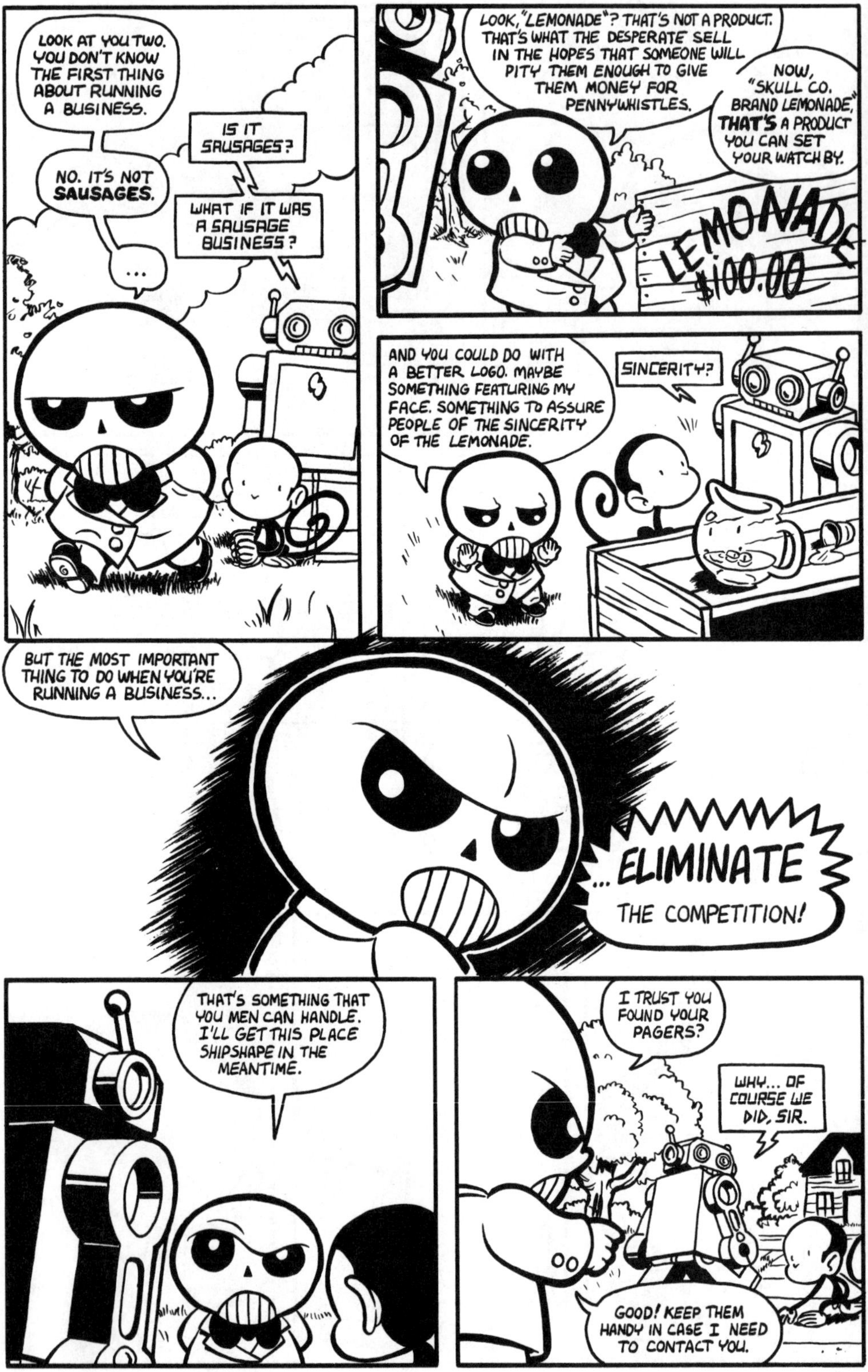
LOOK AT YOU TWO. YOU DON'T KNOW THE FIRST THING ABOUT RUNNING A BUSINESS.
IS IT SAUSAGES?
NO. IT'S NOT **SAUSAGES**.
WHAT IF IT WAS A SAUSAGE BUSINESS?
...
LOOK, "LEMONADE"? THAT'S NOT A PRODUCT. THAT'S WHAT THE DESPERATE SELL IN THE HOPES THAT SOMEONE WILL PITY THEM ENOUGH TO GIVE THEM MONEY FOR PENNYWHISTLES.
NOW, "SKULL CO. BRAND LEMONADE," **THAT'S** A PRODUCT YOU CAN SET YOUR WATCH BY.
LEMONADE $100.00
AND YOU COULD DO WITH A BETTER LOGO. MAYBE SOMETHING FEATURING MY FACE. SOMETHING TO ASSURE PEOPLE OF THE SINCERITY OF THE LEMONADE.
SINCERITY?
BUT THE MOST IMPORTANT THING TO DO WHEN YOU'RE RUNNING A BUSINESS...
...ELIMINATE THE COMPETITION!
THAT'S SOMETHING THAT YOU MEN CAN HANDLE. I'LL GET THIS PLACE SHIPSHAPE IN THE MEANTIME.
I TRUST YOU FOUND YOUR PAGERS?
WHY... OF COURSE WE DID, SIR.
GOOD! KEEP THEM HANDY IN CASE I NEED TO CONTACT YOU.

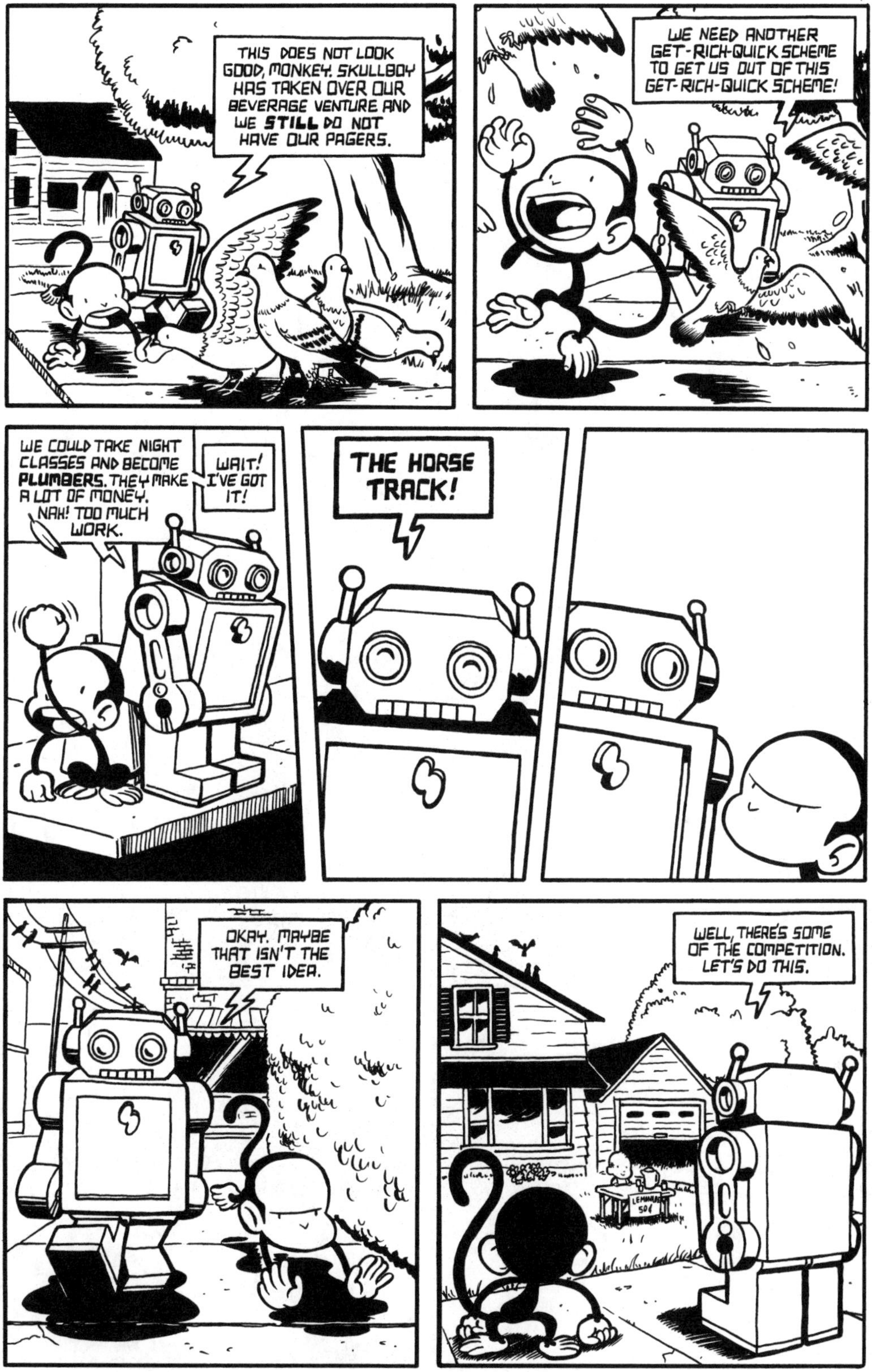
THIS DOES NOT LOOK GOOD, MONKEY. SKULLBOY HAS TAKEN OVER OUR BEVERAGE VENTURE AND WE **STILL** DO NOT HAVE OUR PAGERS.
WE NEED ANOTHER GET-RICH-QUICK SCHEME TO GET US OUT OF THIS GET-RICH-QUICK SCHEME!
WE COULD TAKE NIGHT CLASSES AND BECOME **PLUMBERS**. THEY MAKE A LOT OF MONEY.
NAH! TOO MUCH WORK.
WAIT! I'VE GOT IT!
THE HORSE TRACK!
OKAY. MAYBE THAT ISN'T THE BEST IDEA.
WELL, THERE'S SOME OF THE COMPETITION. LET'S DO THIS.

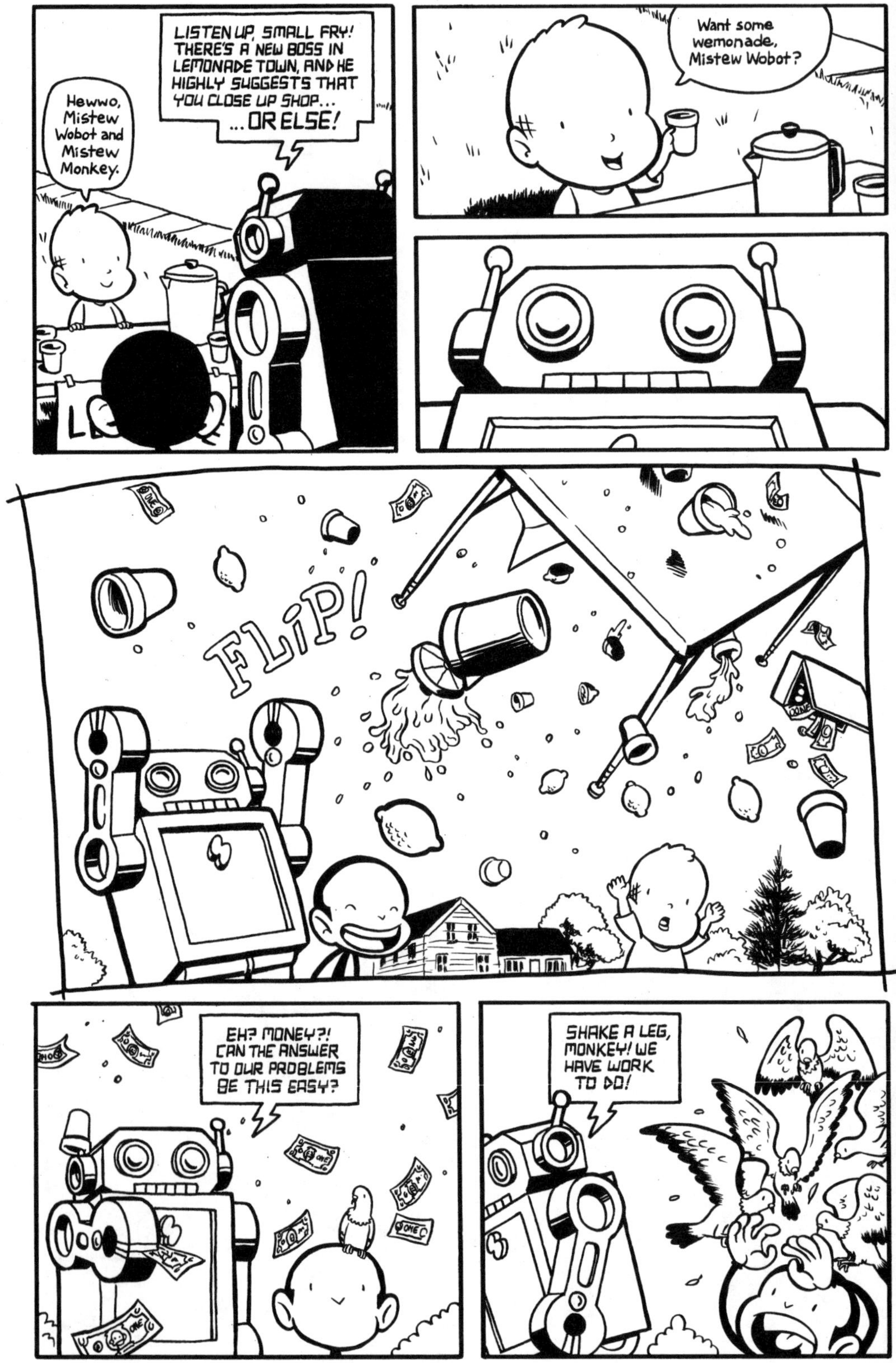
Hewwo, Mistew Wobot and Mistew Monkey.
LISTEN UP, SMALL FRY! THERE'S A NEW BOSS IN LEMONADE TOWN, AND HE HIGHLY SUGGESTS THAT YOU CLOSE UP SHOP... ...OR ELSE!
Want some wemonade, Mistew Wobot?
FLIP!
EH? MONEY?! CAN THE ANSWER TO OUR PROBLEMS BE THIS EASY?
SHAKE A LEG, MONKEY! WE HAVE WORK TO DO!

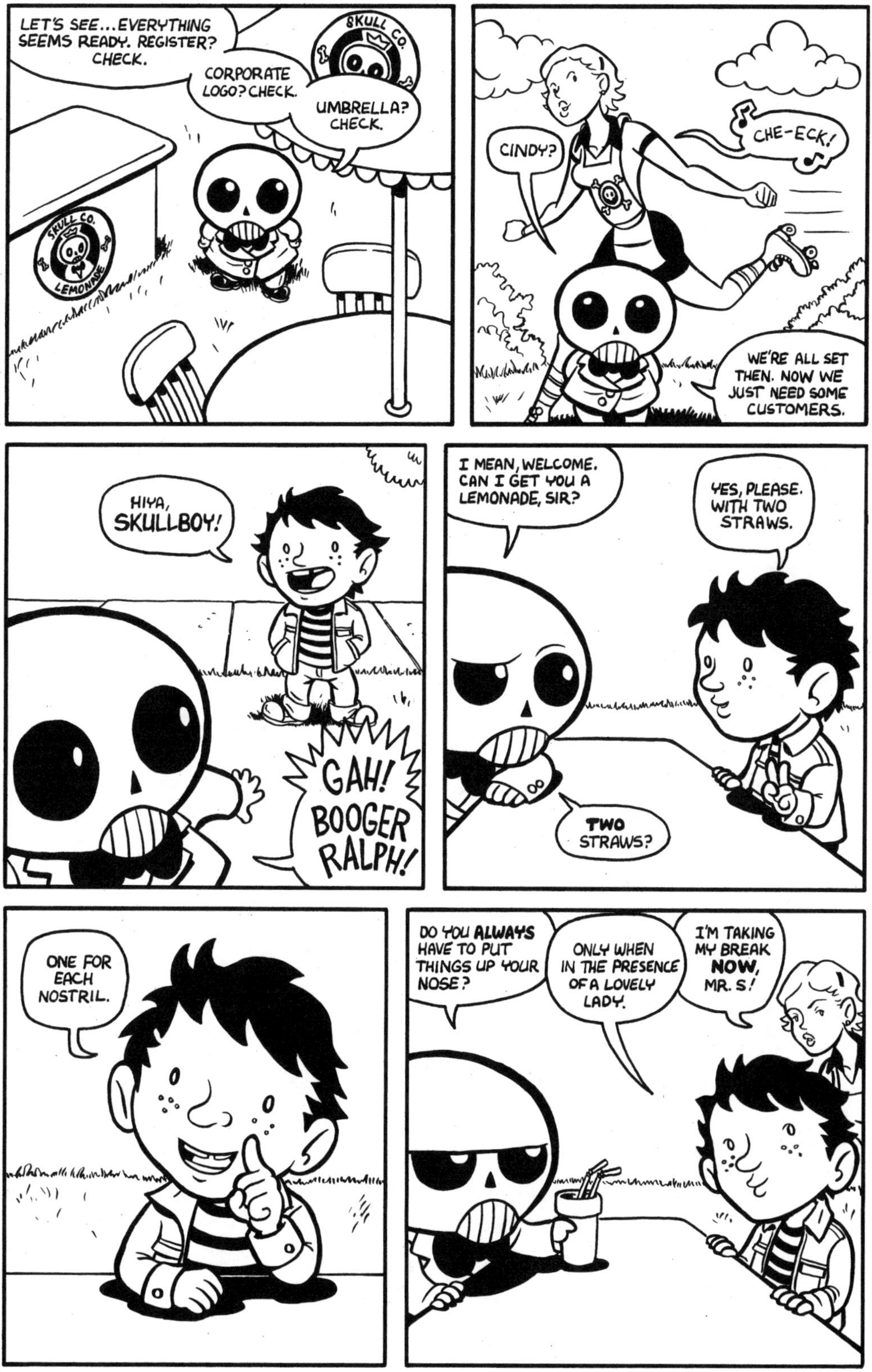
LET'S SEE... EVERYTHING SEEMS READY. REGISTER? CHECK.
SKULL CO.
CORPORATE LOGO? CHECK.
UMBRELLA? CHECK.
SKULL CO. LEMONADE
CINDY?
CHE-ECK!
WE'RE ALL SET THEN. NOW WE JUST NEED SOME CUSTOMERS.
HIYA, SKULLBOY!
GAH! BOOGER RALPH!
I MEAN, WELCOME. CAN I GET YOU A LEMONADE, SIR?
YES, PLEASE. WITH TWO STRAWS.
TWO STRAWS?
ONE FOR EACH NOSTRIL.
DO YOU ALWAYS HAVE TO PUT THINGS UP YOUR NOSE?
ONLY WHEN IN THE PRESENCE OF A LOVELY LADY.
I'M TAKING MY BREAK NOW, MR. S!

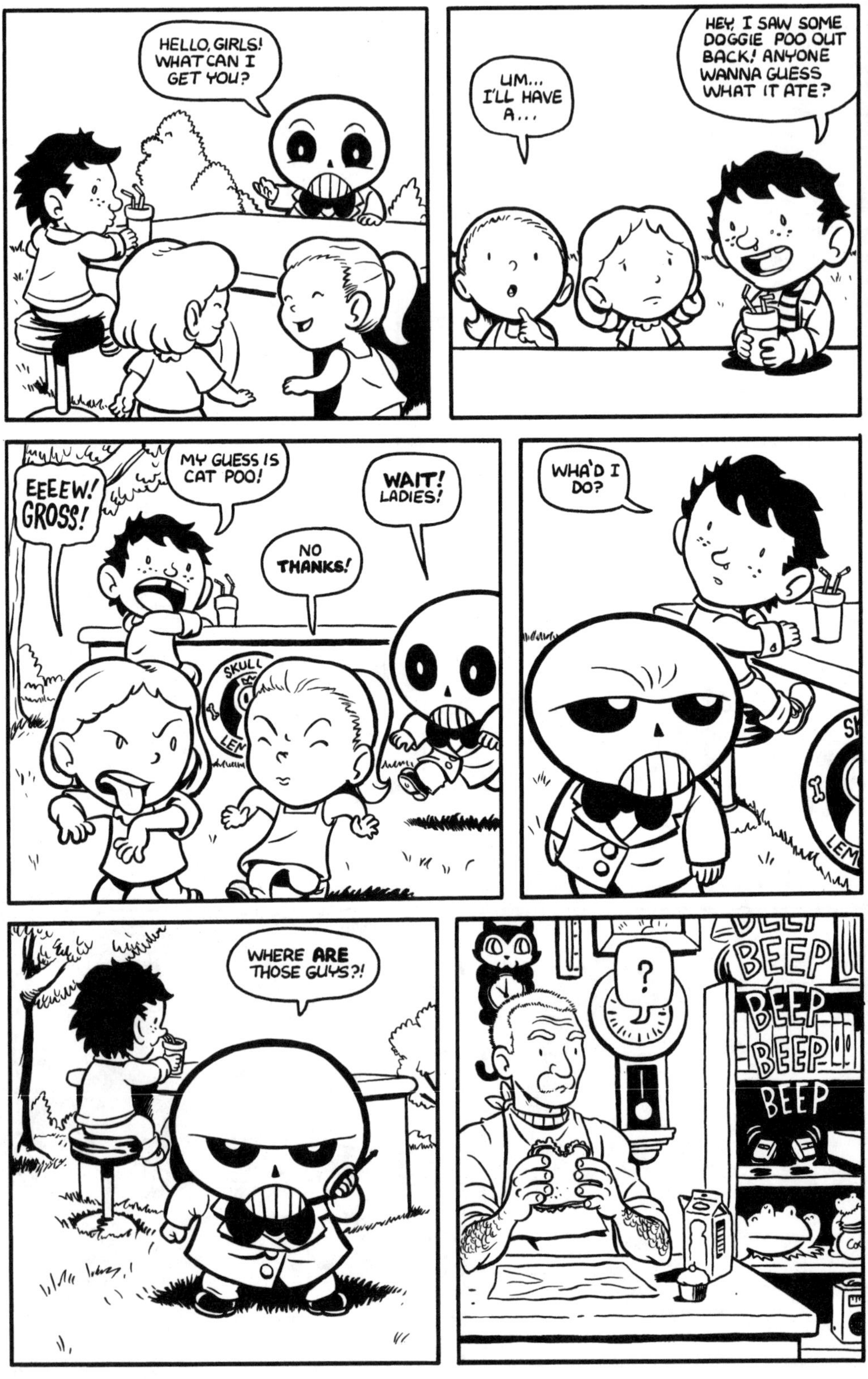
HELLO, GIRLS! WHAT CAN I GET YOU?
UM... I'LL HAVE A...
HEY, I SAW SOME DOGGIE POO OUT BACK! ANYONE WANNA GUESS WHAT IT ATE?
EEEEW! GROSS!
MY GUESS IS CAT POO!
NO THANKS!
WAIT! LADIES!
SKULL
LEM
WHA'D I DO?
WHERE ARE THOSE GUYS?!
?
BEEP
BEEP
BEEP
BEEP

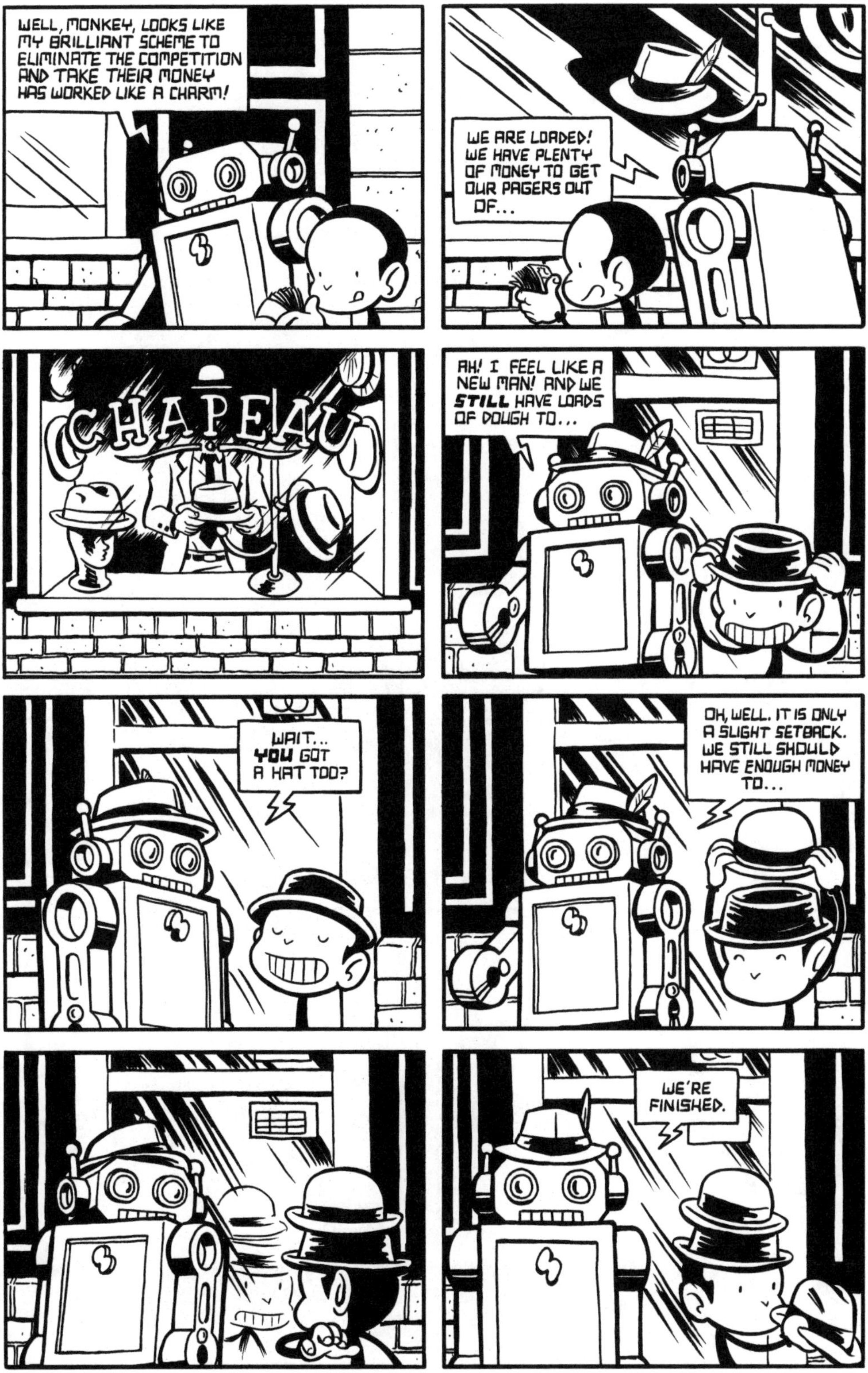
WELL, MONKEY, LOOKS LIKE MY BRILLIANT SCHEME TO ELIMINATE THE COMPETITION AND TAKE THEIR MONEY HAS WORKED LIKE A CHARM!
WE ARE LOADED! WE HAVE PLENTY OF MONEY TO GET OUR PAGERS OUT OF...
CHAPEAU
AH! I FEEL LIKE A NEW MAN! AND WE STILL HAVE LOADS OF DOUGH TO...
WAIT... YOU GOT A HAT TOO?
OH, WELL. IT IS ONLY A SLIGHT SETBACK. WE STILL SHOULD HAVE ENOUGH MONEY TO...
WE'RE FINISHED.

THAT'S IT. I'M **RUINED.** I CAN'T SELL A DANG THING WITH BOOGER RALPH AROUND.

THEN IS IT OKAY IF I GET PAID NOW, MR. S?

AH! LEMON FRESH.

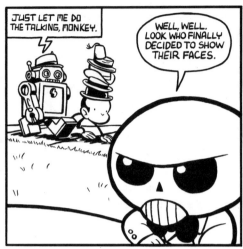

JUST LET ME DO THE TALKING, MONKEY.

WELL, WELL. LOOK WHO FINALLY DECIDED TO SHOW THEIR FACES.

HELLO, SIR!

WHERE HAVE YOU TWO **BEEN!** I'VE BEEN PAGING YOU FOR **HOURS!**

I NEEDED YOU TO GET RID OF **THIS** GOON!

WHOA! THAT'S A LOT OF GUMMI WORMS UP THERE.

I THOUGHT YOU SAID THAT YOU **FOUND** YOUR PAGERS!

WELL, YOU KNOW WHAT THEY SAY, SIR. WHEN LIFE GIVES YOU LEMONS, **MAKE LEMONADE!**

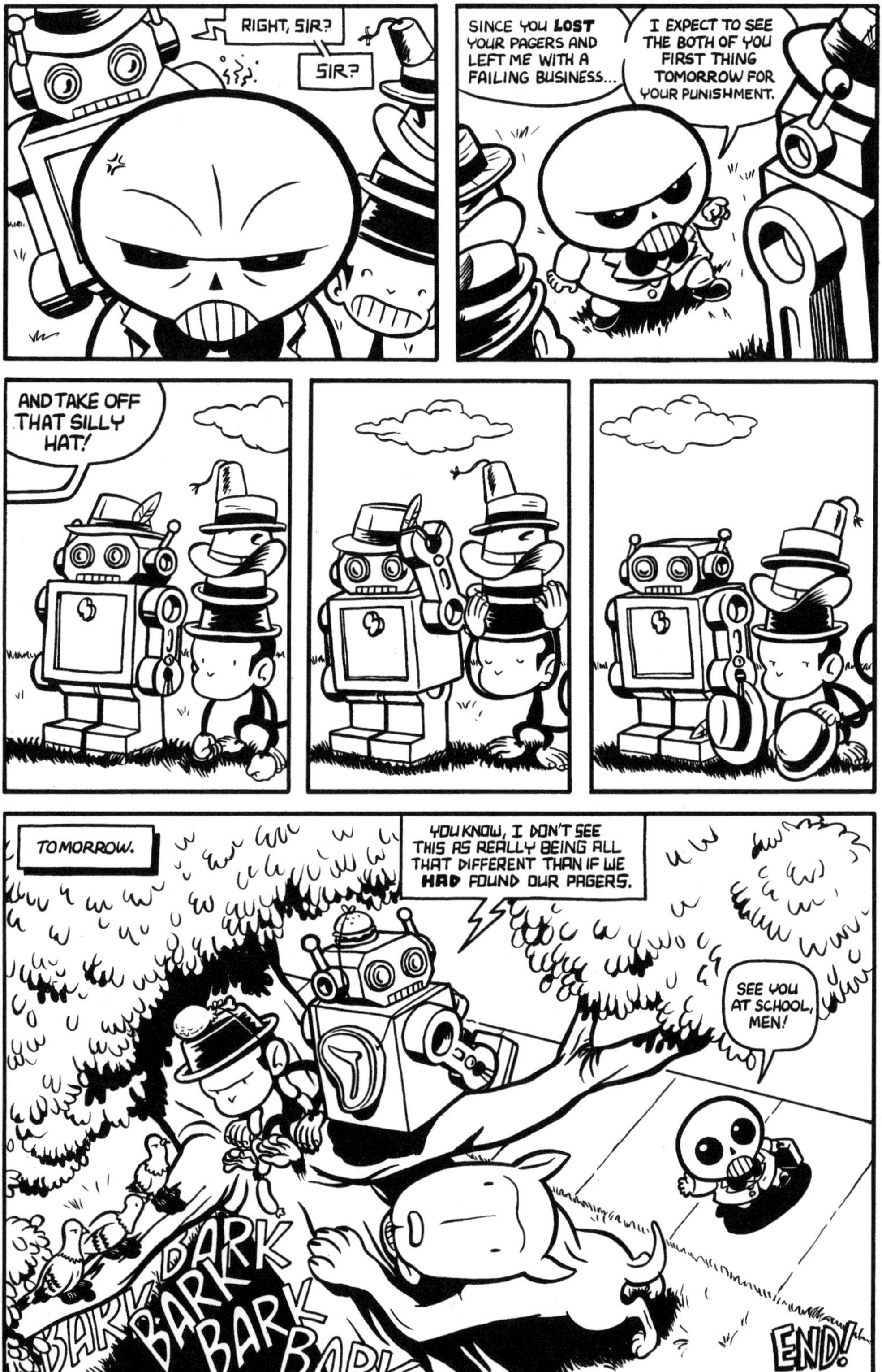
RIGHT, SIR?
SIR?
SINCE YOU LOST YOUR PAGERS AND LEFT ME WITH A FAILING BUSINESS...
I EXPECT TO SEE THE BOTH OF YOU FIRST THING TOMORROW FOR YOUR PUNISHMENT.
AND TAKE OFF THAT SILLY HAT!
TOMORROW.
YOU KNOW, I DON'T SEE THIS AS REALLY BEING ALL THAT DIFFERENT THAN IF WE HAD FOUND OUR PAGERS.
SEE YOU AT SCHOOL, MEN!
BARK BARK BARK BARK BARK BARK
END!

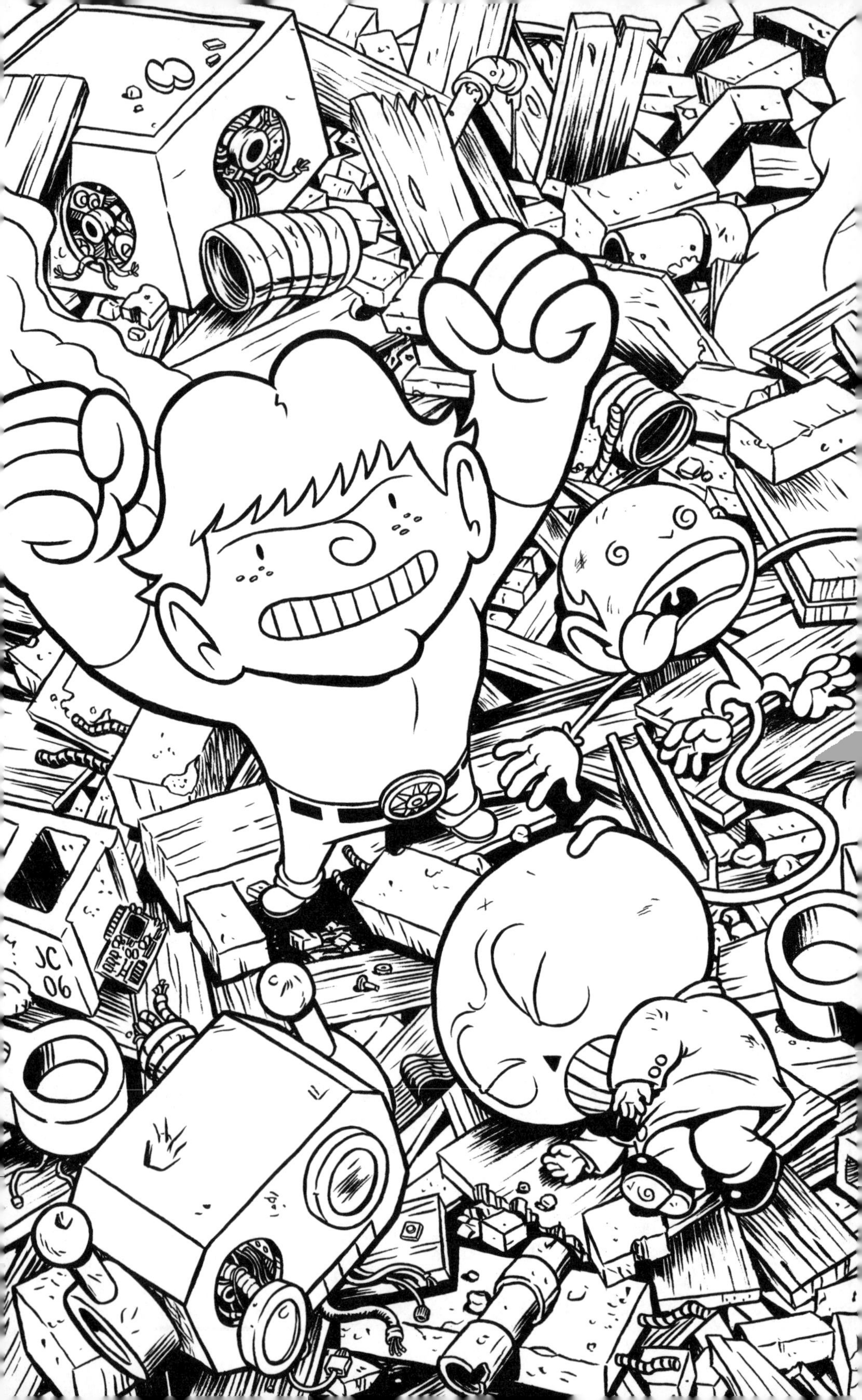
JC
06

A MiGHTY SKULLBOY ARMY ROMP!

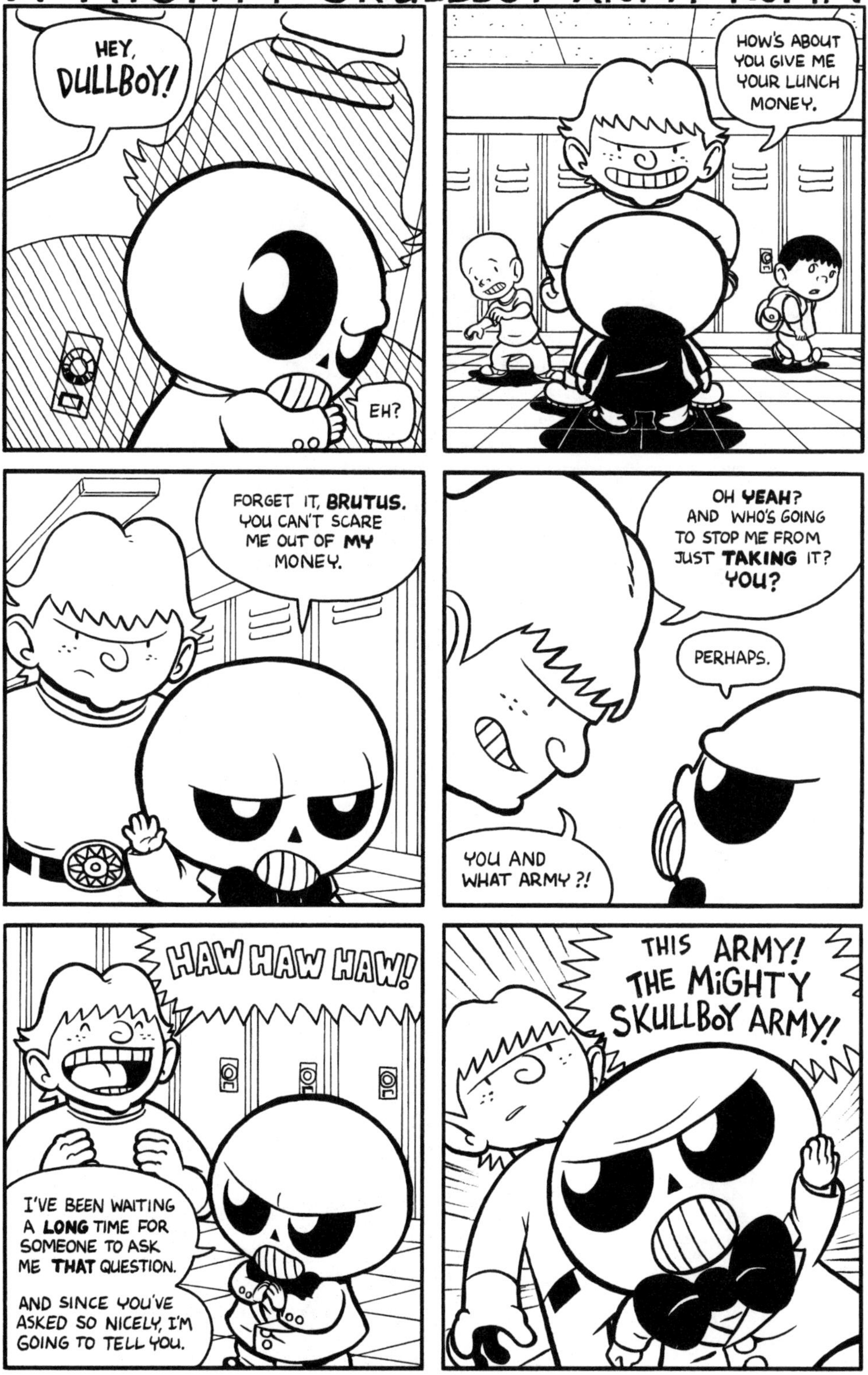
HEY, DULLBOY!
EH?
HOW'S ABOUT YOU GIVE ME YOUR LUNCH MONEY.
FORGET IT, BRUTUS. YOU CAN'T SCARE ME OUT OF MY MONEY.
OH YEAH? AND WHO'S GOING TO STOP ME FROM JUST TAKING IT? YOU?
PERHAPS.
YOU AND WHAT ARMY ?!
HAW HAW HAW!
I'VE BEEN WAITING A LONG TIME FOR SOMEONE TO ASK ME THAT QUESTION.
AND SINCE YOU'VE ASKED SO NICELY, I'M GOING TO TELL YOU.
THIS ARMY! THE MiGHTY SKULLBOY ARMY!

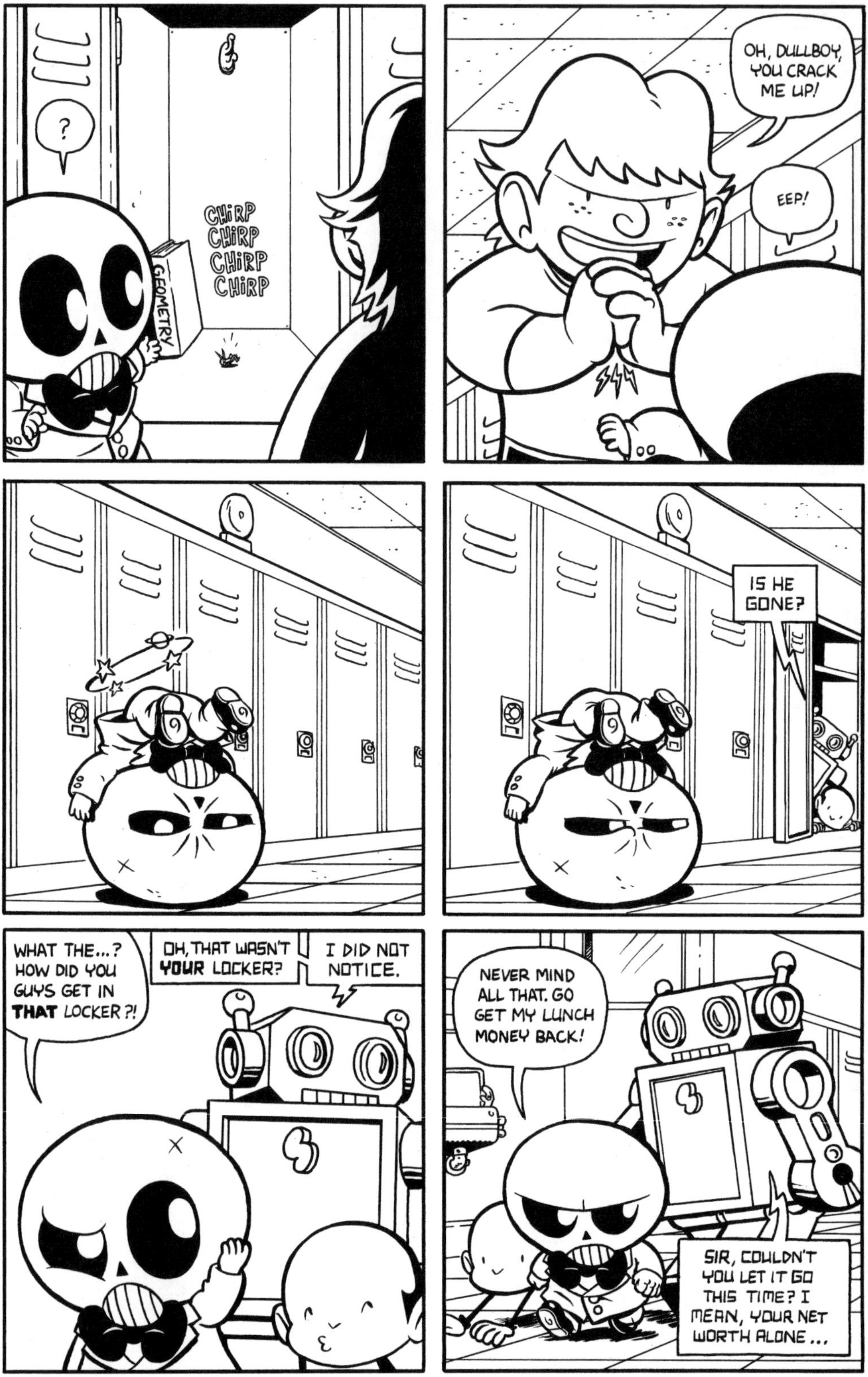
?
GEOMETRY
CHIRP
CHIRP
CHIRP
CHIRP
OH, DULLBOY, YOU CRACK ME UP!
EEP!
IS HE GONE?
WHAT THE...? HOW DID YOU GUYS GET IN **THAT** LOCKER?!
OH, THAT WASN'T **YOUR** LOCKER?
I DID NOT NOTICE.
NEVER MIND ALL THAT. GO GET MY LUNCH MONEY BACK!
SIR, COULDN'T YOU LET IT GO THIS TIME? I MEAN, YOUR NET WORTH ALONE...

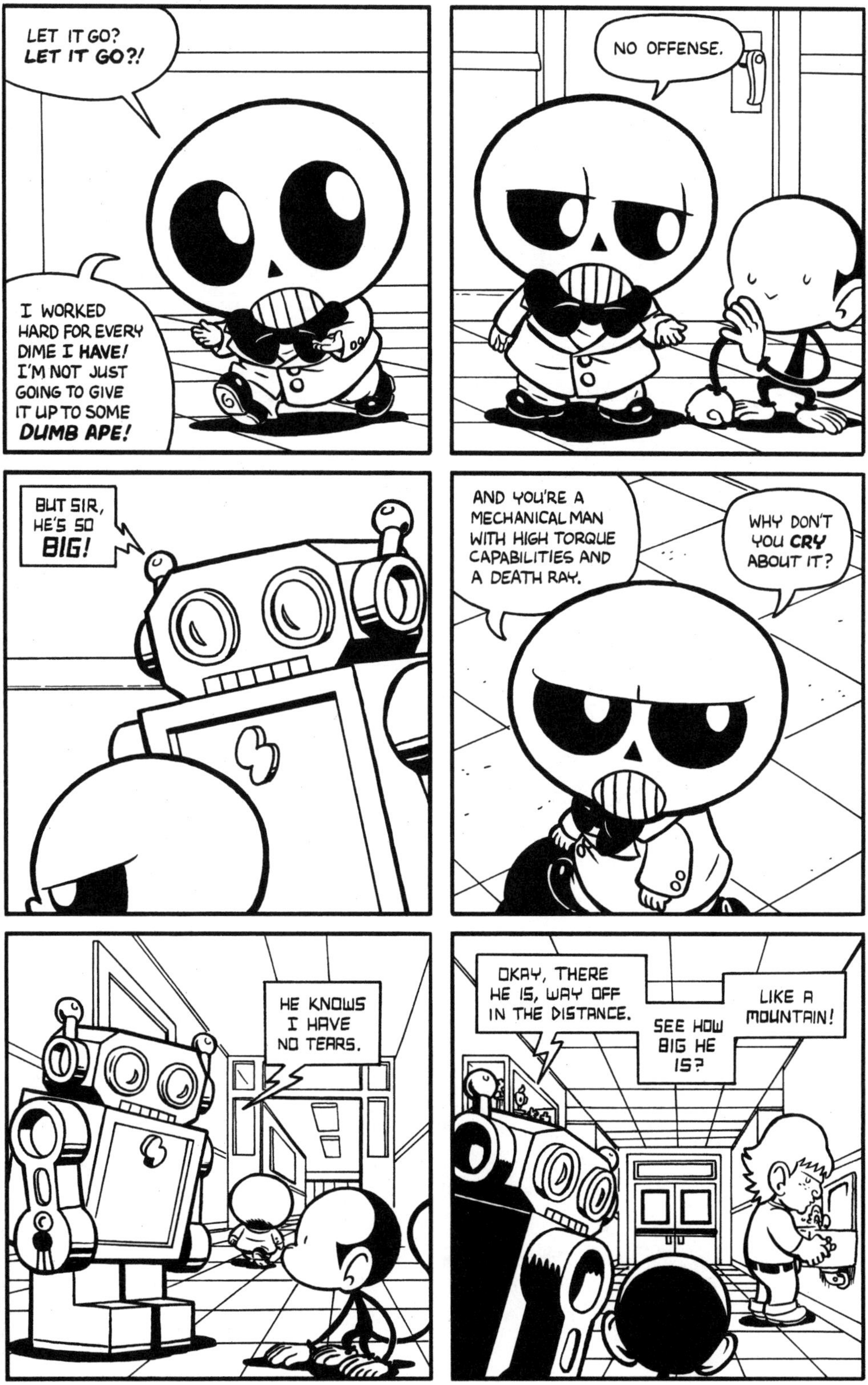
LET IT GO? LET IT GO?!
I WORKED HARD FOR EVERY DIME I HAVE! I'M NOT JUST GOING TO GIVE IT UP TO SOME DUMB APE!
NO OFFENSE.
BUT SIR, HE'S SO BIG!
AND YOU'RE A MECHANICAL MAN WITH HIGH TORQUE CAPABILITIES AND A DEATH RAY.
WHY DON'T YOU CRY ABOUT IT?
HE KNOWS I HAVE NO TEARS.
OKAY, THERE HE IS, WAY OFF IN THE DISTANCE.
SEE HOW BIG HE IS?
LIKE A MOUNTAIN!

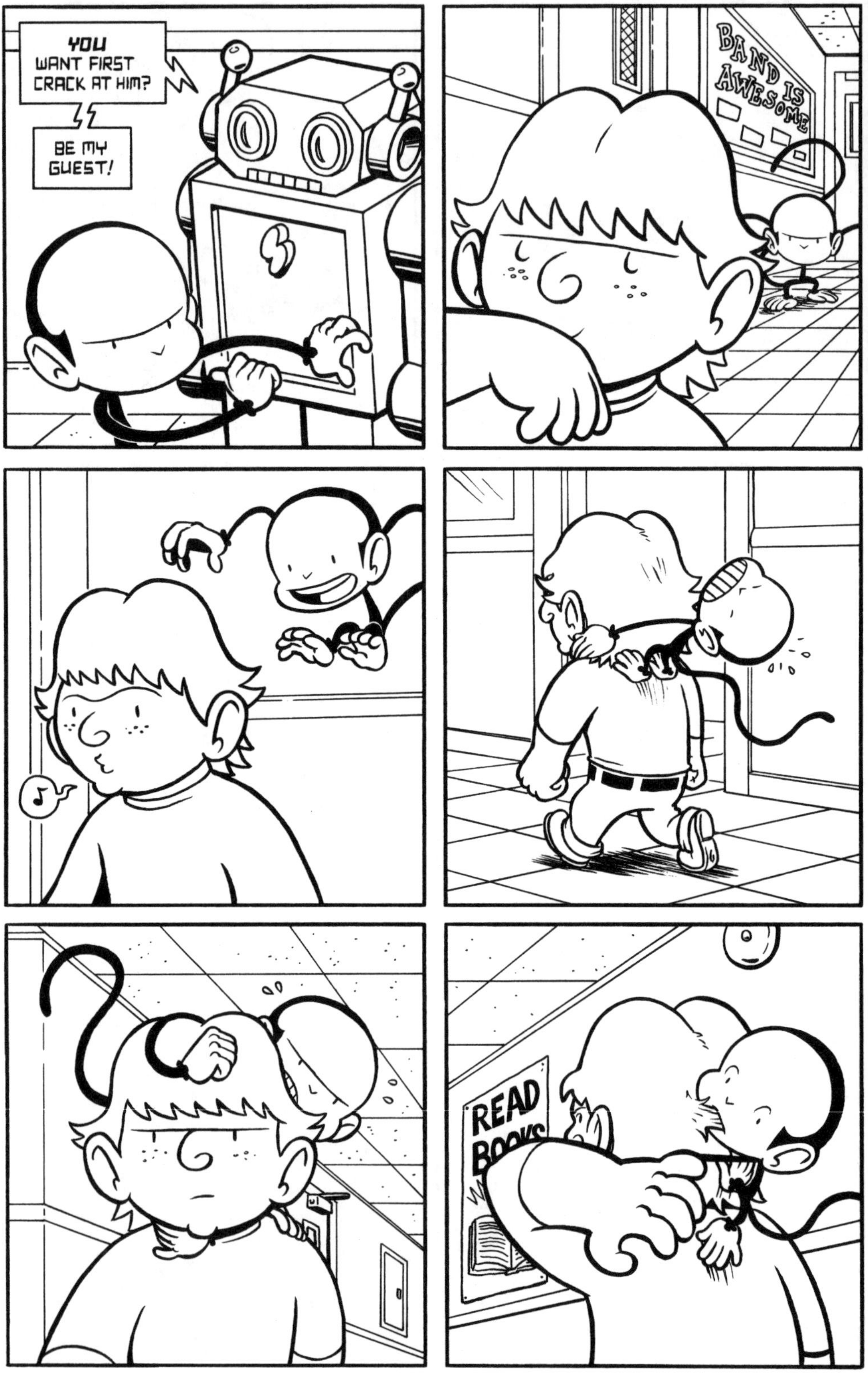
YOU WANT FIRST CRACK AT HIM?
BE MY GUEST!
BAND IS AWESOME
READ BOOKS

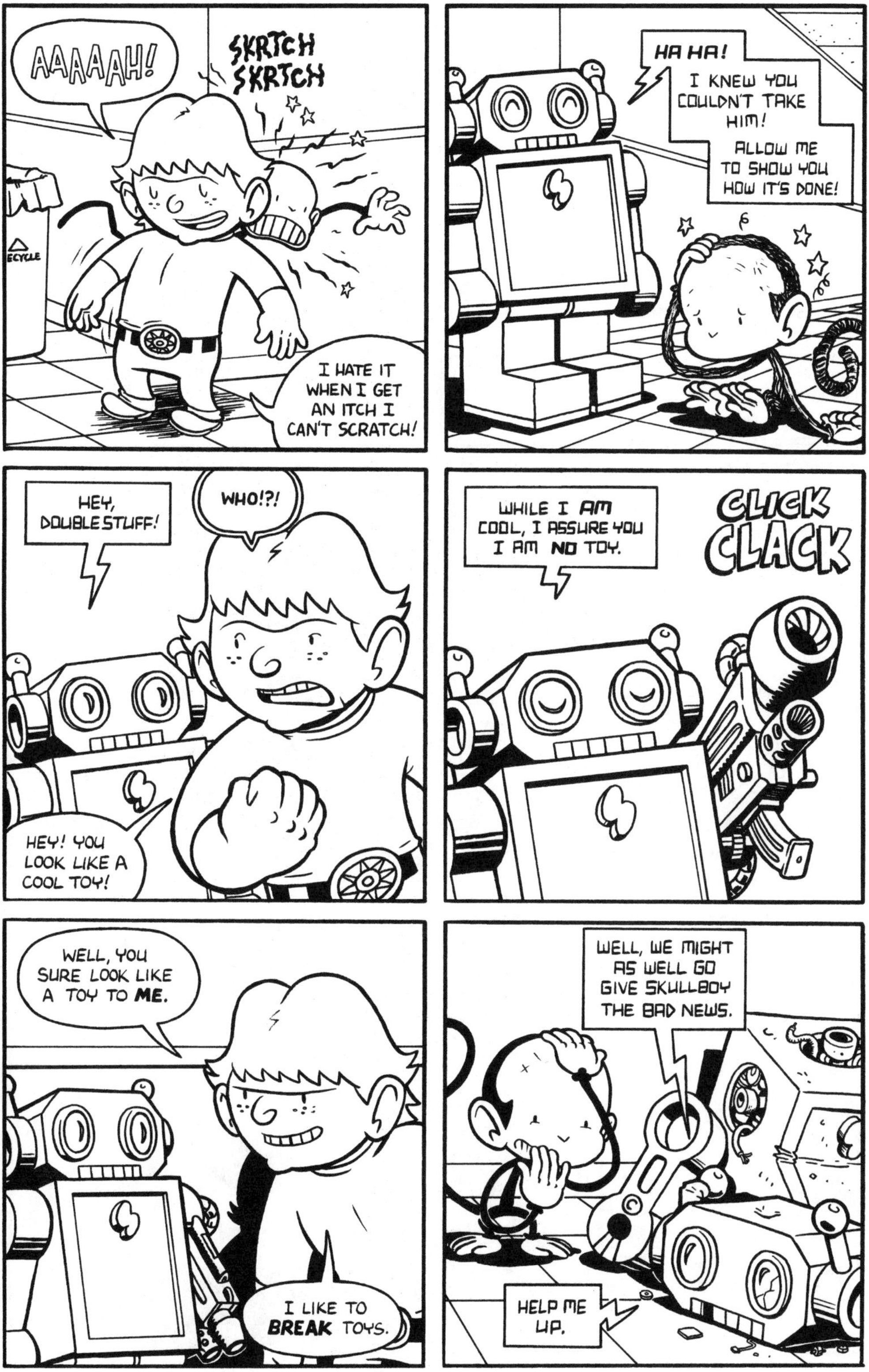
AAAAAH!
SKRTCH SKRTCH
I HATE IT WHEN I GET AN ITCH I CAN'T SCRATCH!
RECYCLE
HA HA!
I KNEW YOU COULDN'T TAKE HIM!
ALLOW ME TO SHOW YOU HOW IT'S DONE!
HEY, DOUBLESTUFF!
WHO!?!
HEY! YOU LOOK LIKE A COOL TOY!
WHILE I AM COOL, I ASSURE YOU I AM NO TOY.
CLICK CLACK
WELL, YOU SURE LOOK LIKE A TOY TO ME.
I LIKE TO BREAK TOYS.
WELL, WE MIGHT AS WELL GO GIVE SKULLBOY THE BAD NEWS.
HELP ME UP.

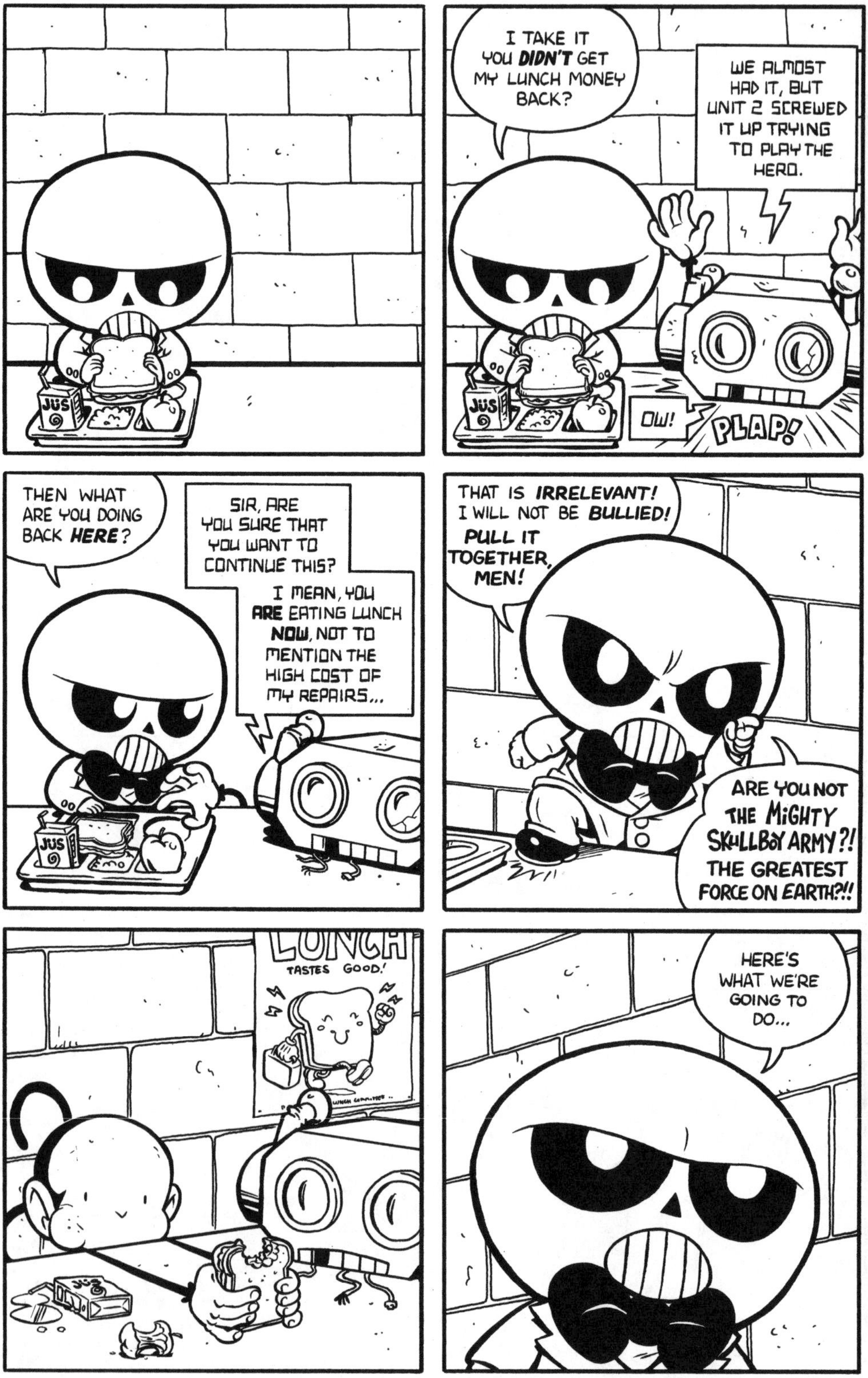
JÜS
I TAKE IT YOU **DIDN'T** GET MY LUNCH MONEY BACK?
WE ALMOST HAD IT, BUT UNIT 2 SCREWED IT UP TRYING TO PLAY THE HERO.
OW!
PLAP!
THEN WHAT ARE YOU DOING BACK **HERE**?
SIR, ARE YOU SURE THAT YOU WANT TO CONTINUE THIS?
I MEAN, YOU **ARE** EATING LUNCH **NOW**, NOT TO MENTION THE HIGH COST OF MY REPAIRS...
THAT IS **IRRELEVANT!** I WILL NOT BE **BULLIED!**
PULL IT TOGETHER, MEN!
ARE YOU NOT THE MIGHTY SKULLBOY ARMY?! THE GREATEST FORCE ON EARTH?!!
LUNCH TASTES GOOD!
HERE'S WHAT WE'RE GOING TO DO...

LATER...

OKAY, MEN, BRUTUS ALWAYS USES HIS ILL-GOTTEN GAINS ON THIS SODA MACHINE AFTER LUNCH.

IT WILL BE YOUR JOB TO MAKE SURE THAT *TODAY* HE'LL BE DRINKING *THIS*.

EXTRA PUNCH!!
PRUNE JÜS
FAST ACTING!
REGULAR! FOR TO BE REGULAR! FOR

PIECE OF CAKE, BOSS.

♪

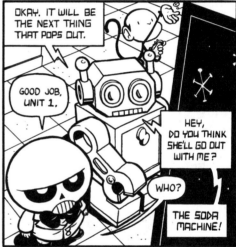

OKAY. IT WILL BE THE NEXT THING THAT POPS OUT.

GOOD JOB, UNIT 1.

HEY, DO YOU THINK SHE'LL GO OUT WITH ME?

WHO?

THE SODA MACHINE!

HER EYES ARE LIKE LIMPID POOLS, PLACED ELEGANTLY BETWEEN HER "R"s AND "N"s.

QUIET, FOOL! HERE HE COMES!

UH-OH...

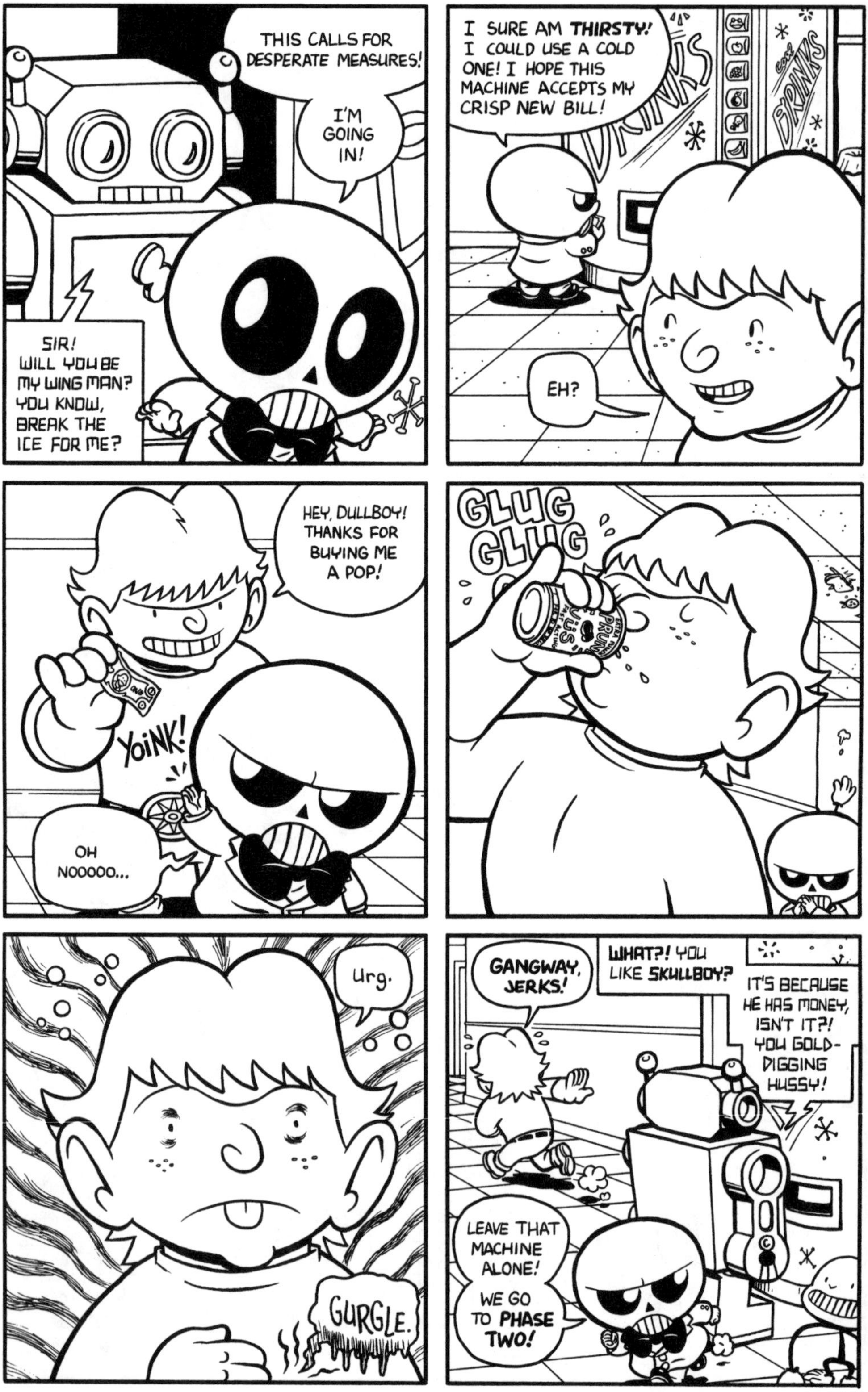
THIS CALLS FOR DESPERATE MEASURES!
I'M GOING IN!
SIR! WILL YOU BE MY WING MAN? YOU KNOW, BREAK THE ICE FOR ME?
I SURE AM THIRSTY! I COULD USE A COLD ONE! I HOPE THIS MACHINE ACCEPTS MY CRISP NEW BILL!
EH?
HEY, DULLBOY! THANKS FOR BUYING ME A POP!
YOINK!
OH NOOOOO...
GLUG GLUG
Urg.
GURGLE.
GANGWAY, JERKS!
WHAT?! YOU LIKE SKULLBOY?
IT'S BECAUSE HE HAS MONEY, ISN'T IT?! YOU GOLD-DIGGING HUSSY!
LEAVE THAT MACHINE ALONE!
WE GO TO PHASE TWO!

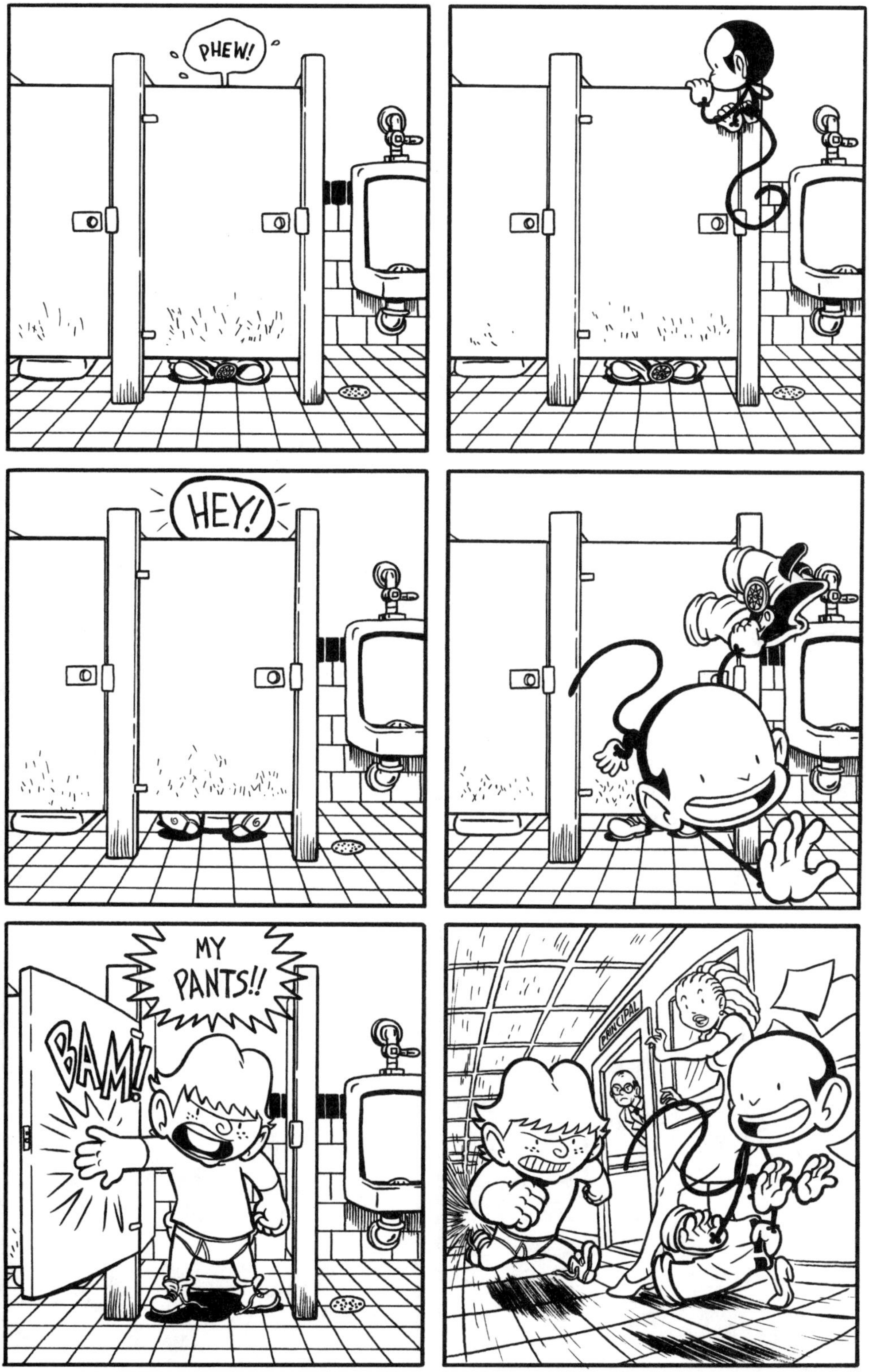
PHEW!
HEY!
MY PANTS!!
BAM!
PRINCIPAL

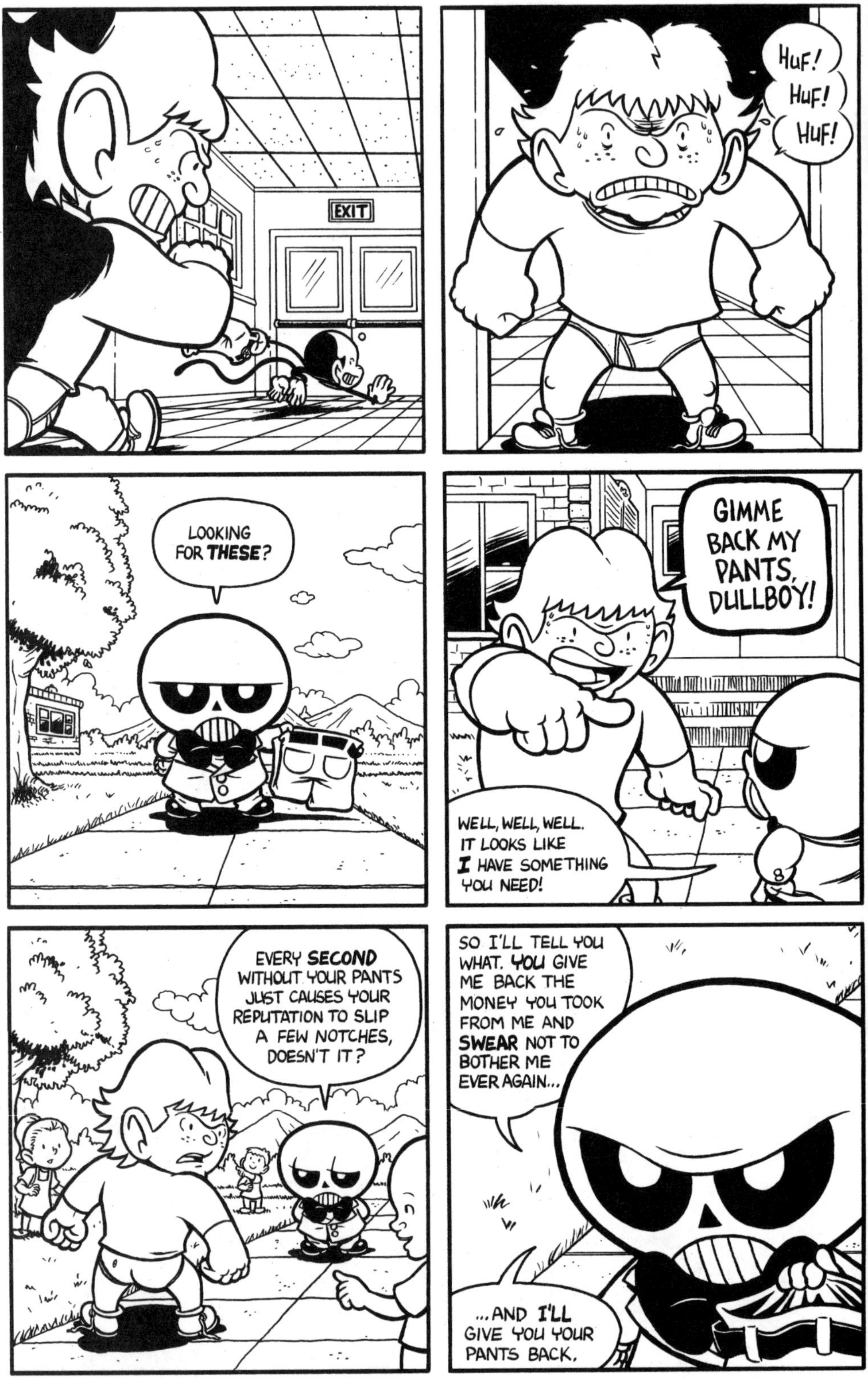
EXIT
HUF!
HUF!
HUF!
LOOKING FOR THESE?
GIMME BACK MY PANTS, DULLBOY!
WELL, WELL, WELL. IT LOOKS LIKE I HAVE SOMETHING YOU NEED!
EVERY SECOND WITHOUT YOUR PANTS JUST CAUSES YOUR REPUTATION TO SLIP A FEW NOTCHES, DOESN'T IT?
SO I'LL TELL YOU WHAT. YOU GIVE ME BACK THE MONEY YOU TOOK FROM ME AND SWEAR NOT TO BOTHER ME EVER AGAIN...
...AND I'LL GIVE YOU YOUR PANTS BACK.

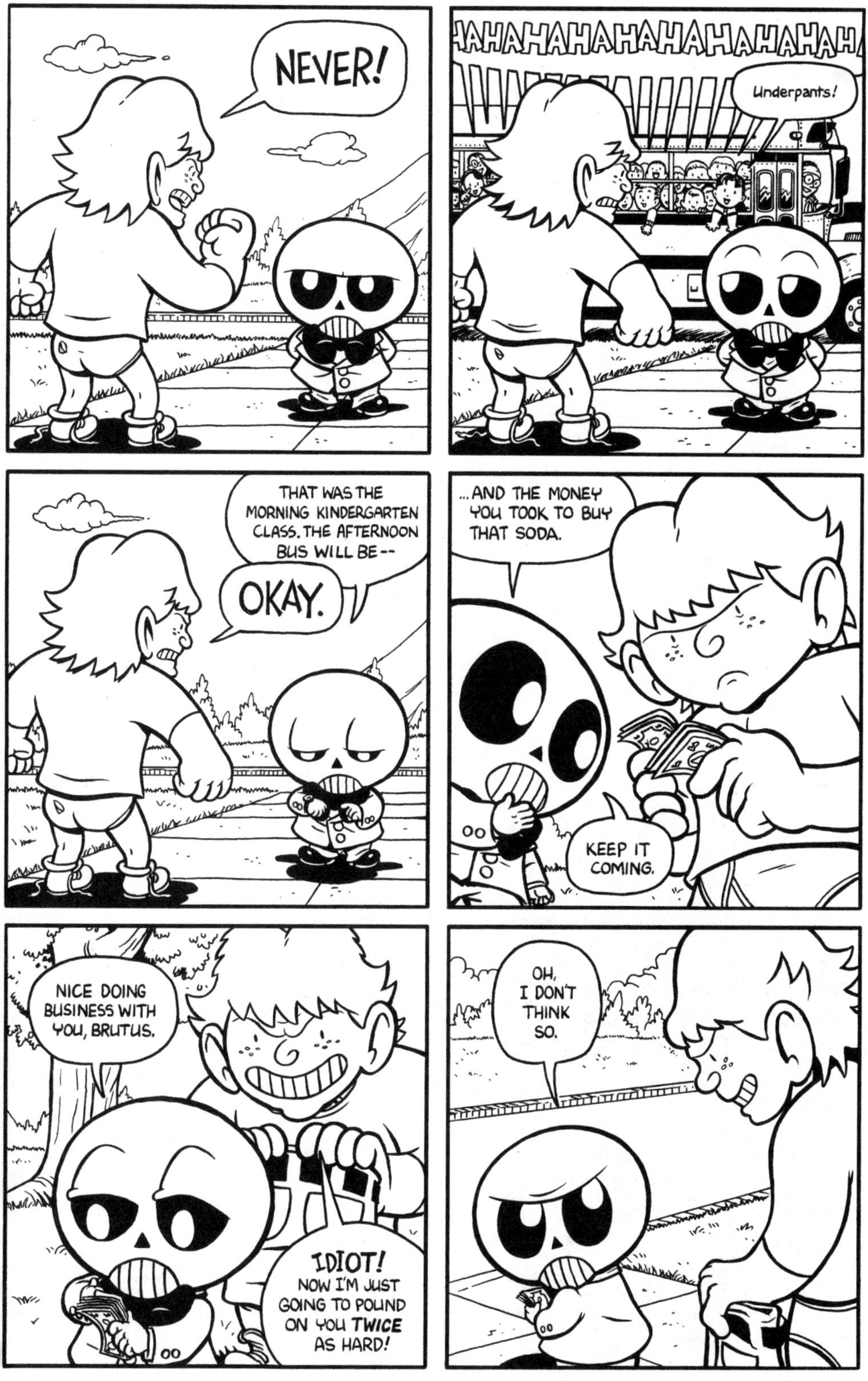
NEVER!
HAHAHAHAHAHAHAHAHAHAHAH
Underpants!
THAT WAS THE MORNING KINDERGARTEN CLASS. THE AFTERNOON BUS WILL BE--
OKAY.
...AND THE MONEY YOU TOOK TO BUY THAT SODA.
KEEP IT COMING.
NICE DOING BUSINESS WITH YOU, BRUTUS.
IDIOT! NOW I'M JUST GOING TO POUND ON YOU TWICE AS HARD!
OH, I DON'T THINK SO.

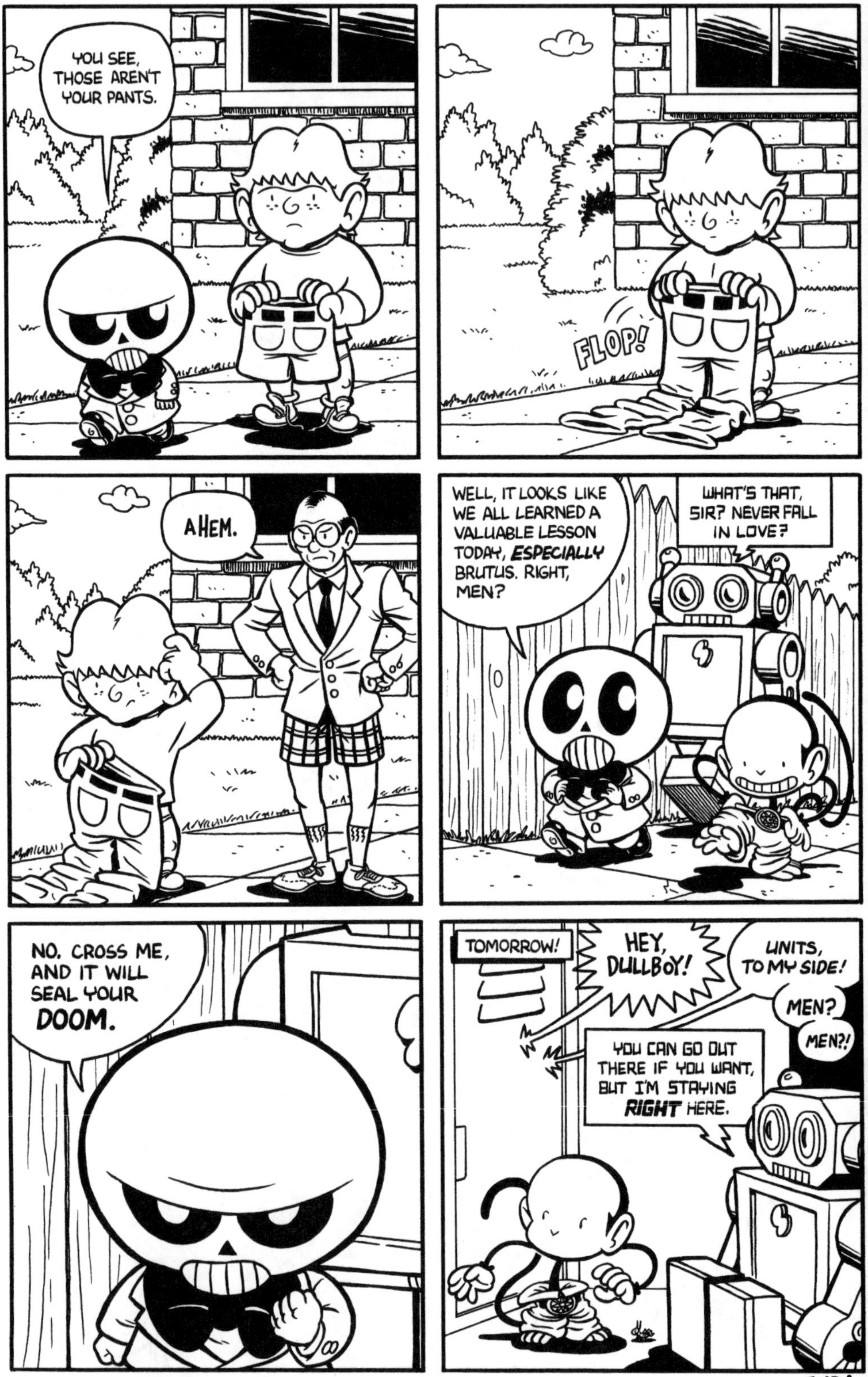
YOU SEE, THOSE AREN'T YOUR PANTS.
FLOP!
AHEM.
WELL, IT LOOKS LIKE WE ALL LEARNED A VALUABLE LESSON TODAY, ESPECIALLY BRUTUS. RIGHT, MEN?
WHAT'S THAT, SIR? NEVER FALL IN LOVE?
NO. CROSS ME, AND IT WILL SEAL YOUR DOOM.
TOMORROW!
HEY, DULLBOY!
UNITS, TO MY SIDE!
MEN?
MEN?!
YOU CAN GO OUT THERE IF YOU WANT, BUT I'M STAYING RIGHT HERE.

END!

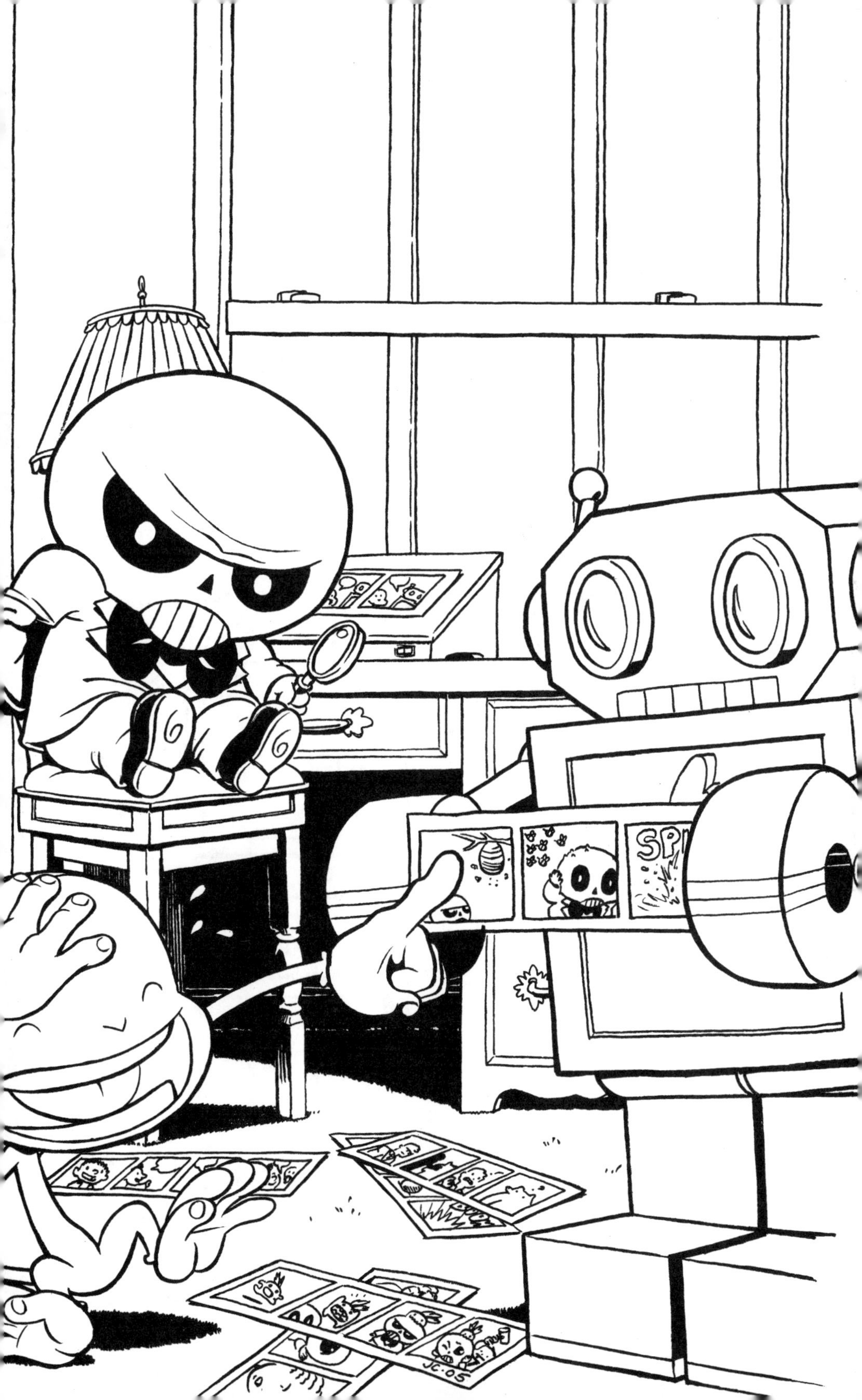

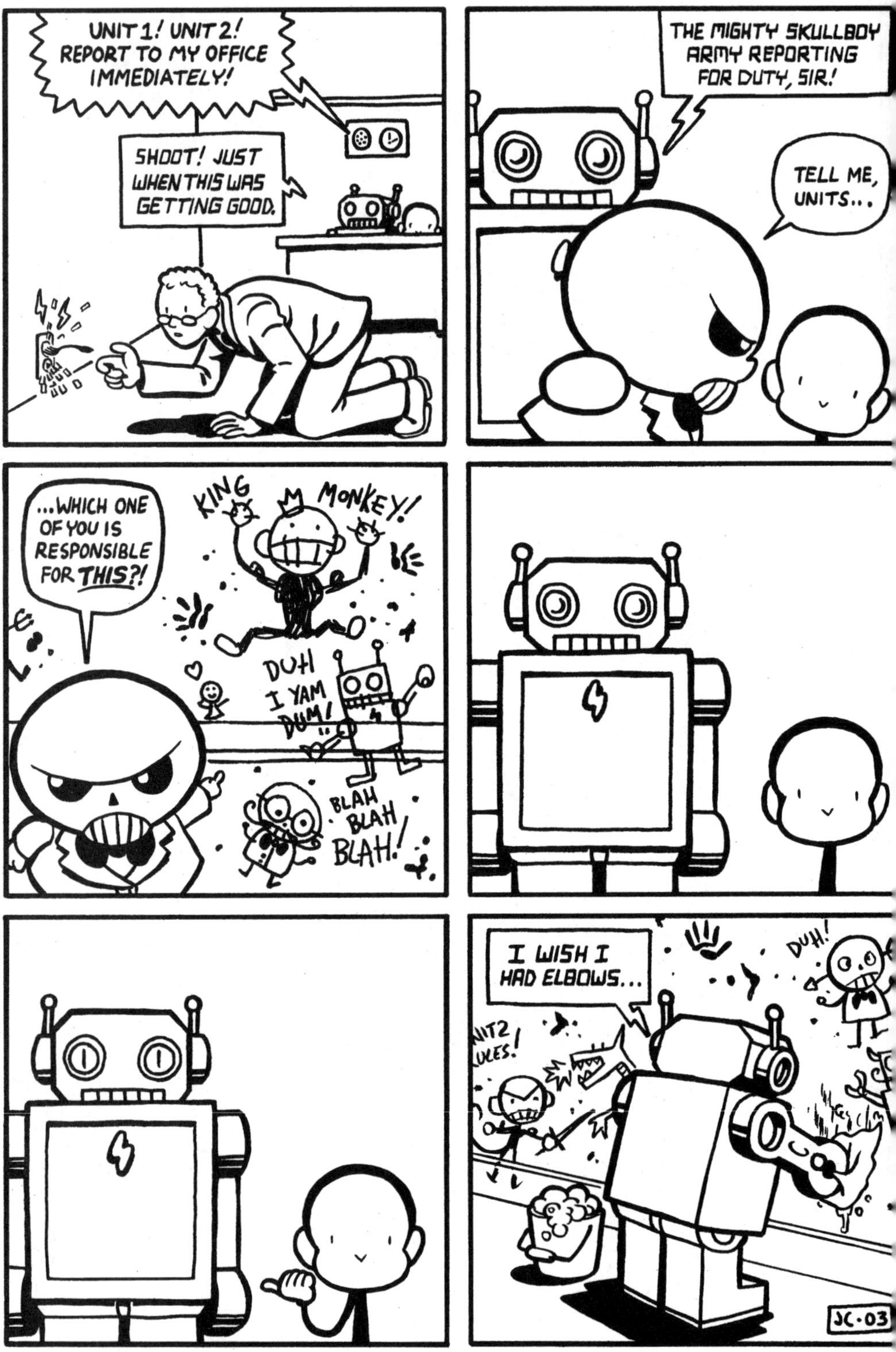
UNIT 1! UNIT 2! REPORT TO MY OFFICE IMMEDIATELY!
SHOOT! JUST WHEN THIS WAS GETTING GOOD.
THE MIGHTY SKULLBOY ARMY REPORTING FOR DUTY, SIR!
TELL ME, UNITS...
...WHICH ONE OF YOU IS RESPONSIBLE FOR THIS?!
KING MONKEY!
DUH I YAM DUM!
BLAH BLAH BLAH!
I WISH I HAD ELBOWS...
DUH!
JC·03

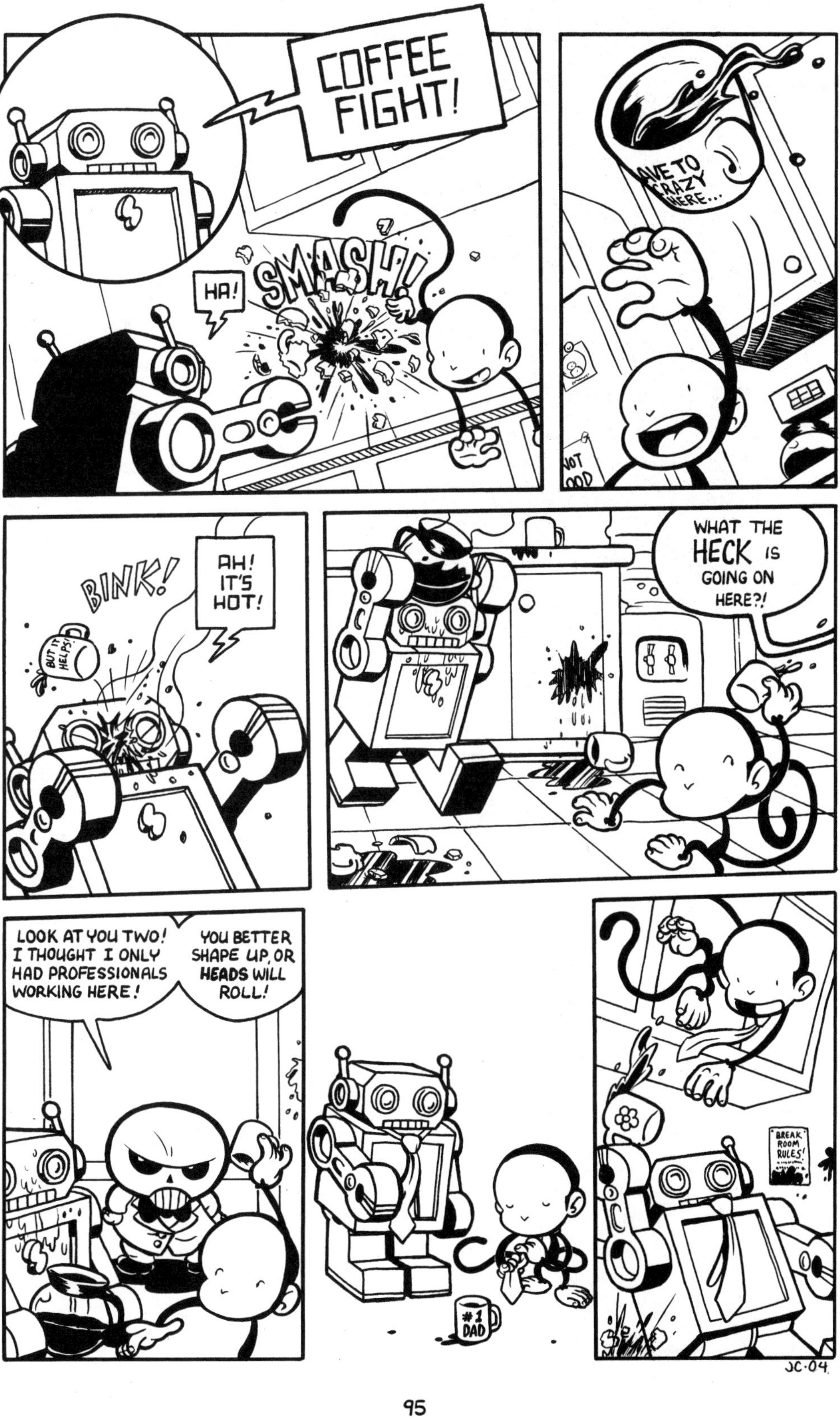
COFFEE FIGHT!
HA!
SMASH!
BINK!
BUT IT HELPS!
AH! IT'S HOT!
WHAT THE HECK IS GOING ON HERE?!
LOOK AT YOU TWO! I THOUGHT I ONLY HAD PROFESSIONALS WORKING HERE!
YOU BETTER SHAPE UP, OR HEADS WILL ROLL!
#1 DAD
BREAK ROOM RULES!
JC·04

THE MiGHTY SKULLBOY ARMY

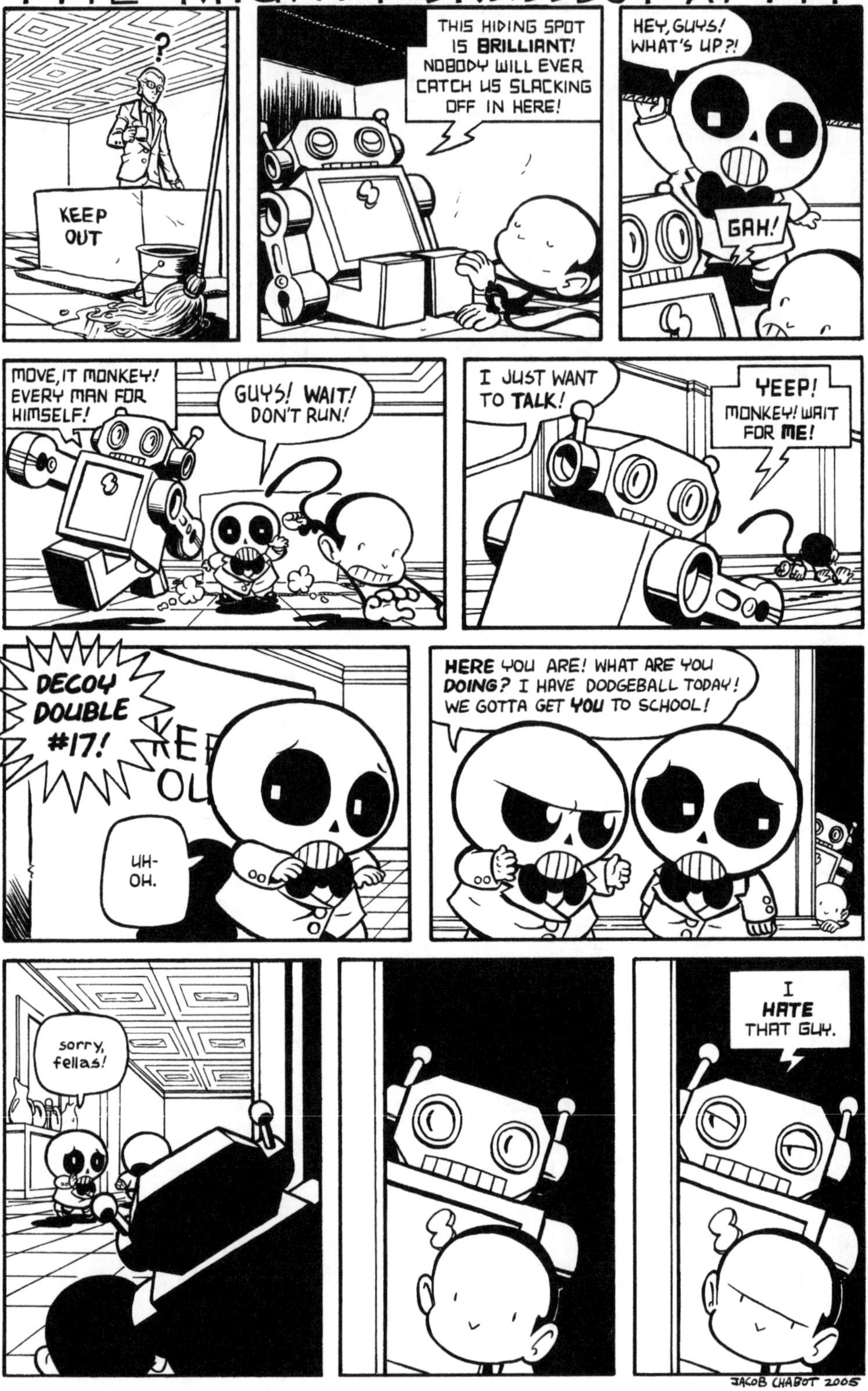
?
KEEP OUT
THIS HIDING SPOT IS BRILLIANT! NOBODY WILL EVER CATCH US SLACKING OFF IN HERE!
HEY, GUYS! WHAT'S UP?!
GAH!
MOVE, IT MONKEY! EVERY MAN FOR HIMSELF!
GUYS! WAIT! DON'T RUN!
I JUST WANT TO TALK!
YEEP! MONKEY! WAIT FOR ME!
DECOY DOUBLE #17!
UH-OH.
HERE YOU ARE! WHAT ARE YOU DOING? I HAVE DODGEBALL TODAY! WE GOTTA GET YOU TO SCHOOL!
sorry, fellas!
I HATE THAT GUY.

JACOB CHABOT 2005

The Mighty SKULLBOY ARMY

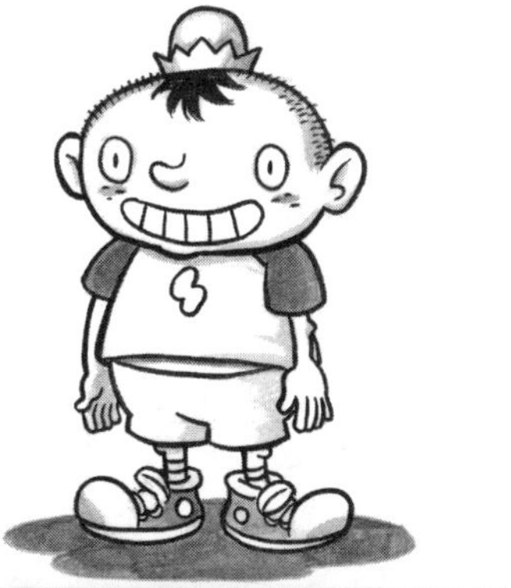

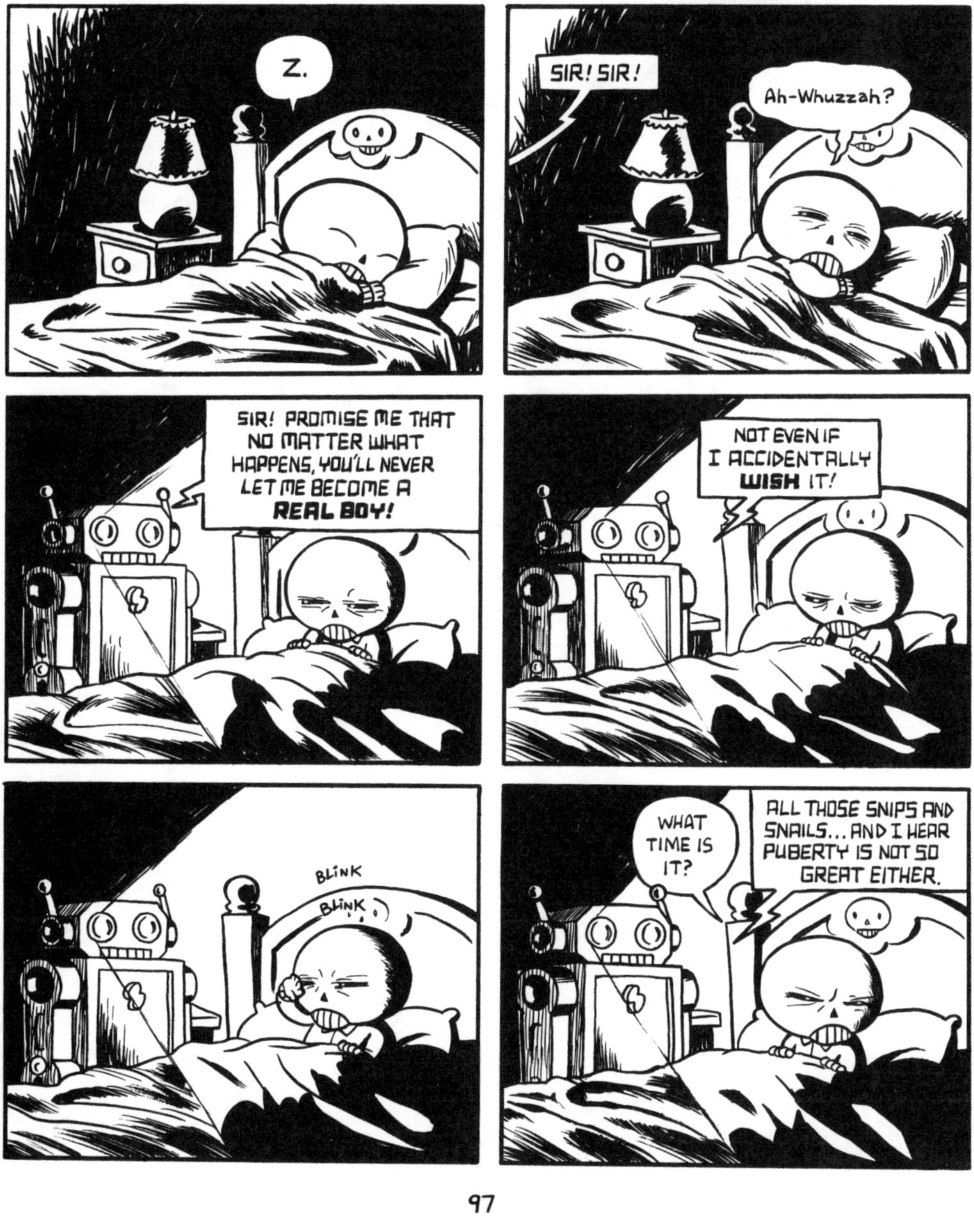
Z.
SIR! SIR!
Ah-Whuzzah?
SIR! PROMISE ME THAT NO MATTER WHAT HAPPENS, YOU'LL NEVER LET ME BECOME A **REAL BOY!**
NOT EVEN IF I ACCIDENTALLY **WISH** IT!
BLINK
BLINK
WHAT TIME IS IT?
ALL THOSE SNIPS AND SNAILS... AND I HEAR PUBERTY IS NOT SO GREAT EITHER.

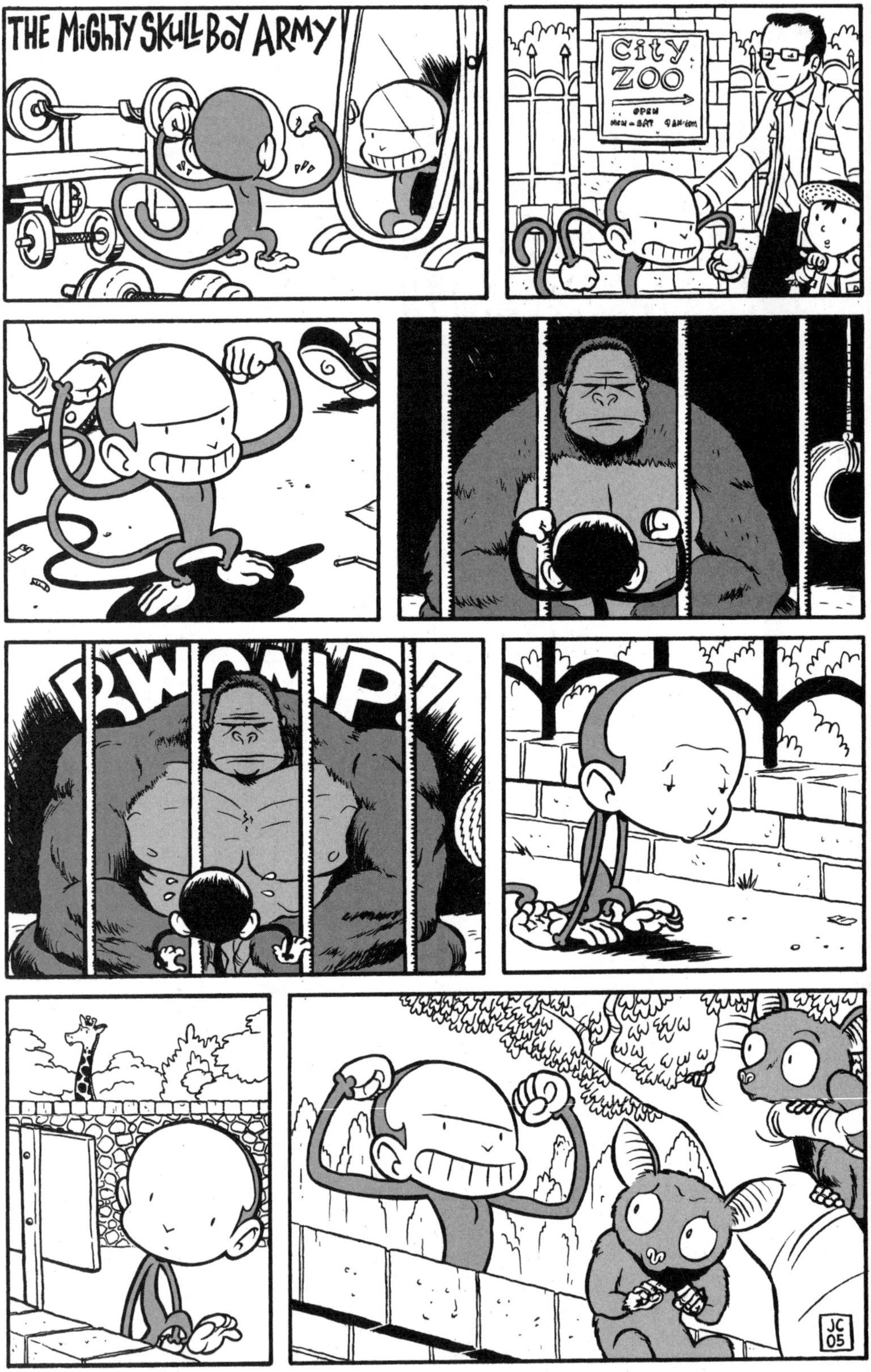
THE MIGHTY SKULL BOY ARMY
City ZOO
OPEN
BWOMP!
JC 05

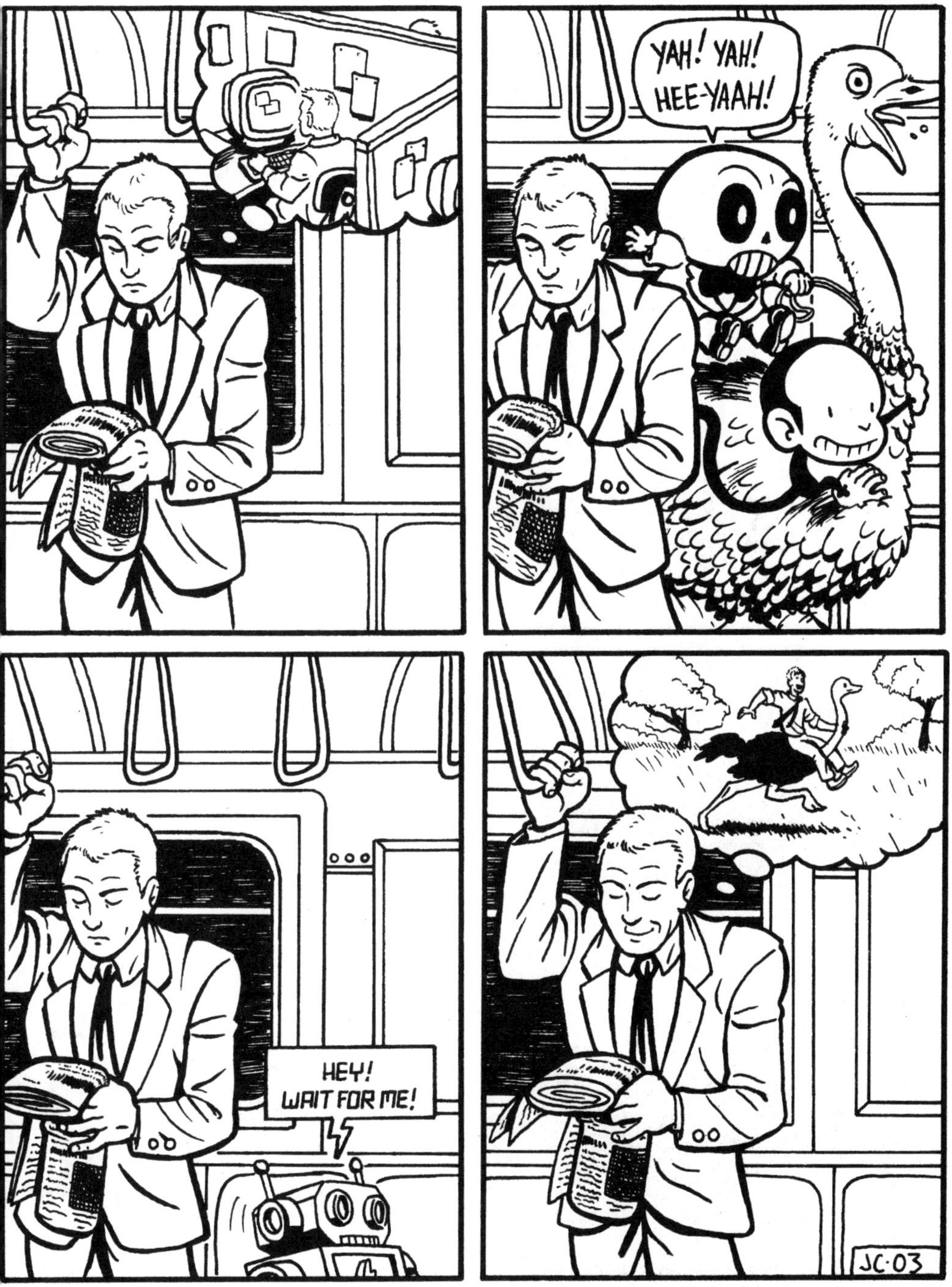
YAH! YAH! HEE-YAAH!
HEY! WAIT FOR ME!
JC·03

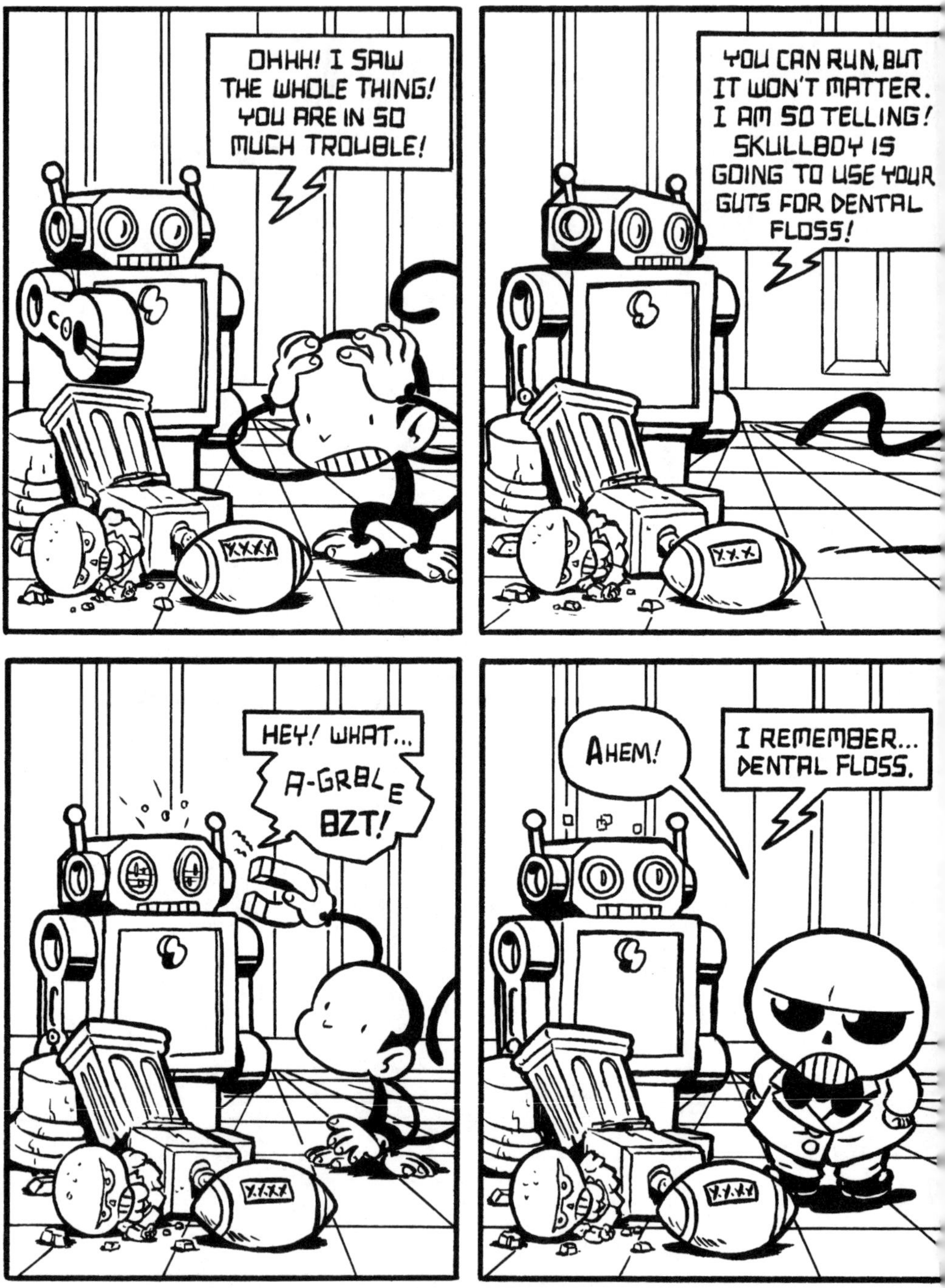
OHHH! I SAW THE WHOLE THING! YOU ARE IN SO MUCH TROUBLE!
YOU CAN RUN, BUT IT WON'T MATTER. I AM SO TELLING! SKULLBOY IS GOING TO USE YOUR GUTS FOR DENTAL FLOSS!
HEY! WHAT... A-GRBLE BZT!
AHEM!
I REMEMBER... DENTAL FLOSS.

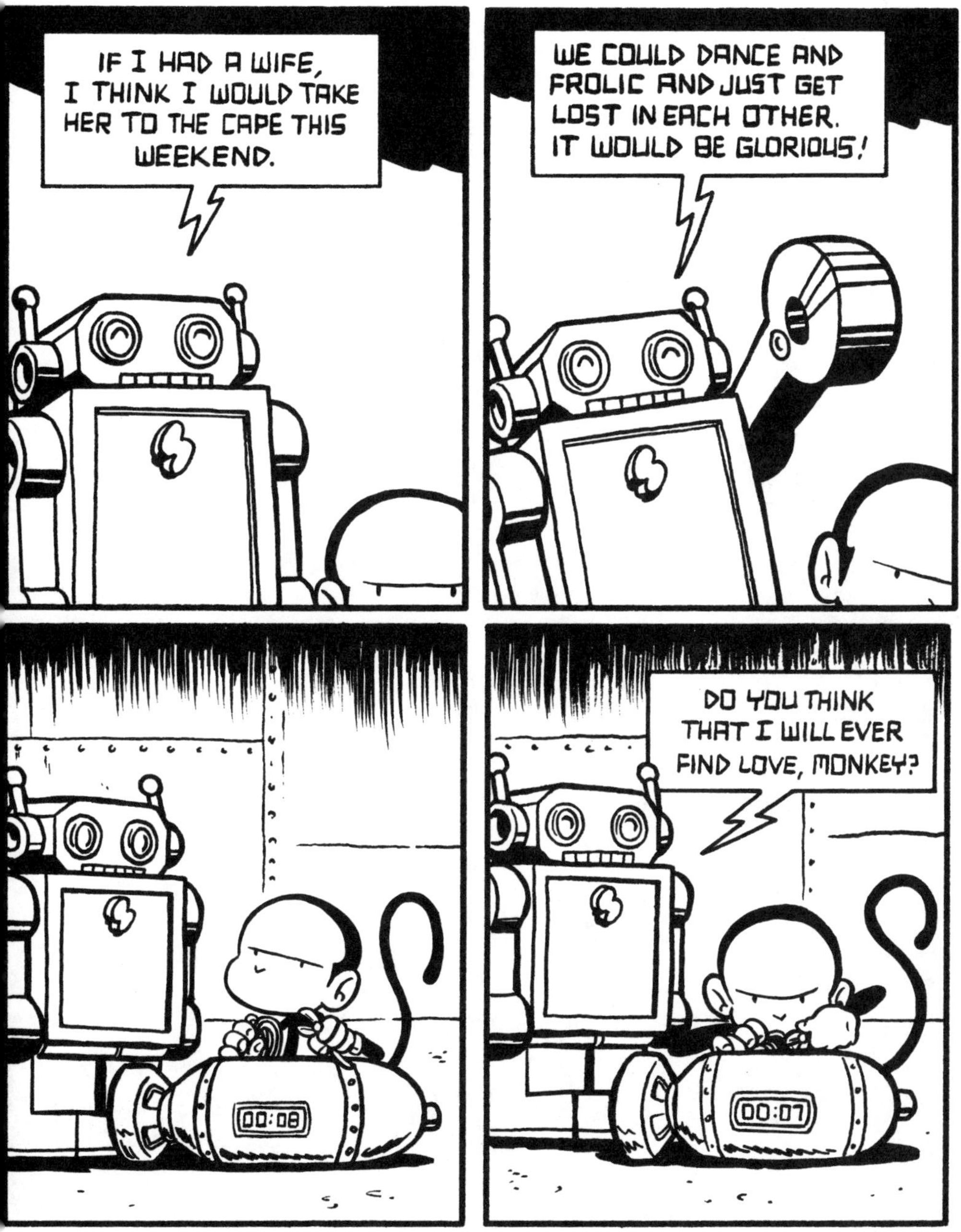
IF I HAD A WIFE, I THINK I WOULD TAKE HER TO THE CAPE THIS WEEKEND.
WE COULD DANCE AND FROLIC AND JUST GET LOST IN EACH OTHER. IT WOULD BE GLORIOUS!
00:08
DO YOU THINK THAT I WILL EVER FIND LOVE, MONKEY?
00:07

MORE YOUNG ADULT TITLES FROM
DARK HORSE BOOKS!

BEASTS OF BURDEN: ANIMAL RITES
Written by Evan Dorkin, illustrated by Jill Thompson

Beneath its surface of green lawns and white picket fences, the picturesque little town of Burden Hill harbors dark and sinister secrets. It's up to a heroic gang of dogs—and one cat—to protect the town from the evil forces at work. Adventure, mystery, horror, and hur thrive on every page!

978-1-59582-513-1 | $19.99

ITTY BITTY HELLBOY
Written by Art Baltazar and Franco, illustrated by Art Baltazar

The characters that sprung from Mike Mignola's imagination, with an AW YEAH COMICS twist! This book has ALL the FUN, adventure, and AW YEAHNESS in one itty bitty packa

978-1-61655-414-9 | $9.99

JUICE SQUEEZERS: THE GREAT BUG ELEVATOR
Written and illustrated by David Lapham

Tunnels made by a legion of giant bugs crisscross the fields below the quaint California town of Weeville, and only one thing can stop them from overrunning the place: the Juic Squeezers. A covert group of scrawny tweens, the Squeezers are the only ones who car into the cramped subterranean battlefield and fight the insects on the frontlines!

978-1-61655-438-5 | $12.99

THE USAGI YOJIMBO SAGA
Written and illustrated by Stan Sakai

Dark Horse proudly presents Miyamoto Usagi's epic trek along the warrior's path in a new series of deluxe compilations. The rabbit *ronin*'s adventures have won multiple awards and delighted readers for thirty years!

VOLUME 1: 978-1-61655-609-9 | $24.99
VOLUME 2: 978-1-61655-610-5 | $24.99

DISCOVER THE ADVENTURE!

Explore these beloved books for the entire family.

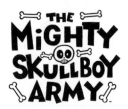

THE MIGHTY SKULLBOY ARMY

VOLUME 2 AVAILABLE NOW!

ANOTHER HILARIOUS COLLECTION OF COMICS BY JACOB CHABOT!

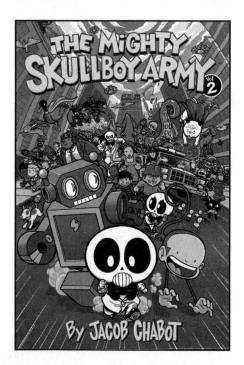

THE MIGHTY SKULLBOY ARMY
Vol. 2
By JACOB CHABOT

THE MIGHTY SKULLBOY ARMY continues! The robotic scoundrel Unit 1 and the super-smart simian Unit 2 await Skullboy's orders—ready to face any challenge that comes their way, from dodge balls to monster brawls. But are *you* ready? Are you ready for necktie-wearing bears in thinking caps, police chases, giant squid action, time travel showdowns, not-so-evil clones, vengeful pigeons, the thrill of banking (banking!), flying dogs, and more? Well, are you?! I don't think you are. Well, when you can finally muster up the courage to fill out that Skull Co. application, maybe you'll be ready for another dose of sharp, all-ages humor and clean, detailed artwork from the mirthful mind of Jacob Chabot!

ISBN 978-1-59582-872-9 | $14.99